Praise for the Work of Annie England Noblin

The Sisters Hemingway

"A fun, quick read for anyone who loves a family drama, with wit and heart to go around."

—*Booklist*

"Noblin returns to Cold River, Mo., in this sweet tale of coming home after life goes awry in the big city. . . . [This] heartwarming story of the strength of family will please fans and newcomers alike."

—*Publishers Weekly*

"Combining sibling rivalry, romantic story lines . . . a strong cast . . . and a realistic, colorful Ozarks setting, this well-paced story will appeal to those who enjoy family dramas. Its warm, engaging tone and happy ending for all will appeal to readers of Susan Wiggs or Mary Alice Monroe."

—*Library Journal*

Pupcakes

"Noblin's tale of self-discovery, populated with a colorful cast of characters, is both lighthearted and life-affirming. Readers are in for a sweet treat."

—*USA Today*

"Fans of Noblin's canine-themed tales will beg for more!"

—*Library Journal*

Just Fine with Caroline

". . . All heart! Noblin knows how to make characters come to life. I was completely charmed on my trip to Cold River."

—Stephanie Evanovich

Sit! Stay! Speak!

"Readers of Debbie Macomber will enjoy . . . Noblin's first novel. It's an enjoyable story full of laughter, tears, and just plain fun."

—*Library Journal*

"A touching and engaging book about friendships, family, and the power of dogs to inspire changes in our lives."

—*The Bark* magazine

"Will delight fans of Mary Kay Andrews and contemporary women's fiction."

—*Booklist*

Maps
FOR THE
Getaway

Also by Annie England Noblin

St. Francis Society for Wayward Pets

The Sisters Hemingway

Just Fine with Caroline

Pupcakes

Sit! Stay! Speak!

Maps
FOR THE
Getaway

A NOVEL

ANNIE ENGLAND NOBLIN

WILLIAM MORROW
An Imprint of HarperCollinsPublishers

P.S.™ is a trademark for HarperCollins Publishers.

MAPS FOR THE GETAWAY. Copyright © 2021 by Annie England Noblin. All rights reserved. Printed in the United States of America. No part of this book may be used or reproduced in any manner whatsoever without written permission except in the case of brief quotations embodied in critical articles and reviews. For information, address HarperCollins Publishers, 195 Broadway, New York, NY 10007.

HarperCollins books may be purchased for educational, business, or sales promotional use. For information, please email the Special Markets Department at SPsales@harpercollins.com.

FIRST EDITION

Designed by Diahann Sturge

Highway road infographic © Tartila / Shutterstock, Inc.
Chinese crested dog © Africa Studio / Shutterstock, Inc.

Library of Congress Cataloging-in-Publication Data has been applied for.

ISBN 978-0-06-291073-8 (paperback)
ISBN 978-0-06-308231-1 (hardcover library edition)

21 22 23 24 25   LSC   10 9 8 7 6 5 4 3 2 1

For Brittany and Nikki, my lifelong, ride-or-die best friends

Maps
FOR THE
Getaway

Prologue

Laurie

May 2000

Laurie smiled for the camera, one arm slung around her best friend Genie, and her other holding on to her high school diploma. Her foster mother, Kitty, struggled with the camera for a moment before heaving a sigh of frustration and handing it over to Laurie's foster father, Dan.

"Okay, girls, let's try it again," Dan said in his rough but gentle country twang.

Laurie shifted on her feet and leaned in again to Genie, forcing her smile to go as wide as her face would allow. She wanted to look happy in this picture for Kitty and Dan. They deserved it, after all, for the years they'd cared for her. When she'd first come to live with them six years ago, she didn't even know if she'd get through junior high, let alone high school. Now she was a graduate with a full ride to the University of Missouri to play softball.

"I'll go get these printed at Walmart tomorrow," Kitty said, taking the camera back from Dan. "We'll add them to your scrapbook."

"Okay," Laurie replied. She pulled at the bobby pins stuck between her hair and the base of her graduation cap. "Can I take this off now?"

"Sure," Kitty said. She smiled, teary-eyed, at Laurie and then pulled her in for a hug. "I'm so proud of you, kiddo."

At nearly five feet eleven, Laurie towered over Kitty, but she folded herself into her foster mother the same way she had that first night—a twelve-year-old girl, trying to be tough, but still so, so scared. That night, Kitty came into the bedroom, the first bedroom Laurie had had in a very long time. Kitty sat down on the edge of the bed while Laurie wept and held on tight to the black trash bag she'd come with, all that was left of her previous life inside.

Kitty hadn't said anything. She just sat on the edge of the bed until Laurie cried herself to sleep. Laurie had known Kitty was there, even though she hadn't looked at her. She didn't know what to say, having used every single curse word she'd learned from her mother's last boyfriend in the car on the way over, hoping she might sound tough enough that nobody in this new place would mess with her. Kitty hadn't said anything then either.

When Laurie woke up later, sometime in the early hours of

the morning, she found Kitty asleep in the chair in the corner of the room. She considered running but realized that her belongings had been taken out of the trash bag while she slept and put into drawers and into the closet. There were pajamas laid out for her, along with a glass of water and a ham sandwich. It was such a nice gesture, and Laurie was so tired of running away, that when Kitty opened her eyes and held out her arms, Laurie collapsed into them.

"Come on, Laurie," Genie said, pulling Laurie away from Kitty. "We've got to go find CiCi and Kate."

Laurie gave Kitty one last squeeze and then took off after Genie. "Wait! I'm coming!"

"Do you really think CiCi is going to marry Brent?" Genie asked Laurie as they walked. "I mean, I know she says she's not going to college, but *Brent*?"

Laurie shrugged. "I don't know. I heard Kitty telling Dan a couple of weeks ago that Brent's dad is going to retire this summer and give Brent the car lot, so maybe."

"I think it's a bad idea," Genie said.

"Why don't you tell her that?" Laurie asked, grinning. "I'm sure that'll go over real well."

"No way," Genie replied. She unzipped the front of her gown. "The last time I said anything to CiCi about a guy, she told me she wasn't taking dating advice from a virgin."

Laurie stopped walking. "Why do you let her talk to you like that?" she asked.

"I don't know," Genie said. "It's easier than arguing with her. Besides, it's true."

"It doesn't matter whether it's true," Laurie replied. "Next time she says something like that, tell her you'd rather be a virgin than the Crossett County Queen of Blow Jobs."

Genie snorted. "You say it, and I'll watch."

"If she says shit like that in front of me, I will," Laurie said. "But Genie, you've got to start sticking up for yourself . . . not just with CiCi, but with everyone."

They both knew the "everyone" Laurie was referring to was Genie's overbearing father, but neither one of them was going to say it. Genie nodded. "Okay," she said. "I'll work on it."

On the other side of the gymnasium was the elementary school playground, and that's where Laurie and Genie found CiCi and Kate—sitting on swings, swaying back and forth. As Laurie and Genie approached, Kate held a bottle half-full of brown liquid out to them.

"Are you guys drinking?" Genie asked. "You can't do that on school property!"

"We're eighteen," Kate replied. "We can't do it anywhere."

Laurie took the bottle and drank. Then she handed it over to Genie. "Liquid courage," she said.

Genie shook her head. "My dad will find out."

CiCi reached into her purse and pulled out a bottle of Listerine. "No, he won't," she said. "Not if you rinse your mouth with this after."

"You don't have to if you don't want to," Laurie replied. She took another drink. Laurie did want Genie to stick up for herself, but she also wanted her to have a little fun. A shot or two of Kate's dad's whiskey wasn't going to hurt her.

Genie snatched the bottle out of her friend's hand and took a sip. It burned all the way down, and she had to shut her eyes tight so she wouldn't cry. She blindly handed the bottle back to Kate. "That's disgusting," she said.

The other three laughed, and Genie couldn't help but laugh with them. She and Laurie sat down on the remaining swings.

"Is everybody going to Brent's party tonight?" CiCi asked.

"I still don't understand why Brent is throwing a graduation party," Kate replied. "He graduated last year."

"It's for me," CiCi said.

"It's an excuse to get a keg," Kate said. "His parents are out of town, and you know his older brother bought out the liquor store."

"So?" CiCi asked, inclining her head to the now-empty bottle in Kate's hand. "It's not like you need an excuse."

Kate rolled her eyes. "I'll be there," she said.

"I can't," Laurie said. "You know I leave tomorrow for Missouri U for softball camp. I have to pack, and I can't show up hungover."

"What about you, Genie?" CiCi asked.

Genie dug her feet into the gravel. "I'm going to try," she said. "Dad is taking me out to dinner, so I'll ask him then."

"You can't ask him," CiCi said. "You know what he'll say. He hates Brent."

"The only thing we agree on," Genie muttered.

"You can't ask him," CiCi repeated.

"I'll sneak out later if I can," Genie replied. "He usually has a few beers on the weekend. It'll be fine."

"God, I can't wait to get out of here," Kate said. "Laurie, I'm jealous you get to leave tomorrow."

"I don't really want to go," Laurie admitted. "I don't feel like I'm ready."

"I feel more than ready," Kate said. "Sometimes I feel like if I have to spend another minute here, I'll go crazy."

"I feel the same way," Genie replied. "I'm eighteen. Eighteen years old, and I have to sneak out of my dad's house just to hang out with my friends."

"Did I ever tell you guys that Kitty and Dan were my sixth foster placement in eight weeks?" Laurie asked.

"I overheard my parents talking about it once," CiCi said. "They said there had been a few."

"More than a few," Laurie said. "I ran away from every home they put me in until this one. That's one reason they sent me out of the county. Well, that and the trial."

"But you stayed with Kitty and Dan for six years," Genie said.

Laurie nodded. "Yep, and it feels weird to be leaving them voluntarily."

"It's not like you can't come back," Kate said. "Kitty and Dan aren't going to rent out your room or anything."

"I'm eighteen," Laurie replied. "And unlike your parents, that alleviates Kitty and Dan's responsibility to me."

"But you know they don't feel that way," Genie said.

"I know," Laurie said. "But I also know I'm leaving tomorrow."

"Aren't you even a little bit glad to be done with high school?" Kate asked.

"So glad," Laurie replied, laughing. "Unbelievably glad."

"Me too," the other three agreed.

"We could have been done in December if you'd all been willing to follow the schedule I made for us," Genie replied.

"There was no way I was going to come in an hour early every morning to take calculus," CiCi said. "I barely made it through Algebra II."

"You didn't even follow your own schedule," Kate pointed out. "And you think we should have followed it?"

"I didn't need to follow it," Genie said. "I was done in December anyway."

"You finished your credits, and you still came to school?" CiCi asked. "Why?"

Genie shrugged. "I like school."

"I don't understand you," CiCi said. She looked down at her watch. "I've gotta go home and change my clothes before the party. Kate, are you coming?"

"Yeah," Kate said, standing up. "We'll see you guys later?"

"I might stop by for a few minutes," Laurie said. "Maybe."

"Bye!" Kate called over her shoulder.

Laurie and Genie stared after them, watching the sun sink

lower in the sky. "You're not going to go tonight," Genie said to Laurie once CiCi and Kate were out of earshot.

"Neither are you," Laurie replied.

"True," Genie admitted.

"Will you come over tomorrow morning before I leave?" Laurie asked. "Kitty says we need to be on the road by about seven thirty."

"Of course," Genie replied. "I wouldn't miss it. And you know I'll be up there in August. We're going to be roommates. Don't worry."

Laurie looked down and nodded, trying to keep control of the tears threatening to spill onto her cheeks. "I know," she said.

"Then we'll graduate, and I'll be a teacher and you'll be a journalist, and we'll live next door to each other and raise our families together, and the only thing that we'll hate are the parties CiCi and Kate will still be inviting us to."

Laurie looked up from her feet and saw Genie's father walking toward them, a crumpled graduation program in his hand. "Your dad's looking for you," she said. "I think you better go."

Genie hopped off the swing and gave Laurie a quick hug. "I'll see you tomorrow morning," she said.

Laurie wanted to believe what Genie said. She wanted to believe they'd all be friends forever—that they'd raise families together and live close and still be having the same arguments well into their adulthood. But the practical part of her knew better, and deep down, she knew her friends knew it too. This night felt much more like an ending to something than a beginning.

Laurie stopped swinging and stood up. She knew Kitty and Dan would be looking for her by now, and for the rest of the night, at least, she knew just exactly where she belonged.

Chapter 1

Genie

Twenty Years Later

Genie walked through the sliding glass doors and signed her name, like always, in the guest book. For the last two years, she'd been coming over every single weekday at four o'clock, half an hour before her father went down to the cafeteria for dinner. She didn't visit at all on the weekends. The weekends, she believed, were her time, and she usually spent them on the couch with a bottle of wine and Netflix, a habit the internet told her was cliché and expected of single women approaching forty.

Harold Walker had a small suite at the end of the hallway, with a living room, bedroom, bathroom, and kitchenette. It was expensive, but Genie's father had always been smart with his money. He could afford it, and it was, after all, the only nursing home with an Alzheimer's unit *and* the only nursing home in their small town of Orchard Grove. Her father, had he known who and where he was, would have liked it, because there were so many rules to follow, and he'd liked rules. Genie liked it because it was close, and since she knew most of the people working there—and even living there—she knew her father was safe.

Genie found him where she always did—sitting in his recliner and dozing in front of the television. She helped him get ready for dinner on the nights when he would let her. Always a snappy dresser, her father liked to wear a bow tie every evening to the cafeteria.

"Dad," Genie said, touching his arm lightly. "Dad, wake up. It's almost dinnertime."

Harold stirred slightly, his eyes rolling back so that Genie could see the whites.

Genie checked her phone. "Dad, it's after four. Look, Andy Griffith is on. You know when Andy Griffith comes on, it's time to get ready for dinner."

"It's been on all day," Harold replied, drawing himself up and out of the chair. Even stooped, he towered over Genie.

"Oh, that's right," Genie replied. "It's a Mayberry marathon. I told you last week."

"You did?"

"Yes, I did."

Harold's bushy white eyebrows furrowed. "I didn't see you last week," he said. "Are you new here?"

"Dad," Genie said. "It's me. Eugenia." She hated referring to herself by her given name, but sometimes using it triggered her father's memory. The nurses told her that she shouldn't get upset when he didn't remember her. They said it wouldn't always work to remind him who she was. Sometimes, they told her, it would even make him angry.

Tonight, however, all her father did was yawn.

"What bow tie do you want to wear?" Genie asked. "I'll get it out for you."

"It doesn't matter," Harold replied. "I'm going to be late to the table, and that old coot Roger is going to be in my place."

Roger, her father always remembered.

"Not if we hurry," Genie replied, grabbing the red-and-white polka-dotted bow tie from the dresser drawer.

"Not that one," Harold replied, ripping the bow tie out of Genie's hands and throwing it back into the drawer.

Genie plucked a navy bow tie out of the drawer and secured it around her father's neck. He refused to wear clip-on bow ties, which he could have managed himself, so she or one of the nurses had to come help him. "There," she said.

Harold knit his eyebrows together and looked into the mirror. "I guess it will have to do," he said.

"You look very dapper." Genie reached out to straighten the bow tie, because her father's fumbling hands had knocked it a bit off-kilter.

Harold swatted Genie's hands away, and a hint of the man

he'd once been flashed in his eyes. "Are you married?" he asked her.

"No," Genie replied. "I'm not."

"It's not surprising," he said. "Men don't like women who weigh more than they do."

Genie sighed. "Dad," she said. "Please don't say that to the nurses."

"You're not my nurse?"

"I'm your daughter."

Genie followed behind her father until they got to the cafeteria, and she gave him a quick peck on the cheek as he sat down. Harold wiped it away with the back of his hand, the same way the petulant five-year-old boys in Genie's kindergarten class did when they thought girls gave them cooties.

"I'll see you tomorrow, Dad," Genie said.

"Not if I die first," Harold replied. "And what a sweet relief that would be."

After she left her father to his dinner, Genie walked over to the nurses' station to chat with Leah, the mother of Simone, a little girl in Genie's kindergarten class. Parent-teacher conferences had been nearly two weeks ago, and Leah couldn't ask for any days off, since she was still new at the nursing home. In fact, she was new to nursing altogether. She'd graduated with her RN only the spring before.

"I'm worried about Simone's reading," Leah said. "Are you sure she's ready for first grade?"

Genie folded her hands together on top of the desk. "She's right where she needs to be," she said. "She shouldn't be reading chapter books by the end of kindergarten."

"I was," Leah replied. "But she doesn't like to read. She doesn't even like me to read to her."

"She likes drawing," Genie replied. "She likes math."

"She can't like reading too?"

"It doesn't make as much sense to her right now," Genie said. "But it will. Trust me, it will."

Leah sighed. "I'm just worried."

"I'm not," Genie said. "She's a smart girl. She's a stubborn girl, but that's okay."

Leah reached out and put her hand on top of Genie's. "Thanks, Genie," she said. "I'll give your dad an extra ice cream after dinner."

"I don't think I'm allowed to accept favors," Genie replied, winking. "But my father thanks you."

Genie left the nursing home and sat in her car for a long time. She was a good teacher; she knew that. She'd always been good at teaching. Her father had been a good teacher too, although she knew that their techniques were vastly different. He'd expected excellence; no, he'd demanded it. The students who were capable rose to the challenge. The students who weren't, well, they knew better than to take his classes. Genie, on the other hand, taught kindergarten and preferred the children who were independent, like Simone. Her father wouldn't have liked Simone, and no amount of extra ice cream would have changed that.

For thirty-six years, Dr. Harold Walker had been a biology teacher at the high school in Orchard Grove, Missouri. Everyone loved him, and he was voted teacher of the year more times than Genie could count. When he retired five years ago, it wasn't because he wanted to go. It was because, more times than not, he'd shown up completely unaware of where he was or what he was doing there, and that's when Genie would have to make the short trek up from the elementary school and take him home. They'd seen his regular doctor, and then seen specialists, and then learned the awful diagnosis. Genie gave up her adorable rental near the historic downtown and returned to her childhood home to help him, but she couldn't manage it alone, and he'd moved into the long-term-care facility. It was odd, the transition from child to caregiver, but the truth was, Genie hadn't been a child in a very long time.

Genie had just turned four when her mother, Christine, died. She didn't remember much of that time, but she learned later that it was ovarian cancer that took her. Genie was an only child, and her father, a geneticist, worked for the government. That's why they'd chosen to settle in the small Missouri town—Christine's grandparents, the people who'd raised her, lived there. Harold could go off for weeks or months at a time, doing whatever it was that he did for the government, and Christine had the help of Nan and Pop.

For the next six years after her mom's death, Genie lived with Nan and Pop while her father continued his big government job. They showered her with love, too much love, her father always said, and it was nearly as traumatizing as her mother's death when, the spring Genie was ten, Nan and Pop both got sick and died, one right after the other.

That left Harold to care for his daughter, and with no more family members to pawn her off to, he was forced to quit his job and return to Orchard Grove for good. The high school felt lucky to gain such an accomplished scientist, and everyone treated Dr. Walker as if he walked on water, which was, of course, the way he'd always expected to be treated in a Podunk like Orchard Grove, where he was the intellectual superior of literally everyone.

Genie, for her part, did her best to make her father proud. She excelled in school, she kept her room tidy, and she was always on hand to do whatever it was Harold asked of her. She tried to keep her mess of thick, auburn hair out of her eyes, and she tried to stand up straight, even though it was in her nature to slouch. She tried to wear clothes that flattered her ample figure. She covered up the freckles that spilled across the bridge of her nose with concealer, because they reminded her father of her mother, and that made him sad. Still, it was hard to please Harold, and when he wasn't berating her for the way she made her bed or the B she'd gotten in physical education, he was completely ignoring her.

And just like that, it was as if the first ten years of Genie's life never happened. Her mother and her beloved great-grandparents were gone. The old Chrysler that Pop drove was sold for scrap, and it was replaced in the garage by her father's classic cars. Nan's piano was donated to the high school music room. Her father sold everything else at auction—all of the farm equipment and the animals; even Genie's beloved Australian shepherd, Skylar, had to find a new place to live. They kept the house, though, because her father saw no point in selling a perfectly good (and free) home. So at least Genie got to keep her bedroom.

Genie had begged her father to let her keep Skylar. She'd cried and cried, because that was the tack that always worked on Nan and Pop. Her father, though, told her to stop sniveling, and so she'd tried to reason with him, explaining that Skylar would be a good guard dog, and besides, he was as old as she was. They were even born in the same month! Who was going to want a retired cattle dog? No, the best place for Skylar was at their house, where Genie could take care of him.

Two weeks after Pop's funeral, Genie came home from school to find Skylar gone, and it was the first time (but not the last time) that Genie realized her father did not love her. At least, he didn't care about her feelings, and for Genie, that might have been worse. All she wanted was for someone, *anyone*, to care about how she felt.

It was around that time when Genie discovered books as an escape from her reality. Although she liked most of the books her father approved on their weekly trips to the library, it was the treasure trove of romance novels she found tucked away in the attic that really ignited in Genie a love for the written word. The books had been her mother's, and all Genie could figure was that her father forgot about them, the pages now yellowed and brittle from age. She spent hours in the attic after school, and she never brought a book downstairs. Her father didn't really care what she was doing, as long as she wasn't bothering him, and so she never had to worry that he'd come up looking for her. She came down at dinnertime, and they ate in silence, and then she'd scurry back up again until it was time to go to sleep.

It was her routine for years and years until she met Laurie in seventh grade. Genie was good at routine. She loved books, but she also loved schedules. She loved notes and charts and itineraries. If she kept herself busy enough with routine, Genie didn't have to worry about the fact that she didn't have any friends. Laurie—a foster kid staying with the Scott family— was brand-new at their little school. The Scotts always had foster children, ever since Genie could remember, but Laurie was different from most of them, who held back and didn't make friends, sure they'd be moving on again soon. Laurie was loud and boisterous, smart and sarcastic, and Genie knew they were going to be friends the moment Laurie told Mr. Dillard, the math teacher, that he could kiss her ass during an algebra test.

Laurie was sent to the office, and Genie invited her over for dinner. Genie knew that her father would be unhappy, but she also knew he wouldn't say anything—Dan Scott sat on the school board. Genie's father wouldn't want it getting back to him that the beloved science teacher had been hateful to one of his foster children.

After that, they were inseparable, and then in eighth grade, they were paired with CiCi and Kate, two popular girls who were already best friends, in gym class. Kate was the smartest student in their grade, and CiCi was the prettiest. Neither girl seemed to be thrilled about being placed with Laurie and Genie, but when Genie suggested they cut gym class the next day and go to her house to read dirty books in the attic, Kate and CiCi decided they hadn't given the scheduled, quiet girl with glasses quite enough attention.

Genie was never really sure how it happened, but by her freshman year in high school, she had three best friends, which was three more friends than she'd ever had, and it was the happiest time of her life.

A lot had changed in the years since, and at the same time, it hadn't. She passed the same places on her way home from visiting her father—the hair salon where she made awkward conversation with a woman she hadn't liked in high school; the grocery store, where she shopped late at night, right before closing, in case anyone saw her and judged her purchases; and the funeral home, where she'd attended her mother's funeral. Genie slowed down as she passed the funeral home, nearly coming to a complete stop. Outside, she saw Kitty Scott talking with Wade Collins, the director and owner of the funeral home. Genie wondered what they could be talking about—surely Dan was fine. If he'd died, the whole town would've heard by now. Still, Kitty looked pretty upset.

When Genie pulled into the driveway at home, she took her phone out of her purse and scrolled through her texts to find CiCi. Maybe she'd know what was going on. Genie typed out a couple of messages and then deleted them. She hadn't spoken to CiCi in a couple of months—they'd only waved at each other in passing. They sent occasional texts and exchanged messages on social media, but being friends with CiCi reminded Genie of orbiting planets around the sun. CiCi was the center of everything, and everyone else sort of spun around her, and Genie, as one of CiCi's oldest friends, was pretty far back in the rotation. She was Pluto. Okay, maybe not Pluto, since Pluto wasn't even a planet anymore, but for sure Uranus. *Great*, Genie thought. *I'm Uranus.*

Genie silently cursed her father for putting scientific metaphors in her head. She really didn't know why she was being so paranoid about Kitty at the funeral home anyway. She was probably there on ladies' auxiliary business. They always made sure that when someone died, there were flowers for the service. It was part of their philanthropic duty, and Genie hoped when she died, there would be people like Kitty around to make sure her funeral wasn't bare.

Genie was so deep in thought that she didn't feel her phone vibrating in her hand until she was inside the house, staring up at the cabinets and wondering what to cook for dinner, knowing full well she was going to have canned spaghetti and a glass of milk like she did every night, and by the time she looked down and realized she had a missed call, she also had four text messages from CiCi, and every one of them read, *S.O.S.*

Chapter 2

CiCi

It wasn't as if CiCi thought the woman flirting with her husband was more attractive than she was. In fact, this woman was hardly attractive at all. Her dark roots were way too long to be fashionable, and her handbag looked like it came from the bargain bin at Walmart. Normally, CiCi would at least try to tell herself that those kinds of thoughts were mean, and she shouldn't be thinking them, but today she wasn't in the mood to scold herself.

She adjusted the lens on the binoculars she'd borrowed from her bird-watcher father and tried to get a better look. Brent, her husband, was still good-looking, but he had a gut where his abs used to be, and the stubble on his chin grew in silver instead of brown. But the woman flirting with him didn't seem to care, and she couldn't have been more than about twenty-five.

"Gold-digging hussy," CiCi said under her breath to the empty car.

Of course, it wasn't like there was much gold to dig for—the car dealership where Brent worked and which he claimed to own was actually his brother's. Their father had figured out years ago that giving it to Brent was a bad bet. But since Brent was the face of the dealership—and had been since he was twenty years old and flunked out of college—everyone, especially women, always assumed he had the big bucks. Hell, CiCi thought that too, once upon a time. She'd married Brent a few years after high school thinking she'd have a perfect life.

She, however, was no longer in her twenties, and she knew the truth after two decades of marriage.

CiCi hid the binoculars under the seat and drove across the street to the dealership. She loved the way she looked behind the wheel of her pearl-white Tahoe; with her blond hair (devoid of discolored roots) pulled back into a steep ponytail and her larger-than-necessary sunglasses, CiCi Rogers looked every bit the rich man's wife. Gold or no gold, it was the only part she was willing to play. She'd worked hard all these years, unlike Brent, to maintain her figure. She'd even had a tummy tuck after their second daughter was born, and she spent at least an hour on her Peloton every day. She looked good, and she knew it, even if she was every single soccer mom cliché that ever existed. Cliché looked good on her.

CiCi turned off the Tahoe and hopped out, attempting to make her gait casual, even though she could feel a spring in her step that would give her away to everyone at the dealership. They knew what she looked like when she was pissed off, because that was her only mode lately.

Brent saw her coming and attempted to pawn the other woman off onto one of his salespeople, but the woman wasn't having it. She stayed firm, stuck like glue to Brent's side, despite CiCi's approach.

"What are you doin' here, babe?" Brent asked her. "Did you call? I didn't hear my phone ring."

CiCi sidled in next to Brent and filled the narrow space between him and the woman, forcing the woman to back up when CiCi's large Chanel bag knocked up against her hip.

"Hey! Ow!" the woman said, backing away.

CiCi ignored her and leaned in to kiss Brent. "I just thought I'd stop by before I headed to pick up Lily from dance."

"I thought you usually stayed for practice?"

"Oh, I just had a couple of errands to run," CiCi said airily. "Mom and Dad wanted me to pick up a few things for them while I was out."

CiCi watched as Brent resisted the urge to roll his eyes. It wasn't that he disliked her parents exactly, but he resented the fact that her parents moved in right next door to them nearly ten years ago, and Brent had basically been their gardener and mechanic and handyman ever since.

"So are we going over there for dinner tonight?" Brent asked. "Because I think I might be a little bit late." He looked past CiCi to the blonde with the cheap handbag.

CiCi dug her fingernails into her palms and replied, "We go over there every Wednesday, Brent."

"Well, I'm gonna be late tonight."

"I really wish you wouldn't be."

Brent tried to smile, but it came out as more of a grimace, and everyone except the woman with the cheap bag had the good sense to back away slowly and head for safety. "Darling, it's nothing I can help."

"Well," CiCi said, turning her gaze slowly away from Brent and to the woman. "It doesn't look like it'll take long to change her oil, and dinner starts at seven. If you're not home in time to eat, maybe you should consider not coming home at all."

On the way home, CiCi took a detour and pulled into the parking lot across from the funeral home. She always parked there, in the little parking lot with the bakery and the flower shop, so that nobody would know she was actually across the street with Wade Collins at the funeral home. People might assume—and assume incorrectly—that the two of them had taken up an affair. They hadn't, although CiCi would have been lying if she said she hadn't thought about it. Wade, despite the awkward phase that lasted all of his childhood and teenage years, turned out to be incredibly attractive as an adult, and if a woman could get past the dead bodies in the mortuary, Wade was quite the catch.

But what CiCi had going on with Wade was much more innocent than that. For the last few months, she'd been secretly doing hair and makeup for the main attraction at every funeral, which was just a nicer way of saying she'd been coiffing the hair and painting the lips of the local corpses. It was Wade who called the bodies "the main attraction." He had a wonderful sense of humor, but he was also patient and so kind with everyone in a way that made CiCi realize that it was possible for men to care about the feelings of others.

He'd posted an ad in the local paper looking for a stylist, and CiCi overheard the only four stylists in town talking about it at the salon, and when she realized that none of them were going to apply for the position, she went to see about it for herself. At first Wade said he wanted to hire a licensed stylist, but once CiCi showed him pictures of her daughters at pageants when they were little girls, he'd taken her on on a trial basis. Last week, Wade asked her to stay on full-time. He'd been hurt when she said she wasn't sure if it was a job she could tell people about, because what would they think? Wouldn't they gossip about her behind her back? Wade clamped his mouth shut and hadn't said the thing she knew he was thinking—*everybody already gossips about your philandering husband behind your back.*

Philandering was totally a word that Wade would use.

Now, instead of getting out and sneaking into the funeral home, CiCi watched as Wade spoke to Kitty Scott just outside the doorway. There had been a time in her life when CiCi spent more time at Kitty's house than her own, and sometimes she missed it. She hoped everything was okay with Dan. He'd been in poor health the last few years—not that Dan or Kitty would have admitted it. No, that information came from Laurie, who still loved them like her own parents.

CiCi looked down at her phone. She hadn't talked to Laurie in a while. Come to think of it, she hadn't spoken to Kate or Genie much either. They sometimes had four-way chats on social media, but they rarely bothered unless there was some big news to share. She figured Dan dying would have been big enough for Laurie to share, and besides, it'd be all over town by now. She double-checked her messages just in case.

After a few minutes, Kitty reached out to hug Wade, and he awkwardly reciprocated before waving her off. He caught sight of CiCi and trotted across the street and over to her Tahoe. CiCi sat up in her seat and did a quick mirror check to make sure she didn't have mascara smeared under her eyes before she rolled down the tinted window.

"Are you going to come inside?" Wade asked. He leaned his elbows up against the door.

CiCi shook her head. "No, I have to go get Lily from practice. I was just going to stop in and say hi while I had a few minutes, but then I saw you talking to Kitty. Is Dan all right?"

Wade furrowed his brow. "Have you talked to Kitty?"

"No," CiCi replied. "Why? Wade, what's wrong?"

"I think you better talk to Kitty," Wade said.

CiCi let out a sigh of frustration and said, "Wade, I swear to God if you don't just tell me what's happened, I'm going to scream. I've had the worst day, and I don't have time . . ."

Wade reached inside the Tahoe and took one of CiCi's hands

in his, stopping her cold. He was looking at her with such pity that CiCi felt her heart drop down into her stomach.

"Seriously, Wade," she said. "What is it?"

"I'm so sorry to have to be the one to tell you," Wade replied. "But it's not Dan; it's Laurie. CiCi, Laurie died yesterday."

BY THE TIME CiCi arrived home after retrieving Lily from dance practice, she was numb. She hadn't even heard anything Wade said after *died*. She couldn't remember anything, really, about the last hour of her life. She told Lily she had a headache.

At her parents' house, CiCi let Lily run in ahead of her; Lily was excited to tell her Grammy about the solo she'd secured for the Fourth of July recital. She listened to the excited voices spill out of the house and let them wash over her. She took a deep breath. She needed to call Genie and Kate. She needed to tell them, but she didn't know how.

Her mother was waiting for her at the front door and embraced her. "Oh, honey," she said. "I just heard. Oh, baby, I'm so sorry."

CiCi blinked back tears. If she started crying now, she knew she would never stop. "Who told you?" she asked, pulling away. "Was it Kitty?"

CiCi's mother nodded. "She didn't have your number, but Wade called to tell her that he'd told you. . . . Honey, where did you see Wade?"

Before CiCi could answer, she felt her phone vibrate in her

hand, and she unlocked the screen to read the text message, expecting it to be Genie or Kate. *Tell your parents sorry. Don't wait up.*

It was Brent. Of course it was.

CiCi shoved her phone down deep into her jeans pocket. "I'll be right back," she said.

"Where are you going, Mom?" Lily asked.

"Stay here," CiCi said, turning around. "I said I'll be right back."

"Let her go," CiCi's father said, putting his arm around Lily. "She just needs some time to be alone."

CiCi walked next door to her own house and opened the door—Brent always forgot to lock the door when he left in the morning, despite CiCi's attempts to remind him—and stepped inside. She looked around the entryway. She always kept the house neat as a pin, but living with two teenagers and a husband meant that there was nearly always something lying around to make things look messy. She bent down and picked up Brent's running shoes and proceeded up the stairs.

She took a left at the top and pushed open the door to the bedroom they shared and continued picking up his dirty clothes. Finally she opened up the hamper and dumped it all in. Surveying the now clean floor in front of her, she picked up the hamper and set it down by the window.

It was a large window, meant for gazing out into the rolling Missouri hills while sitting at the window seat. It took only a second to get the window open, and it took even less time for

CiCi to pick up the hamper and throw it out the window. She watched as it landed with a crack on the patio. Before long, nearly everything of Brent's was outside.

Returning downstairs, CiCi poured herself a drink from the crystal decanter that Brent kept in his office—the special whiskey, for special occasions or special car clients. She downed the first glass and poured another. After the third glass, she picked up the decanter and carried it with her to the garage, where she retrieved the lighter fluid from Brent's grill.

As she poured the lighter fluid all over the tangle of belongings outside, she could see her parents and daughters watching her from the terrace of her parents' house. Ignoring them, CiCi put the can down on the wrought iron patio table and went in search of her pack of emergency Marlboro Lights. She hadn't smoked a cigarette since Lily's last dance recital, when Melissa Bennett, the dance coach, had pulled CiCi aside and told her she thought Lily was gaining a bit of weight. It had taken all of CiCi's willpower not to punch Melissa right then and there. Instead, she'd pulled out her emergency pack of cigarettes and smoked behind her car while the competition danced to a Cardi B song.

Tonight, though, as CiCi lit a cigarette and then lit a fire of her husband's clothes, it wasn't about willpower. It was about destruction.

"Cecile! My God! What are you doing?" CiCi's mother said, running into the yard. "Have you lost your mind?"

CiCi took a drag and wished she'd thought to grab her Prada sunglasses from her purse to watch the carnage.

"CECILE!"

CiCi didn't acknowledge her mother. She wasn't acknowledging anyone. If she slowed down to think about it, if she gave her concentration to anyone else but the fire raging in front of her, she knew she'd break down. She wasn't ready to cry—not about Laurie, not about Brent. Besides, Laurie couldn't be dead. She'd heard wrong. Everyone heard wrong.

"CiCi!"

CiCi turned slightly when she heard a new but not unfamiliar voice behind her calling her name. It sounded a lot like Genie.

"CiCi!" Genie was flailing her arms and running toward CiCi.

For a moment, CiCi didn't know what was going on, where she was, or what she was doing, but when Genie embraced her, she felt herself melt against her, and they sank to the ground.

"She's gone," CiCi said.

"I know," Genie replied. Her voice was soft, muffled by a pain that CiCi recognized as her own. "I know."

They sat together and watched the fire blaze. Neither of them said anything for a while, until there was the faint sound of sirens in the distance.

"How did you find out?" CiCi asked.

"Kitty called me," Genie said.

"So it's true."

Genie only shrugged.

CiCi looked away from Genie and back to the fire. "Brent is cheating on me," she said. "And I thought this would make me feel better."

"Did it?" Genie asked.

CiCi sniffed. "I mean, yeah. A little."

"I think someone called the fire department," Genie replied.

CiCi stood up and grabbed the crystal decanter. She took a swig, and then, sitting back down, handed it over to Genie. "Here," she said. "Take it."

Genie smelled the decanter. "Jesus, CiCi, what is this?"

"Shut up and take a drink," CiCi replied.

Genie did as she was told.

CiCi looked out into the crowd that had gathered around them, the faces slightly warped from the flames. It looked as if the entire neighborhood had turned out to watch the scene unfold, and she could see the town's only two fire trucks pulling up to the curb. This was going to be a topic of conversation in Orchard Grove for a long time. She wondered if they all knew about Laurie.

Laurie.

Laurie was dead.

Genie handed the decanter back to CiCi. "I think I see your husband."

"Genie," CiCi said. "I don't think I can do this tonight."

"You set his clothes on fire," Genie said. "I think you may at the very least need to tell him to get a hotel room."

"Can't you tell him for me?"

"No," Genie replied.

"Have you talked to Kate yet?" CiCi asked.

"I left her a message on her cell and at her office to call me," Genie replied.

"Do you think she knows?"

Genie sighed and watched as the crowd of onlookers parted down the middle for three men carrying a giant hose, followed by a bewildered-looking Brent. She reached over and patted CiCi's arm. "If she doesn't know by now," Genie said, as the flash of a camera went off somewhere in the distance, "she will soon, I promise."

Chapter 3

Kate

Kate was sitting in the waiting room at the St. Louis County Jail when she first saw the video. She was there to see a client who'd just been denied an appeal, and as she scrolled through social media on her phone, she saw that nearly every one of her friends from Orchard Grove had shared the same video.

At first Kate wasn't sure what was happening. There was clearly a fire, but she didn't know who the people were. The video was blurry, and it was shot from too far away to recognize anyone. Then the video zoomed in on one of the people, taking a drink from what looked like some kind of jug, and Kate realized—the people in the video were people she knew, people she'd known a very long time. The two women in the video were two of her childhood best friends—CiCi Rogers and Genie Walker.

What are they doing? What are they burning? Why are people watching them and taking a video?

Kate closed her social media app and then went to her messages. There was nothing new from either Genie or CiCi. In fact, she'd been the one to send the last message nearly two months ago, humblebragging about one of her sons making first-string lacrosse, but clearly *something* was going on.

There was a knock on the waiting room door, and Kate shoved her phone down into her briefcase and tried to look blasé when her client was brought in.

"How have you been, Loraine?" Kate asked after the woman had settled in across from her at the metal table.

"Fucking fantastic, thanks," Loraine replied.

Loraine was the kind of woman that most men would have said had "resting bitch face." She had a permanent sneer on an otherwise pretty face, and Kate knew that was something they were going to have to work on. She didn't like telling her clients they had to smile or change their expressions for the benefit of the judge or jury—it offended every feminist fiber of her being—but she was also a smart attorney who knew that judges and juries were often men, and those men would make an assumption about the women she defended before she'd even had a chance to, well, defend them.

"Well," Kate began. "The good news is that one of the key witnesses backed out, which will weaken the state's case, should our final appeal for a new trial be accepted."

"Bobby backed out, did he?" Loraine asked.

Kate looked down at her paperwork. "Robert Tilson, yes."

"I told Eddie that if he didn't light a fire under his ass about this witness bullshit, that when I got out, I was comin' for 'em both," Loraine replied smugly. "They listen to me, ya know."

"Loraine," Kate whispered, leaning in closer to her client. "You can't talk like that."

"You're my lawyer, ain't ya? Anything I say to you is privileged, right?"

Kate was about to respond when she felt her phone vibrate from inside the pocket of her briefcase. Hoping it was her assistant with the results of another jury trial from the day before, she held up a finger to Loraine and retrieved her phone.

Instead, she saw a missed call from Genie. Before she could put her phone away, a message popped up from Genie as well. It read—Please call me ASAP.

Quickly, Kate typed out—I'm with a client. Is everything okay?

There was just a one-word response—No.

Kate turned her phone over and nestled it between her legs and then looked up at Loraine. "Listen," Kate said. "You can't go around talking about that kind of stuff. Do you understand? If your cell mates hear you talking about intimidating witnesses, you'll be looking at more than an eighteen-month sentence for aggravated assault, Loraine, and it won't matter if Jesus Christ himself is your lawyer, he won't be able to get you out of that."

"How many times do I have to tell you, it wasn't no aggravated assault? I was *defending* myself," Loraine replied, pushing back in her chair.

Kate sighed. "I know, I know. But the county prosecutor doesn't see it that way. Your husband needed forty-eight stitches."

"He fell into the countertop," Loraine replied. She crossed her arms over her chest.

Kate's phone buzzed again, and she sighed. She didn't actually blame Loraine, not really, because it probably *was* self-defense. Loraine's husband had done serious time in the nineties for assault and battery and drug charges. He wasn't a good guy by any stretch of the imagination. Hell, Kate herself had considered doing the same thing when, nine months ago, Austin had come home from work and announced he wanted a divorce. She'd thought about it every day since, as one humiliation after the next plagued her life, from hiring a lawyer she knew to losing the house to her boys deciding they'd rather live with their dad and his new live-in, cookie-baking girlfriend. Forty-eight stitches seemed like a pretty small price for Austin to pay, actually.

"Hey, lawyer lady, can you hear me?" Loraine was waving her arms in front of Kate, who'd apparently been staring off into space for quite some time. "You all right? You can't quit on me like the last guy. I have the right to an attorney, and not a damn crazy one neither."

Kate's phone continued to buzz as she tried to concentrate on Loraine. A small shiver of panic ran through her when she considered that maybe Genie and CiCi had found out about her divorce. Had Laurie told them? Had her father?

Kate tried to grab ahold of her phone, but her hands were so clammy that it dropped down onto the concrete floor, face-down, and both women heard the crack of glass as the screen shattered.

"Ah, shit," Loraine said. She bent over to get a better look at the phone. "Should have gotten a screen protector. Ya know, my cousin Freddie sells them for five bucks apiece down at the Snap Mart off the bypass. You can tell him I sent ya, and he'll give you a discount. Just don't ask about his glass eye. He don't like talkin' about it."

Kate bent down onto the concrete floor to collect her phone, ignoring Loraine. Despite the cracks in the screen, the phone continued to buzz, and this time, it was a text message from her assistant. It was a screenshot of a news article, and the text read—Isn't she your friend?

Kate clicked on the screenshot to enlarge it and read the headline—"Award-Winning Novelist and St. Louis Native Laurie Lawson Dies of Apparent Heart Attack."

There was nothing else except a list of the books Laurie had written and a small note that this was a developing story and would continue to be updated. Kate stared hard at her phone. It didn't make any sense. She'd just spoken to Laurie the week before, and everything was fine. They'd even made plans to meet for lunch one day soon.

"You all right?" Loraine asked. Her tone was genuinely concerned.

Kate had to hold back the flood of tears she knew was coming. "Loraine," she said, standing up. "I've got to go. I'm so sorry. I've got a personal issue to see to."

Loraine cocked her head to one side as Kate pounded on the door for the guard to release her. "Freddie can take care of personal problems too," Loraine called after her. "Cost you more than five bucks, but he'll throw in a screen protector for free!"

By the time Kate got back to her house in Arnold, about forty-five minutes and a whole lot of traffic away from St. Louis, it was late. She still hadn't gotten used to driving all the way to Arnold, and she still hadn't gotten used to the townhome she'd rented after the divorce. The boys didn't like it, because it was small, and they openly balked at coming to visit on the weekends. They were eleven, and they didn't think they needed their mother anymore, but it was a deep wound that Kate didn't like to acknowledge or address. She knew that their decision had a lot to do with the fact that she worked long hours as a public defender, while her ex, Austin, had a lucrative personal-injury firm in St. Louis. Not only did Kate make less than half of what Austin made, but he and his live-in girlfriend, Angie, could be there for the boys' school and sports activities.

Truly, it was a no-brainer. *Of course* they wanted to live with their father. Hell, half the time, *Kate* wanted to live with Austin. *More* than half the time, if Kate was being honest. She hadn't wanted the divorce, not at all, but just like the boys' decision to live with their father, Kate understood why Austin wanted a divorce. Her work as an attorney came first. It always had. It probably always would.

To add insult to injury, Kate liked Angie. She was calm and reserved and completely unassuming in ways that Kate would never, ever be. Kate's appearance matched her personality— hard to miss. She was tall and leggy with dark, glossy hair and wide-set green eyes.

In the courtroom, Kate knew she could be menacing, and it was a character trait she often forgot to leave at the door. Kate thought, most days, it was probably better to live alone.

But that didn't mean she didn't get lonely. When her coworkers and friends suggested she get a dog after the boys moved out, Kate scoffed at the idea. Really, a dog? Was she that desperate? She knew all about women her age who got dogs after their divorces—they were the women she saw having brunch alone on Sunday, feeding a tiny Yorkie pieces of turkey bacon. No, she was definitely *not* that woman.

Then, six months ago, she'd run into Laurie at a charity event. Although they went to lunch at least once every couple of months, Kate hadn't divulged the details of her separation until that night, and even then, it was only after they'd escaped their dates and had a few drinks. Kate was there on the arm of the district attorney, since he was also recently divorced. Laurie was there with a man at least fifteen years her junior who had bleached-blond tips that reminded Kate of a boy band she'd been obsessed with in high school.

Laurie not only insisted Kate get a dog but also demanded that Kate rescue one of the dogs at the shelter Laurie worked with. Before the night was over, Kate found herself agreeing not only to adopt a dog but to come by the next afternoon at five o'clock for a private viewing of all the adoptable animals. Apparently, when you donate a lot of money to a rescue, you can do things like schedule private viewings. Laurie, ever modest, hadn't told Kate how much she'd donated, but Kate heard through the grapevine that Laurie often gave hundreds of thousands of dollars to charities and this one in particular.

At the rescue, Kate walked past each kennel, surprising herself by how sad it made her to realize that none of the animals there had homes. She'd always been of the opinion that homeless animals came in at a far second to homeless people, and she'd never really been inside an animal shelter. She felt a bit overwhelmed, but when she walked past the kennel of a dog sitting up on his hind legs and staring at her, one furry ear cocked to the side, Kate knew that she'd found the right one.

He was a Chihuahua mixed with a Chinese crested, a "Chi-Chi," as Laurie told her. He was just a year old, and he'd been for sale at a designer pet store before they went out of business and released all of the dogs to the rescue.

He was the ugliest dog Kate had ever seen in her entire life. He was hairless everywhere except for his ears, head, and tail.

He had a tremendous underbite, and he somehow managed to look startled all the time.

Kate took him home right then and there, and later that night, as she was sitting in front of the television reading over court documents and mindlessly listening to *Wheel of Fortune* in the background, the strange little dog began to bark every time the host, Pat Sajak, was on the screen. For the next week, Kate presented the dog with a myriad of game show hosts—Alex Trebek, Drew Carey, Howie Mandel, Steve Harvey, and even Ellen for good measure, but the only time the dog ever barked was during *Wheel of Fortune*.

From that moment on, Kate and Pat Sajak were inseparable. He went with her everywhere but to court, and he slept in her bed at night right where Austin used to sleep, except on a much fancier pillow. Kate even made friends with some of the brunch ladies and their designer dogs, and even though she'd never admit it to anyone but her therapist, at Christmas, Kate had treated Pat Sajak to a $560 Moncler hooded puffer vest from Saks and brought him to the local pet store to have his picture taken with Santa Paws.

Kate's sons thought the dog was hilarious, and they liked to take pictures of him to post on their Instagram page. Austin, of course, thought Kate's new pet was ridiculous, and his contempt was obvious after the dog pissed in one of his Armani loafers one afternoon when Kate came by to pick up the boys for a weekend at her house.

Pat Sajak got an extra treat that night for his efforts.

Kate sat her briefcase down on the table and collapsed into the couch. Pat was curled up in her lap within seconds, and all she could do was sit and stare at the message from Genie. She knew she should call her back, but she didn't even know what she was supposed to say.

She kicked off her heels, hardly noticing the way the balls of her feet throbbed with the day's efforts. Most nights, the first thing Kate did was soak in a bathtub full of Epsom salts, but tonight, she simply curled her feet up underneath her and turned on the television—anything for a moment's distraction from processing the fact that one of her oldest friends was dead.

Ten minutes into the channel 4 news, and Kate realized that a distraction was going to prove more difficult than she'd anticipated. Laurie's picture was splashed all over the screen with a voice-over from the newscaster, announcing that bestselling novelist and St. Louis philanthropist Laurie Lawson was dead at the age of thirty-eight, and the apparent cause of death was cardiac arrest, although there would be no official cause of death until the coroner issued a report.

Kate stared hard at Laurie's picture, a picture Kate knew had been the headshot for her latest novel just a year ago. Laurie looked radiant. Her auburn hair was cut into a sharp bob, its natural curl smoothed, and her blue eyes sparkled. She had a smattering of freckles across the bridge of her nose that made her look younger than she really was, although the subtle crease of lines around her mouth gave her away. She just looked like . . . someone you'd want to know. She'd always been that way, Laurie. No matter where she was or who she was with, she had ways of making everything seem amazing. And then she opened up her mouth and whatever was in her head just fell out, and even the most shocked witness would be won over in no time. She'd even won over Genie's horrible Grinch of a father, and that was no small feat.

Kate looked down at her phone again, and, taking a deep breath, she returned Genie's call.

Chapter 4

Genie

Genie tried to focus on the book she was reading, but she couldn't. Her thoughts kept going back to Laurie. Her clothes smelled like smoke from the fire. Her chest still burned from the few drinks she'd had from the decanter. She didn't know what kind of alcohol it had been. Genie had never been very good at knowing the difference between drinks, especially hard liquor. She had a glass of pinot noir with dinner once in a while, but that was it. Her father had never approved.

Distracted, Genie did what she always did when she was stressed or upset—she reached for the notepad on her night-stand and made a list. She started with things she needed to do the next day, like call Kitty and Dan. She should ask if there was anything she could do to help with the funeral. Kitty told CiCi's mom that they were having the funeral here, in Orchard Grove, which surprised Genie a little. Of course, Laurie often said that the only family she ever really had were Kitty and Dan. Regardless, the polite thing for Genie to do was ask if she could help, and it didn't really matter that even the mere thought of attending Laurie's funeral, let alone helping with it, made Genie want to run to the bathroom and throw up.

Beyond being polite, Genie also knew that Laurie would do the same thing for her. She'd been taking care of Genie since junior high—sticking up for her and encouraging her and easing her into the transition of becoming an adult when all Genie really wanted to do was hide under the covers in her bedroom. Genie guessed that was why Laurie, and even Kate to some extent, treated her like she was fragile—a bird with a broken wing or some other metaphor often used for people who couldn't take care of themselves. At least CiCi, even though she could be really mean sometimes, treated Genie like she did everyone else.

Genie let out a silent curse when she bumped into her glass of milk with her notepad and the milk went sloshing out of the glass and onto the notebook and her shirt, and then she smiled to herself. She was wearing her faded old Boyz United shirt, a throwback to a time in her life when all she'd cared about were boy bands and her senior year of high school. She hadn't even realized she'd taken it out of the drawer and put it on. They all had one—Genie, CiCi, Kate, and Laurie. Well, Genie didn't know if everyone else still had them, but she did, and it was her favorite, softest shirt to wear to sleep. In high school, they'd all worn the shirt on the same day, except for the last time, and Genie was reminded that she hadn't always hated it when Laurie stuck up for her. In fact, there had been times when she'd been very, very grateful.

The last time Genie wore her Boyz United shirt in high school, they'd been in eleventh grade. She hadn't gotten the memo that they weren't going to wear the shirt anymore, and so she'd come to school in it, only to find that Kate, Laurie, and CiCi were much more interested in the football game that night than matching outfits.

That afternoon, Genie had found CiCi perched on a picnic table outside the high school, flirting with some idiotic football player whose name Genie hadn't bothered to learn. It was just such a cliché, the cheerleader and the football player, and the whole thing made Genie want to throw up.

Laurie and Kate had gone to the vending machines on the other side of the school campus, because lunch that day had been disgusting. Genie almost walked past CiCi, but CiCi saw her and motioned for her to sit down. CiCi told her all about the football player, who'd ambled off to stand in a circle of his own friends a few feet away. Every so often, the boys would look over at them and make some kind of remark that Genie never quite understood. CiCi understood, though, and she was clearly enjoying the attention.

"So, what do you think?" CiCi was asking her. She was leaned back on her elbows, staring at Genie upside down.

Genie furrowed her eyebrows. "What do I think about what?"

CiCi rolled her eyes. "You know, about me going out with Justin Friday night."

Genie looked over at Justin, who was staring straight at the gap in CiCi's silk tank top. "Uh, I don't know. I guess if you like him, you should go out with him."

CiCi stuck out her bottom lip and pretended to pout. "I told him I couldn't go out with him unless you said it was okay."

"Why would you tell him that?" Genie asked. She'd never known CiCi to ask her opinion *ever* when it came to the boys she dated.

CiCi sat up and turned to look at Genie. It was clear she was trying to communicate something to her friend, but Genie wasn't quite sure what it was until Laurie appeared behind them and said, "CiCi wants you to tell her she can't date Justin over there because she's too afraid to tell him she thinks he smells like her brother's gym socks."

Kate set a king-sized package of Twizzlers and a Diet Coke in front of Genie, plopping down beside her on the picnic table bench. "I don't think he smells like gym socks," she said, pretending to sniff the air. "It's more like a wet dog smell."

She'd said it just loud enough for Justin and his group of friends to hear, and they collectively moved closer to the girls. "Shut up, Kate," Justin said. "Nobody asked you."

"I don't need to be asked for my opinion before I give it," Kate replied. "Especially not by you."

Justin hesitated. This happened a lot with people when Kate spoke. Even at seventeen, Kate had a verbal prowess that was intimidating. Finally, he crossed his arms over his meaty chest, looked away from Kate, and said to CiCi, "I liked it better when you were just hanging out with your fat friend."

Genie felt her face flush crimson, but she didn't respond. She didn't even look at him. He was one to talk about being fat. His neck was the size of her thigh. She wasn't going to give him the satisfaction of knowing that he'd hurt her feelings, and it didn't make any sense to her why he'd make such a hateful comment about her as if she wasn't even there—*she* hadn't been the one to insult him.

Standing next to CiCi, Laurie took a step closer to Justin. "What did you say?" she asked.

"You heard me," Justin sneered. "You and Kate are both bitches. You always have been. I wouldn't screw either one of you with my buddy's dick. I'd rather take a pleasure ride on the SS *Genie*."

Genie's eyes flicked up to Justin at the exact same moment that Laurie's fist made contact with his nose. He let out a howl like a feral animal caught in a trap and stumbled backward, landing square on his ass on the concrete.

By now a small crowd had begun to gather around them, while Justin sat, bleeding and cursing. He at least had the good sense not to attempt to get up, because Laurie most assuredly would have knocked him down again.

Justin's mouth was full of blood. "I think you broke my goddamn nose," he moaned.

"Good," Laurie replied, crossing her arms. "Maybe next time you'll think before you insult someone for no fucking reason."

Kate and CiCi grabbed Laurie, one at each arm, and guided her through the crowd. Genie got up and followed, resisting the urge to kick Justin while he was down. Her father was going to kill her as it was, for even being a part of a fight at school. She couldn't imagine what he'd do if he heard she'd actually kicked someone, even if it was a jerk like Justin.

Genie trailed behind her friends. She already knew where they were heading. They were going to the gymnasium to find the softball coach, Mrs. Horton. Laurie was a star softball player, and there were several good colleges scouting her. Since ninth grade, Mrs. Horton had been running interference for Laurie at school, keeping her from being suspended several times when she should have been for fighting or skipping class or something similar, but Genie knew that if Laurie didn't get control of her temper, even when she was sticking up for her friends, she'd never make it on a college softball team.

"I just see red, ya know?" Laurie was saying as Kate and CiCi eased her down onto a chair in Mrs. Horton's office. "Justin is such an asshole. He never should have said anything to Genie."

"Not again, Laurie," Mrs. Horton said, resting her forehead on the palms of her hands. "You've already got one strike against you, and it's just September."

"He deserved it," Laurie replied, sullen.

"I don't know how many more times we can use the mother-in-prison excuse."

Laurie bit at the corners of her mouth, and Genie sat down beside her and put her hand on Laurie's arm. "I appreciate you sticking up for me, Laur," Genie said. "But you just can't do stuff like that. You're going to get expelled this time for sure."

"I went to see her last weekend," Laurie replied. "She wrote Kitty a letter and asked to see me, and Kitty told me I didn't have to, but I had to go so I could tell her to her face that I didn't want her to write anymore. I don't ever want to see her again."

Everybody in the room except for Genie looked away—down at their hands, at paperwork on Mrs. Horton's desk, at the clock on the wall—anywhere to keep from having to look at Laurie. But not Genie, and that was why she and Laurie were best friends. Genie never looked away. She simply leaned over and gave Laurie a hug.

Everybody in Orchard Grove knew the story of Laurie's parents. Laurie had grown up two towns over, closer to the St. Louis side of the county. Her mother had been a secretary for the elementary school and her father had worked for the railroad. By all accounts, it was a comfortable life. Then one night while Laurie was asleep in her bed upstairs, Laurie's mother shot Laurie's father in the living room of their house. Her mother had immediately called the police, and they came and arrested her mother and took Laurie away. That's how she'd come to live with Kitty Scott and her family halfway through Genie's seventh-grade year.

The rumor always was that Laurie's father used his wife as a punching bag every chance he got, but Laurie's mother would never admit to a motive for the murder, and so she was sentenced to life in prison. Laurie, for her part, never spoke about it except to talk about how much she hated her mother.

It was no wonder that Laurie sometimes lashed out, and most of the time people were understanding and kind. Still, punching a football player in the nose probably wouldn't garner her much sympathy from the powers that be at school. She was going to get suspended for sure this time, which could affect her ability to play softball.

Mrs. Horton stood up. "I want you girls to stay right here. *Right here*, do you understand me? I'm going to go and find the principal."

CiCi, Kate, Genie, and Laurie nodded in unison.

"Maybe we'll get to stay down here for the rest of the day," CiCi said once Mrs. Horton was gone. "How awesome would that be? I heard that Mrs. Horton watches *As the World Turns* every day at one o'clock."

"CiCi," Kate replied. "Don't you think we have bigger things to worry about than watching some stupid soap opera?"

CiCi shrugged. "Well, I didn't punch anybody."

"This is all your fault!" Genie said. "If you hadn't been flirting with that absolute Neanderthal, none of this would have happened."

"I didn't do anything!" CiCi replied, plopping down on one of the beanbags on the opposite side of the room. "*I'm* not the one who went all *Armageddon* on Justin."

"That's right," Kate said. "You didn't do anything when

Justin was flirting with you, because we all know you have it bad for Brent and want to make him jealous by flirting with the grossest guy on the team."

"Justin Wilson is the grossest guy on the team," CiCi replied pointedly.

"And you dated him too."

"I did not," CiCi said.

"You did too," Genie replied. "I have a list. Do you want to see it?"

"You have a list?" CiCi asked. "That's creepy."

"You asked me to keep a list," Genie said. "Remember? You said if you had a list, you could avoid dating the same guy more than three times."

"Fine!" CiCi said, throwing her hands up in the air. "Fine. I'm sorry. It's my fault. I suck."

"It's okay," Laurie said, getting up from the chair where she was sitting and plopping herself down beside CiCi. "I hate that guy. I've been looking for an excuse to punch him since junior high."

"He does have the most punchable face in the senior class," Genie admitted, a small smile creeping across her face.

"So, really," CiCi said, shoving Laurie from the beanbag onto the floor with a giggle, "I did us all a favor."

Chapter 5

Kate

Kate hated going back to Orchard Grove, even on happy occasions like Christmas, which was something she did faith-
fully ever year for her father. She spent twenty-four hours
there with the boys, which was just long enough for her to see
half the town (usually the half she didn't like) and just short
enough for her brothers to complain that she didn't visit them
because she was a fancy lawyer now and thought she was better than they were.

Today, Kate knew, she'd see everyone. Every single able-
bodied person in Orchard Grove would be coming to pay their
respects to Laurie, who, like Kate, probably hadn't liked them
either.

It turned out that Kitty hadn't wanted anyone's help with
the funeral and, in fact, planned to have a completely private
service, which had apparently been at Laurie's request. She'd

left written instructions that, in case of her unexpected death, everything be left low-key. She feared a public funeral might bring droves of her fans to Orchard Grove, and to be quite honest, the tiny town was completely unprepared. Instead, there was a planned family night, and it wasn't even mentioned in the local newspaper. Everyone in town found out through word of mouth, and the mouth had of course been CiCi's. The only thing Kitty asked for Genie, CiCi, and Kate to do was to come to the family night and be there with her and Dan to welcome people as they arrived.

Kate wanted to do anything other than that. But Genie insisted that they all three be there, and she wasn't about to refuse to show. She guessed it was better than having the funeral in St. Louis—because then people would be asking her where her husband was, and she couldn't very well tell them that he'd left her for someone who worked *less* and probably gave *more* blow jobs.

Ugh, that was such an antifeminist thing to think. (And she reminded herself she liked Angie.) But damn, supporting all women sure was hard sometimes, especially when at least one of those women was living with her ex-husband and playing house with her children. Even though Laurie hadn't had any children, and she'd never kept a husband for longer than a couple of years, she seemed to understand the desperation Kate felt. Laurie hadn't pitied her like Genie would have or been secretly happy about it like CiCi. Laurie just listened as Kate drank more wine than she should have and said things that made her cringe when she woke up in the morning and remembered.

So, Kate thought, leaning her forehead against her steering wheel. *I can do this for Laurie.*

She felt the tears well up, and she blinked rapidly. God, what was she going to do without her? What were any of them going to do without her?

When she looked up, Genie and CiCi were standing under the awning of the funeral home, waiting for her. When Genie caught her eye, she gave her a tentative wave. Kate got out of the car and walked over to her friends. She couldn't help but think about how the day was too pretty and too warm for something like this to be happening. It was an odd feeling for everything around her to be warm and cheerful when she felt so cold on the inside.

She let out a little sigh of relief when Genie reached out to hug her. Genie was good at hugs, and Kate supposed it was because Genie was a kindergarten teacher. Lord knew Genie hadn't learned to hug from her father.

"We should go inside," CiCi said. "I think Kitty and Dan are waiting for us, and everyone else will be coming in soon."

Kate hesitated. "Is she in there?"

"Who?" CiCi asked. "Laurie? Yes, she's in there. Where else would she be?"

"Is the casket . . ."

CiCi shook her head. "There isn't a casket. Laurie wanted to be cremated. So there's just a picture of her, an urn that Kitty and Dan picked out, and a copy of her first book."

"How do you know all of that?" Genie wanted to know. "Did I miss a town memo?"

The tips of CiCi's ears turned pink, which Kate knew from experience meant she was about to lie. "I ran into Wade yesterday," she said. "He told me."

"So she's gone," Kate said. She didn't even have the heart to wonder why CiCi would lie about how she found out. Laurie wasn't even inside, and she didn't know why, but for some reason, that felt worse than knowing she'd have to look at a casket.

"Come on," Genie said gently, ushering her forward.

Kitty and Dan were indeed inside, and they were talking to a man who Kate took more than a few seconds to recognize.

"Holy shit," Kate said under her breath to Genie and CiCi. "Is that Wade Collins?"

"Yeah," replied CiCi. "Didn't you know he came back to take over for his parents?"

"I knew he came back to take over for his parents," Kate said. "What I didn't know is that he got *hot*."

"I swear the single women in this town are killing their relatives just to spend time with him," Genie whispered. "Last month Old Man Kennecott died, and I've never seen as many low-cut black dresses in my life as I did at his funeral."

"Funeral Floozies," CiCi said. "Every single one of them."

Kate had to bite down on her tongue to keep from laughing, and when she noticed Genie was doing the same thing, she felt the weight of their reality lighten just enough so that she could breathe.

Kitty looked up from Wade and gave the women a weary smile. Her eyes were slightly red-rimmed, and she was clutching what looked like a very soggy tissue in one hand. "Oh, girls," she said, hurrying toward them and snuffling slightly. "I'm so glad you're here."

"Of course," CiCi said, leaning in to hug her.

"What can we do?" Genie asked.

"Just be here," Kitty said. "I know there will be so many people tonight, and I can't . . ." She trailed off, tears welling up.

"Don't worry," CiCi replied, hugging Kitty again. "We're here to help."

Kate marveled at CiCi's natural ability to comfort Kitty. It wasn't, Kate knew, an ability she herself possessed. She wondered if that was because she'd been raised by a single father, but looking at Genie, who seemed to have the same instincts as CiCi, Kate doubted that was it. Maybe it really was like Austin told her on the boys' first day of kindergarten when she hadn't cried at all—she lacked maternal instinct. She was broken somewhere deep inside. Laurie had felt the same way; they'd discussed it more than once, but at least Laurie had the good sense not to have children.

"Oh, CiCi," Kitty said. "How are you? Are you making it okay?"

Kitty wasn't asking how CiCi was taking Laurie's death. She was asking about something else entirely, and Kate knew it had everything to do with Brent, a fire, and a video circulating around all of Orchard Grove.

"I'm fine," CiCi said, smiling. "Everything is fine."

"Well," Kitty replied, squeezing CiCi's arm. "I'm glad to hear it."

By now people were beginning to stream in, and Kitty wandered off to tearily greet them.

"I don't want to do this," CiCi admitted.

"Nobody does," Genie replied. "Nobody likes this part."

"No," CiCi said. "No, I mean yes, I hate *that*, but I also don't want to do this because people are going to be asking me questions about Brent and whispering about me behind my back all night."

"Nobody is going to do that," Genie said. "Not here."

"Kitty did."

CiCi looked so miserable right then that Kate nearly told her about her own divorce, just to make her feel better, but when she opened her mouth, all that came out was, "We'll go get a big drink after this, okay?"

CiCi nodded. "A really, really big one."

Chapter 6

CiCi

CiCi hoped that it looked like she was close to tears because her friend was dead and not because she was upset that people in town were gossiping about her. Of course she was upset about Laurie. *Of course she was.* More than anything, she wished she could muster some of Laurie's strength and pretend she didn't care about anything anyone was saying—that her marriage was over, that her husband was a cheater, and that it was probably no wonder about either of those things, because she was batshit crazy. She'd made that clear in the video that was circulating around town and social media. She couldn't even go to the grocery store without someone stopping to pepper her with questions or pass by her with a sidelong, sympathetic glance.

She'd always been a worrier about what other people thought, even as a kid, and she'd found that the best way to keep that worry at bay was to just conform to what everyone else was doing, and if she was going to stand out, it needed to be for something positive, like being the head cheerleader or the prom queen. It was easier to quell the fears if she could tell herself people gossiped about her out of jealousy.

It was easier once she found Kate, and then easier still after Genie and Laurie. She was part of a group, a package deal, and it didn't matter what anyone else said, because they were her friends. But she'd really screwed up this time. Brent moved out. The girls were staying with her parents, and she was alone in a house she'd never really liked, anyway, worried that people she'd never really liked, anyway, were gossiping about her behind her back.

CiCi felt Genie squeeze her hand. *God, even Genie feels bad for me. This is the worst.*

"Did you see old Ms. Pills is here?" Kate whispered, bending down to CiCi's and Genie's height. "She hated Laurie."

"She hated everyone," Genie replied.

"Not as much as she hated Laurie," CiCi said. "Remember how she would make Laurie's essays an example to the class about what not to do?"

Genie and Kate both nodded. "She was the best writer in the class," Kate said.

"The whole school," Genie added. "That's why Ms. Pills hated her, I bet."

"What was it that she said to Laurie that time she gave her an F on that report about *Lady Chatterley's Lover*?" CiCi asked. "Something about crawling?"

"Oh my God," Kate said. "I forgot about that."

"She told her," Genie said, scrunching up her nose and trying to remember. "She said . . . she said Laurie had to learn to crawl in her class before she could walk."

"What does that even *mean*?" CiCi asked.

"Shhhh," Genie hissed. "She's coming over here."

Automatically, as if back inside the old woman's English classroom, all three of them stood up a little bit straighter as Ms. Pills marched toward them, still pretty spry for a woman of such advanced age.

"The pen at the guest book is out of ink," she said.

"Okay," Genie replied, looking between Kate and CiCi. "I'm sorry about that."

"Someone needs to fix it," Ms. Pills continued.

"We don't work here," Kate said.

"I simply cannot sign the guest book if there is no pen," Ms. Pills said. She continued to look up at them expectantly.

Kate opened her mouth to speak, but CiCi held up a hand and said, "I'll take care of it, Ms. Pills. I'm sure Wade has an extra."

CiCi turned and hurried toward the back of the funeral home and the office. She didn't turn around to see Kate or Genie staring after her, although she knew they were. She'd figure out a way to tell them later, about what she'd been doing here. Right now she just wanted an excuse to leave the room, which was filling up like a balloon full of hot air.

She breathed a sigh of relief when she got to the office and closed the door behind her. She knew right where Wade kept the extra guest book pens, but she sat down in the big leather chair and rested her forehead against the cool wooden desk.

"Are you all right?"

CiCi looked up to see Wade standing in the doorway of his office, his brow creased with concern.

She sat up and straightened the collar of her silk blouse. "Uh, Ms. Pills says the pen at the guest book is out of ink," she said. "I came back here to find another one, and I just . . ."

"Needed a break?" Wade finished.

"Need an exit strategy," CiCi said, trying to smile and failing miserably. "Or need a drink."

"You know we haven't kept alcohol on the premises since Mr. Belcher found my dad's bottle of whiskey in the desk drawer and got so drunk he knocked over his wife's casket during the funeral," Wade replied. "She rolled right out of the coffin. I don't think the poor pastor ever recovered from all that."

"I thought that was just a rumor," CiCi said.

Wade walked into the room and leaned up against the desk, positioning himself across from CiCi, and replied, "All rumors have at least a kernel of truth. But I won't tell you which kernel."

"Ugh, that's what I'm afraid of," CiCi said, putting her head back down on the desk. "It's so much easier to enjoy rumors when they aren't about you."

"I haven't heard any rumors about you," Wade said.

CiCi sat back in the chair. "That's because you spend all your time with dead people."

"The dead talk more than you think they do," Wade replied.

"You're so weird," CiCi said. She was smiling now. She couldn't help it, and for a moment, she considered apologizing to Wade for not seeing him for who he was in high school. Life, she thought, might have been a little different if she had.

"Here." Wade reached around her and pulled open the drawer on the right side of his desk. He took out a heavy black pen and handed it to her. "Take this out to Ms. Pills before she makes us stay after class to write sentences."

"I'd rather write sentences than go back out there," CiCi grumbled.

Wade closed his hand over CiCi's as she accepted the pen and said, "When you're ready, we'll give them something they can *really* gossip about."

CiCi felt her heart in her throat. She wanted to tell him she was ready, but even saying it in her head felt like a lie. She was so lonely it hurt, and she couldn't remember the last time she'd been touched or even looked at the way Wade was looking at her right then, but she wasn't ready. Not yet, and CiCi wished she could say how much the fact that he knew it meant to her.

By the time she got back out to the guest book, Ms. Pills had already gone. CiCi was trying to figure out how she was going to explain herself when Kate and Genie rushed up to her, her absence already forgotten.

"Ms. Pills escaped from the nursing home," Kate said.

"What?"

"She snuck out during dinner in the cafeteria," Genie said. "I've been in that cafeteria during the dinner rush, and it is nuts. Old people pushing and shoving to be first in line. Anyway, I guess she slipped out and actually *called a cab* to come and get her to take her here. She didn't even like Laurie! Anyway, the staff at the home called the police and everything."

"We all got Silver Alerts on our phones," Kate said.

"What's a Silver Alert?" CiCi asked. "I don't think I've ever seen one."

"It's like an Amber Alert," Genie replied. "Except for old people."

"God, Laurie would have loved this," Kate continued. "I bet she would have put it in a book."

CiCi grinned. "Yeah, she would have."

"CiCi," Genie whispered, elbowing her friend in the ribs.

"Hey, ow!" CiCi exclaimed.

"No," Kate said, stepping in front of CiCi's line of vision. "Don't look."

CiCi knew what was happening before she saw it, but that didn't stop the swell of anger she felt rising from the pit of her stomach. *How dare he.*

Just inside the doorway, in line to sign the guest book, was Brent, and he wasn't alone. He had on his arm the woman CiCi had seen at the dealership the week before. She'd known about the woman, of course, months before she'd seen her in person.

That was usually how it worked with Brent—as long as he kept the other women out of sight, CiCi didn't have to acknowledge that they existed. It was different this time, though. This woman had been at the dealership, and now, *NOW,* she was with him here, the one place Brent should have had the good sense to avoid.

"Ignore him," Kate whispered to CiCi. "Don't give him the satisfaction of a reaction."

"I think I'm going to be sick," CiCi said.

"Let's get out of here," Kate replied.

Genie glanced from CiCi to the front door and back again. "The only way out is through the front," she said. "We'll have to walk past them."

"That's okay," Kate said. She looped one of her arms through CiCi's. "Genie, you get her other arm. We'll just pretend we don't see them."

"I'm going to be sick," CiCi said again.

"Keep your head up," Kate replied. "Just put one foot in front of the other."

CiCi allowed them to guide her toward the door. She kept her eyes straight forward, even as she knew people around her were buzzing with the excitement of it all. Their whispers felt like waves crashing into her ears, and all she could hear was a dull roar, like putting her ear up to a conch shell at the beach.

Brent saw them as they approached, and he drew himself up to his full height, all five feet nine inches, and puffed out his chest when they paused in front of him and the woman he was with, to allow the congestion around the doorway to dissipate.

CiCi tried not to look at him. Her stomach was roiling, and her only thought was about making it outside before she threw up. She'd never been a crier. She could think of only a few times in her life she'd ever cried. She could count them on one hand, in fact. Instead, when she got upset or angry, CiCi threw up, and there was no stopping the tidal wave of vomit that was coming.

"You guys," CiCi said. She tried to swallow, but she couldn't.

Brent's eyes widened when he realized what was about to happen. He'd lived with her long enough—nearly twenty years, after all—to know what was about to happen. He glanced from CiCi to Kate and said, "You need to—"

"We don't *need* to do anything," Kate said, cutting him off. "You don't get to come here and tell us anything. I can't even believe you have the audacity to show up here. We're trying to *grieve* our friend. A friend who, by the way, couldn't stand you."

"But—" Brent began, his free arm, the arm that wasn't intertwined with the other woman's, motioning toward CiCi.

"This isn't her fault!" Kate replied, her voice near fever pitch. "Don't you dare blame her!"

CiCi couldn't control what came next. She twisted out of Kate's and Genie's grips and lurched forward, one hand clamped over her mouth. But not even her hand could stop the tidal wave of vomit that spewed out, landing directly, to her horror, all over Brent.

They all stood there for a few seconds, too stunned to say or do anything. It was as if the entire room was watching them, and despite the fact that CiCi was absolutely mortified by what just happened and still felt sick to her stomach, the image of Brent standing there covered in vomit, one hand still outstretched, was hilarious, and she began to giggle.

"Oh God," CiCi said, unable to hide her laughter. "I'm so sorry."

"Ew!" the woman beside Brent squealed, backing away from him. "Ew!"

Genie looked up and over the top of CiCi's head to Kate and said, "We've got to get her out of here."

Kate looked away from Genie and over to Brent. "I'd get myself cleaned up if I were you," she said to him. "And while you're at it, call a lawyer. You're going to need a good one, trust me."

And with that, Kate and Genie each took hold of one of CiCi's arms and helped her out of the building, tears of laughter, humiliation, and sadness streaming down her face.

Chapter 7

Genie

By the time Genie pulled into the driveway, it was completely dark outside. They'd made a quick stop at the liquor store, where Genie had refused to go inside, since someone from the school might see her. She knew it was silly, but one rumor that she was an alcoholic, and that would be her legacy. Nearly everybody, even the teetotaling Baptists, drank, but it's one thing to drink in secret behind closed doors and quite another to roll up to Pat's Party Pantry on a Friday night.

After that they'd made their way to Sonic, where they'd ordered Route 44 slushes. It had been their tradition in high school—they'd find someone, usually CiCi's stoner older brother, to buy them gin at the liquor store, and then they'd order slushes from Sonic for what they called "gin and Sonic."

Genie rushed CiCi and Kate inside, bottles of gin clanking in their handbags.

"Why do you care what the neighbors think, anyway?" Kate asked. "I don't even *know* my neighbors."

"I know all of my neighbors," CiCi replied. "I wish I didn't, but I do."

"Didn't your neighbors leave you outside in the snow when you broke your ankle?" Kate asked Genie.

"They did," CiCi said before Genie could reply. "She had to drag herself to where she'd dropped her phone and call me to come and get her."

"I said I know my neighbors," Genie grumbled. "I didn't say they weren't assholes."

"Wow," Kate said, stepping through the threshold and into the dimly lit house. "It looks the same as it did in 2000."

"That was probably the last time you were in here," Genie replied. She tried to keep the annoyance out of her voice. She'd been to Kate's house several times over the years, but Kate never came here, not even after her father went to the nursing home.

"Yeah, I don't understand why you don't make it more your own," CiCi said, glancing around. "You could, you know, now that your dad is at Shady Oak."

Genie shrugged. She couldn't tell them that she kept it the same because she still worried her father would come busting in the door one day demanding to know what *she'd* done to *his* house. "I guess I just hadn't thought about it."

"Well, you should," Kate said, twisting the lid off one of the bottles of gin. "Here, hand me your slush."

"No," Genie said. "You always put too much in it."

"I do not," Kate said, grinning.

"I'll do it," CiCi replied, taking the bottle from Kate. "Here, Genie, give it to me."

Genie sighed and handed her slush over to CiCi. "Not too much, not too much," she said.

"Are you sure you're even okay to drink?" Kate asked CiCi. "After your stunning performance earlier, I wasn't sure."

"I'm fine," CiCi said. "Totally fine. I don't want to talk about it."

"He's probably going to have to throw those shoes away," Kate continued, ignoring her. "And the look on that woman's face!"

"Just one more reason for my daughters to be embarrassed of me," CiCi muttered. "Lily won't even speak to me. She's staying with my parents, and she won't answer any of my texts or calls. She told my mother I was ruining her life, and I'm starting to think she's right."

"Oh, that's not true," Kate said, putting down her drink to wrap an arm around CiCi. "She's seventeen. Everyone is ruining your life at seventeen."

Genie felt pangs of guilt in her rib cage. She knew if she took her phone out of her purse, she'd have several texts from Lily asking her what happened earlier. She and Lily were especially close, and even though CiCi never came out and said it, Genie knew that CiCi was jealous. They were just so much alike, the two of them—shy and bookish and awkward, and CiCi, no matter what she said, wasn't any of those things. Lily had been texting Genie since the night of the bonfire, and Genie hadn't said anything to CiCi about it, for fear that she'd be upset and feel betrayed.

Genie absently took a drink of her slush and nearly gagged. "CiCi, this is all gin!"

"Sorry," CiCi said. "Hey! Let's go up to the attic!"

"How much have you had to drink already?" Kate asked. "Why would we go to the attic?"

"Like we used to, remember?" CiCi asked, pulling Kate along. "We'd sneak up there after school to eat snacks and look at those dirty books that belonged to Genie's mom."

"Romance novels," Genie corrected her. "They were romance novels. And they weren't dirty."

"They were soft-core porn," CiCi replied. "And I feel like they really set me up to be disappointed in sex and adulthood," she added. "I mean, I thought I'd have at least ten orgasms a day after reading that stuff."

Genie and Kate laughed, and Genie pulled down the door and stairs connected to the attic so that they could climb up.

"Uuuuugh," CiCi groaned. "This is not as easy as it was twenty years ago."

Once they were all three up the steps and crowded into the little attic, Genie flipped the switch to the little lamp beside the window and was surprised to find that it still worked. The room, now illuminated, looked almost exactly the same as it had the last time they'd been up there, only with a whole lot more dust.

"I haven't been up here for a couple of years," Genie said. "And that was just to store some boxes when I moved back in. I didn't even think to look around."

Kate picked up a dusty pillow and sneezed. "You know the drill," Kate said once she'd recovered. "Grab a pillow and sit down."

CiCi and Genie did as they were told. For a moment Genie forgot herself and looked around the room for Laurie and then remembered she wasn't coming. She wasn't ever coming.

"It feels weird without Laurie, right?" CiCi said, reading Genie's thoughts. "Even this tiny room feels too big without her here."

"It feels like yesterday we were up here," Kate said, folding her legs in front of her.

"Remember how we used to buy those teenybopper magazines and bring them up here to read?" CiCi asked.

Genie held up a dusty copy of *Tiger Beat* between her thumb and forefinger. "I do remember," she said. "You guys made me buy them, because you were too embarrassed."

"Give me that," Kate said, snatching the magazine away from Genie. The cover, once glossy, was now faded, but there was no mistaking the six faces staring back—they were the members of Boyz United.

"They were so hot," CiCi said, taking the magazine from Kate. "So, so, so hot."

"Now they're old like us," CiCi lamented. "Have you seen pictures of them now?"

"Haven't they all been to rehab?" Kate asked. "I swear I remember reading a story about how they'd been to rehab."

"The twins went," Genie said. "Cory and Caleb."

"Oh, that's right."

"I wish we'd gotten to see them the summer after graduation like we planned," CiCi said.

"Laurie had softball camp at MU," Kate reminded her. "And you were planning a wedding."

CiCi rolled her eyes. "I think the concert would have ended up being more productive."

"And cost less," Kate replied. "I bet your parents are still paying off that reception."

"It was a gorgeous wedding," CiCi said, her tone wistful.

Kate and Genie shared a look. "Well," Genie said, hoping to stave off a wave of nausea. "I read in *People* that they're doing a reunion concert in Las Vegas."

CiCi looked up. "Really?"

"Yeah," Genie replied. "In a couple weeks, at the end of the month."

"Oh, we should go!" CiCi said, waving the magazine and causing dust particles to fly around the room.

After they'd all finished sneezing, Kate said, "We can't do that."

"Why not?" CiCi asked.

"Uh, because we're adults . . . with responsibilities?" Kate asked.

"Maybe *you* are," CiCi said.

"Brent is probably one signature away from having a restraining order taken out on you," Kate said to CiCi. "And Genie has her father to think about. I have cases to defend. I mean, I wish we were still eighteen, but we aren't."

"You're not the president of the United States," CiCi replied. "St. Louis will not fall apart without you for a few days."

Kate looked to Genie for help, but all she could do was shrug. Yes, it was true she had her father to think about, but he was in a nursing home. He was being taken care of. He probably wouldn't even notice if she was gone for a few days. She doubted anyone would notice. "I don't know," she said finally. "It sounds kind of fun."

"Right?" CiCi asked. "It would be so fun!"

"What about the kids?" Kate asked.

"It's not like either one of mine is speaking to me," CiCi said. "Besides, it's just a few days."

Kate sighed. "Can we even still get tickets?"

"Let's go check," Genie said, pulling herself up from the floor. "My laptop is downstairs."

"Perfect," CiCi replied.

They all three clomped back down the stairs and into the kitchen while Genie retrieved her laptop from the nightstand in her bedroom. She quickly logged out of Netflix before presenting her laptop to her friends, so they wouldn't see the sappy Hallmark movie she'd been watching the night before.

"So?" CiCi asked, taking a drink of her refill. "Anything?"

Genie squinted at the Google search. "It's sold-out on Ticket-master," she said a few minutes later. "But we can buy them from a third party, it looks like, for twice the price."

"How much?" Kate asked.

Genie clicked around for a while before finally replying, "A couple hundred is the cheapest . . . for the nosebleeds."

"I don't care if it's the nosebleeds," CiCi said. "Please, you guys. We've got to do this. I'll pay."

Kate and Genie looked at each other. "We'd still have to pay for hotel and gas, unless we wanted to fly," Kate said.

"Road trip!" CiCi said, clapping her hands and spilling her drink onto the tile floor. "Oops."

"I think you've had enough of that," Genie said. She inwardly cringed at the mess on the floor. It was a leftover habit, the immediate worrying about messes, from when she'd lived with her father. With the exception of her bedroom, which was always a disaster, she kept the house neat as a pin. She couldn't help it, and it was all she could do not to start cleaning up the spill right then.

"I'm serious," CiCi said. She was pleading now, her lower lip set into a pout. "I need this. I need to get out of here for a little while."

Genie sighed. "Summer school doesn't start until the second week of June," she said. "I guess I don't really have a reason to say no."

"You're supposed to be on my side," Kate said to Genie.

"Laurie would want us to go," CiCi said. "She would want us to do something together to honor her memory."

"That's not fair," Kate replied. "You can't bring our dead friend into this."

"Yes, I can!" CiCi replied. "I'm *grieving*. I can do whatever I want."

"That's not how it works!" Kate called to CiCi as CiCi turned away from them and wandered into the living room, clutching the dusty copy of *Tiger Beat*.

"Like she's the only one grieving," Kate muttered.

"Look at her," Genie replied, pointing to CiCi. "How would you feel if your marriage fell apart like that? It can't be easy for her, especially not right now."

Kate didn't reply. She was studying her fingernails—perfect red ovals on slender hands—and for a moment, Kate looked very, very sad.

"Kate?" Genie asked. "Are you okay?"

Kate looked up. "I'm fine," she said. "But I swear, when are we going to stop giving in to her?"

Genie shrugged. "I don't know. Never, probably."

They both laughed.

"She's right, though," Genie continued. "Laurie would want us to go. She was always talking about the four of us taking a vacation together."

"It never happened," Kate said. "I just thought it would eventually, you know?"

"I know."

"Okay," Kate said finally. "CiCi, get in here and buy our tickets."

"Really?" CiCi squealed. "I mean, really? For real?"

"We'll split the hotels," Kate said. "And the gas, but you're going to buy our tickets."

"Done," CiCi said. She disappeared and then reappeared seconds later with a credit card in her hand. "They're on Brent." She winked. "His treat."

Later that night, after CiCi had fallen asleep on Genie's couch and Kate had set off for St. Louis, Genie sat up, awake, in bed. Because she couldn't sleep, she'd been working on their trip itinerary, mapping out hotels and sending a quick email to the only travel agent in town for a few pointers. When she'd offered to make the plans for the trip, she hadn't realized that she'd never really been anywhere to speak of. She wondered if Kate or CiCi considered this when leaving her in charge, or if they simply knew she needed to make plans in order to quell her anxiety.

Either way, she was grateful. The job kept her from worrying about being gone from her father, and it kept her from thinking too much about Laurie. She felt guilty about enjoying her time with Kate and with CiCi, and she felt guilt about how rarely they'd all, the four of them, seen each other over the last few years. Text messages and an occasional phone call had seemed like enough before. Now, well, it seemed like much less than enough.

It was nice, though, she thought, not being alone in the house for the night. She wished CiCi hadn't thrown up in the bathtub, but other than that, it was nice. Genie understood why CiCi hadn't wanted to go home to an empty house, even after Kate offered to drive her. Even though most of the time Genie enjoyed her solitude, it could be difficult knowing that the one thing that remained consistent in her life was that she went to bed alone and woke up alone. She couldn't really imagine what that reality was like for CiCi—someone who'd always had family there for her. At least Genie was used to being alone.

Genie shut her laptop and placed it on her nightstand. She took her glasses off and put them down next to her laptop. Maybe she ought to get a cat. Of course, she'd let the first-grade teacher take the kindergarten class fish home for the summer, because Genie always managed to kill it. No fish had survived a May-August vacation at her house, and it was unlikely that a cat would fare better.

Maybe, she thought, drifting into sleep, *there will be more to my life one day than dead fish and imaginary cats.*

Chapter 8

Kate

A week later, Kate sat outside Austin's house with Pat Sajak in his doggie car seat, his tongue lolling in and out of his mouth as he panted. He'd never enjoyed car rides, and Kate already felt the guilt not only of forcing him into the car that morning but also for what she was about to do—leave him in the care of her ex-husband for the next week.

She could have had him boarded, she guessed, but the last time she'd done that, just a month after adopting him, he'd contracted kennel cough. Kate had been in Arizona at the time, visiting her mother and getting Botox injections in her face and neck (a routine less painful than seeing her mother), and Laurie had gone and picked Pat up herself, taken him to the vet, and had him almost as good as new by the time Kate returned.

Now that wasn't an option, and Kate had to admit that Austin had been more than gracious about agreeing to watch her dog while she went gallivanting off to relive her senior year in high school. He'd always been such a fucking nice guy, and Kate wondered jealously if her dog would choose her ex-husband over her the way her own children had.

The front door opened, and the twins came bouncing out, wearing soccer cleats and throwing a slightly flattened soccer ball at each other's heads.

Shit, shit, shit. She'd forgotten about the soccer game this morning.

Kate got out of the car, leaving Pat in the back seat, intermittently panting and barking his displeasure about being ignored. When the boys saw her, they both waved, and Evan jogged over to give her a hug. Unlike his brother, Evan wasn't too cool to express his affection for her, and Kate reveled in it, squeezing him so tightly that he wriggled away from her, laughing.

"Mom! You're crushing me!"

"Sorry," Kate said. She grinned at him and then over at Eli, who was standing next to Angie near the door. He smiled back, but he didn't come over to where she stood with Evan.

Angie whispered something to him, and he rolled his eyes and stomped over toward Kate, with Angie trailing behind him.

"Hey, kiddo," Kate said.

"Hey," Eli mumbled. "You were supposed to bring snacks today. But I bet you forgot."

"I'm sorry," Kate replied. "I can go get some right now and be back before your game even starts."

"Oh, it's okay," Angie piped up. "I know you've been really

busy, and with everything else going on . . ." She trailed off, and placed her hand lightly on Kate's shoulder. "Anyway, I took care of it, so you're off the hook!"

Kate did her best to smile at Angie. The woman was, like Austin, genuinely kind, and there wasn't a hint of malice or judgment in her voice. Kate wanted to hate her.

"Dad says you're leaving the rat with us," Evan said. "Can he sleep with me?"

"Don't call him a rat to his face," Kate said, ruffling Evan's hair. "But sure. I think he'd love that."

Evan ran to the car and retrieved Pat, carrying him like a baby to the front door of the house. Eli followed sullenly behind, but Kate had seen his eyes light up at the mention of the dog.

"I really appreciate this," Kate said to Angie as the boys disappeared back into the house.

"Oh, it's fine!" Angie chirped. "The boys love him and so does Austin."

"I've got his bed and his food in the trunk," Kate said, turning around.

"Don't worry about it," Angie called after her. "We've already got both inside!"

Chapter 9

CiCi

CiCi looked over the itinerary that Genie emailed her the night before. It was . . . in-depth. Not only had Genie mapped out their route, made hotel and dinner reservations at every stop, plotted out pit stops for gas; she'd also marked various points of interest along the way and exactly how long they could spend at each one if they wanted to make it to their destination, check into the hotel, and eat dinner before it got too late.

CiCi's phone pinged. It was Kate. Did you see this itinerary? It's ridiculous.

She will expect us to follow it, CiCi texted back.

I am not prepaid, came the response from Kate.

Prepaid?

Sorry, Kate replied. I'm driving. Voice to text. Running late.

CiCi smiled to herself. Kate was always running late. It had to be part of her DNA or something, because in all the years

CiCi had known her, Kate had never once been on time for anything. She wasn't entirely sure how Kate could be late to court, but she guessed her friend was a good enough lawyer that it didn't matter. She could argue nineteen ways to Sunday about why her lateness was an advantage, and you'd end up thanking Kate for it in the end.

CiCi looked back down at the itinerary. Genie's spelling and grammar and punctuation were perfect, and she found herself wishing that Lily was there to appreciate it. Lily, her oldest, and Genie were so much alike. Half the time CiCi secretly wondered if Lily really belonged to Genie. Lily was quiet and studious and calm. She was nothing like her mother, and Lily would have appreciated the attention to detail in a way that CiCi, looking at the itinerary, would never even see, let alone enjoy. Right now Lily and her younger sister, Sophie, were staying with CiCi's parents next door. Lily was furious with CiCi, not for kicking Brent out of the house, but for making such a spectacle of herself when she did it. Sophie, on the other hand, had always been a daddy's girl, and she was struggling with the fact that her father might be responsible for tearing the family apart and was taking it out on CiCi.

In other words, both her daughters hated her right now, and CiCi didn't really blame them. She wasn't a fan of herself much either, and she was really glad to be getting out of town for a while. Her parents had assured her the girls would be fine with them. And Brent, though a lousy husband, had always been a concerned dad, so she knew her daughters were in good hands.

Anyway, she was tired of getting sympathetic looks or curious stares from people she'd known all her life each time she went to the supermarket. She was tired of searching for Brent's car in every parking lot, just to make sure she wouldn't have to see him in public. For the first time in CiCi's whole life, she wished she'd gotten out of Orchard Grove like Kate and Laurie.

Later, as she made the short drive through town from her house to Genie's, she wondered just how many people had known about Brent's infidelities—because this wasn't the first one—and looked the other way. How many years had she been lying to herself thinking it was a secret, continuing to hold her head high while everybody already knew the truth? Why had she stayed for so long? Would she stay even now, if he came home and apologized? Promised, as he had so many times in the past, that it would never happen again?

She didn't know the answer to that. Right now, the thought of going back to the way things were before sounded nice. At least then her world made sense. At least she had a modicum of control over her own life. Would that be better, she wondered, to give up a part of herself and let it die in exchange for the security of knowing what comes next?

CiCi was so deep in thought that she drove right past Genie's house, even with Kate and Genie waving at her from the driveway. She had to make a loop around the cul-de-sac, before finally rolling to a stop in front of the neat little bungalow.

She was surprised to see that Kate was already there, since she'd said she was running late.

"How is it that I beat you here?" Kate asked, once CiCi emerged from her Tahoe. "You live like five minutes away."

"I thought you would be here an hour ago," Genie said.

"Didn't we say noon?" CiCi asked.

"Yeah, and it's nearly one o'clock," Kate replied.

CiCi looked down at her Apple Watch, the watch that she'd bought to help keep her accountable for exercise and that only ended up making her feel mocked at the end of the day, and realized that *she* was the one who'd been late. "Oops," she said after a few seconds of staring down at the watch face. "Sorry."

"I'm glad you're here now," Kate said, taking CiCi's arm. "I need your help. Tell Genie we've got to take the car."

"What car?" CiCi asked.

"*THE* car!" Kate said, pointing to the garage. "Her dad's car."

CiCi's eyes widened. "Genie, you still have it?"

"*I* don't have anything," Genie replied stubbornly. "It's my father's car."

Kate rolled her eyes. "He's in a *nursing home*," she said. "The man doesn't even have a valid driver's license."

"It doesn't matter," Genie said. "It's not my car."

"Yes, it is," Kate replied.

"I wouldn't feel right about it," Genie said. "What if something happened to it?"

"Nothing is going to happen to it," Kate said. "You're being paranoid."

"I don't have the mileage figured out," Genie continued. "It will mess up the whole itinerary."

"Oh no, what will we do if the itinerary is messed up?" CiCi asked, finally cutting into the conversation with a falsetto.

Genie glared at her. "I put a lot of work into that itinerary," she said.

"We know," Kate said.

CiCi sighed. "We can just take the Tahoe. It's clean, and there's plenty of room for all of us."

"But it's so boring," Kate whined. "It would be so much fun in a classic car. I mean, your father's car is a Lincoln Continental convertible, for cryin' out loud. We'd feel just like Thelma and Louise, but without Brad Pitt and dying at the end."

Genie laughed, and then CiCi said, "You're one to talk about boring." She glanced around, and then continued, "Hey, where's your station wagon?"

"I traded it in," Kate replied. "The mileage was awful. The Prius"—she pointed to a sleek black car in the driveway—"is much better."

"How did you convince Austin to trade it in?" Genie asked. "I thought you said he loved it, because he could fit all of the boys' soccer gear in the back."

"Yeah, and how do you fit two preteen boys in a *Prius*?" CiCi added. "One of Lily's friends drives an older model, and her boyfriend barely fits in the *front*."

"They aren't in it all that much," Kate replied airily. "And Austin never had to drive that tank."

"That picture you posted of him in it after you bought it," CiCi said, beginning to laugh. "He looked like such a tool."

Kate gave her a lopsided smile. "Yeah, it was pretty funny."

"Speaking of posting pictures," Genie said. "Did you and Austin disable your Facebook accounts? I tried to send him a birthday message last month and couldn't find either of you."

Kate nodded and then said, "It's just until a couple of his more sensitive cases are over. You can never be too careful, you know."

CiCi raised an eyebrow but didn't respond. She'd never known Kate *or* Austin to post anything on social media that might make them look bad. In fact, Austin never posted anything at all, and all Kate did was post pictures of her beautiful home and beautiful children. CiCi had no idea how much Kate spent on professional photography, but it was probably more than Brent brought home in a year at the dealership.

"It's for safety reasons," Kate added, as if reading CiCi's mind.

"Gotcha."

"Let's get this show on the road," Kate said, picking up her bags and heading toward the Tahoe.

Genie stopped her. "No," she said. "We can take the Lincoln. You're right. It would be more fun."

"Are you sure?" Kate asked, shooting CiCi a look. "It's really not a big deal."

"It's fine." Genie went back into the house, and after a few moments, the garage door opened. She held up the keys. "Come on," she said. "Hurry up, before I change my mind."

CiCi and Kate let out a squeal and lunged for the car, nearly knocking into each other as they called out, "Shotgun!"

"You have to sit in the back, CiCi," Kate said, throwing her bags into the trunk. "You're shorter than I am."

"What does that have to do with anything?" CiCi demanded. "You know my legs cramp easily."

Genie rolled her eyes. "We'll take turns," she said. "CiCi, you sit in the back first, and then when we stop for gas, you and Kate can trade."

"Fine," CiCi replied. "You two always gang up on me."

"You can pick the music," Genie offered. "I think there are still a whole bunch of tapes in the glove compartment."

"Tapes?" CiCi asked. "Is there an iPod hookup or XM radio or something?"

"In this car?" Genie asked. "Please, the tape deck was a huge adjustment for my dad."

"Maybe we should've taken CiCi's car," Kate mumbled.

"Hey," CiCi replied, folding herself into the backseat. "When we're fifty miles down the road and listening to 'Dancing Queen' by ABBA for the thousandth time, don't forget that this is all your fault."

As THEY DROVE down the main strip in town, people were filling up the streets. Orchard Grove was a small community— just about five thousand people—but on Saturdays, it was as if the whole town came alive. There were exhausted parents taking their kids to soccer or T-ball or whatever sport was in season. There were teenagers wandering the streets taking selfies. There were hipsters walking around in their scarves and lensless glasses and sipping their skinny half-caf mochas. It was an eclectic combination, and CiCi loved Saturday in Orchard Grove.

As they drove past the nursing home, CiCi said, "Genie, I thought you said you needed to go by and see your dad before we left."

Genie's grip on the wheel tightened for a moment, but all she said was, "No. I don't think I'm going to."

"Well, should we put the top down?" Cici asked. "If we're going to be Thelma and Louise?"

"Thelma and Louise and Louise," Genie replied. She pulled the big car to a stop.

Getting the top down was only a little awkward in such an old car, and a small and curious crowd had gathered, watching them from the opposite side of the street. CiCi realized that Genie had stopped right in the middle of town.

Once the three women were safely back inside the car and situated, CiCi said, "Half of those people watching us are going to call my mother the minute we're out of sight."

Kate craned her neck to get a look from her position in the front seat. "Bitches," she said under her breath. "They're all a bunch of bitches."

"The bitchiest bitches to ever bitch," CiCi replied.

"They're just jealous," Kate said. Then, sitting up a little straighter in her seat, she yelled, "You're all just jealous!"

"That's right," CiCi said, feeling her spirits rise. She stood up in the back seat and ignored Genie's protestations and demands for her to sit back down. "Bye, bitches! I'm going to Vegas!"

Both Kate and CiCi threw their arms up in the air, and for the first time all morning, Genie broke into a broad grin as they cruised out of the city limits and into the great expanse of highway ahead of them.

Chapter 10

Kate

Kate eased back into the passenger seat and rested her heels against the dashboard. She willed herself to stop thinking about cases and clients and briefs and all the work she was missing and the fact that her colleagues were, at this very minute, probably discussing her utter lack of dedication to her job, even on a Saturday. They'd all be in the office. She willed herself to stop feeling guilt over the soccer matches she'd missed and was going to miss and felt a familiar wave of sadness wash over her when she realized how likely it was that her sons wouldn't notice that she wasn't there. They were used to that by now, weren't they? Clearly Eli was still angry with her about the divorce, and she knew that was likely to continue. The family counselor told her to be patient, that each boy would have a very different reaction to their new reality, and to be ready for things to get worse before they got better.

It was somewhat comforting to know that CiCi was going through something similar with her children, even if at the same time Kate wouldn't wish that kind of pain on anyone. She'd pledged to tell both of her friends about the divorce at some point during the trip, but now she wasn't so sure that she could. It was easier for them to continue thinking she was in a happy marriage. She was honestly amazed she'd been able to keep the divorce secret at all. Though the women had tried, it was difficult to stay as close as they'd once been.

Kate wondered if either Genie or CiCi felt as nervous as she did about spending a week away from what they were used to, to go on a road trip with two other premenopausal women to see a not-so-teenage boy band who fell out of favor right around the time the flip phone was invented.

What were they even doing, anyway?

She really did know how to give herself a good guilt trip. That was, according to her therapist, one of her greatest talents. Maybe if she'd stayed in Orchard Grove, she'd be happier. Her father seemed to be plenty happy in the shack he'd called home for the last fifty years. When Kate had first gotten married, before the kids, and she and Austin were doing well, she'd made the drive to Orchard Grove and offered to buy her father a house. Whatever he wanted, she'd told him, but she suggested a one-story ranch so that he didn't have to fight with his degenerative disc disease every time he went up and down a flight of stairs. He'd been a carpenter, and a damn good one, for years and years, but his back would no longer allow for the constant bending, and he'd had to go on disability the year before Kate got married.

"Katie, I'm fine," he'd told her. "Your brothers help me out, and I've got no cause to want to leave."

"Dad, you can't live here," she'd said. "You just can't. This place is falling down around you."

Her father had stiffened then, as much as his back would allow him, and said, "It's good enough. Always has been, always will be. I don't need a fancy house like you have."

Kate's house then had hardly been fancy. It was a starter home in the northern part of St. Louis County, in a town called Florissant. It wasn't where they wanted to be, but they were happy. She'd just wanted to help her father, but he was having none of it. He thought she was trying to put on airs, lie about who she was and where she came from, but all she really wanted to do was have something she could be proud of. She was grateful for her father and the life he'd struggled to provide, but she didn't want that life, and she couldn't understand why her father seemed mad at her about her accomplishments instead of proud. He *was* proud, she knew that, inside, but he had a strange way of showing it in that he hardly showed it at all.

"Fine," she'd said, tired of fighting. "But the offer stands, if you ever change your mind."

He hadn't ever changed his mind, and Kate stopped asking. Eventually she stopped visiting too. When the boys were little, she hadn't visited because her father got upset if they stayed in a hotel, but Kate couldn't spend the visit worried one of her children might fall through a rotting floorboard or give themselves tetanus on a rusty nail. By the time they were old enough to know how to navigate the house, neither of them knew their grandfather well enough to *want* to visit.

This, too, had been the subject of many, *many* conversations with her therapist.

"Hey," CiCi said, leaning up from the back seat and forcing Kate out of her thoughts. "I have to pee."

"I saw a sign for a truck stop up ahead about three miles," Genie said. "It's not as close to the first stop on the itinerary as I'd like, but I guess that's okay."

"I'm sorry that my bladder can't read the itinerary," CiCi replied sarcastically.

"Where are we?" Kate asked. "It feels like we've been on the road for hours."

"We're about to cross into Oklahoma," Genie said. "Haven't you been paying attention? You're in charge of the GPS. Your phone is the newest."

"Oh, uh, yeah," Kate replied. "Sorry."

"This is why I should have been in front," CiCi said. "You know Kate can't read a map."

"I don't have to read a map," Kate shot back. "The damn thing talks to you." She held up Google Maps on her phone. "See?"

"Yeah, I know how Google Maps works," CiCi replied. "But your sense of direction has always been questionable."

Genie took the next exit, and they drove down the ramp to a

truck stop called the State Line. She pulled up to the gas pump and cut the engine.

"You two can go on in," she said. "I'll fill it up."

"Okay, but I'll get the next one," Kate said.

CiCi hopped out of the back seat and handed over her debit card. "This one's on me," she said.

Genie tried to wave her off, but CiCi ignored her and pushed her card into the slot and stuck her tongue out at her friends.

Kate couldn't help but laugh. Together, she and CiCi walked inside the truck stop, both of them glancing around for the bathroom.

"My eyeballs are floating," CiCi groaned. "I've gotta pee so bad."

"Excuse me," Kate said to the cashier behind the counter. "Where's the restroom?"

The clerk, who was staring down at her phone, said, without looking up, "It's on the other side in the restaurant."

"Where is that?"

The clerk pointed toward French doors at the far end of the station. "Down there," she said, eyes still glued to the screen.

As if on cue, Kate's stomach growled. "Maybe we should eat too," she said.

"Go tell Genie," CiCi said. "I'll meet you in the restaurant."

After they'd all gone to the restroom and CiCi had tried unsuccessfully to tame her windblown hair, they were ready to eat. After a few minutes, a woman in a baby-blue waitressing dress, a throwback to another time and in complete contrast to the vinyl-and-plastic aesthetic of the restaurant, greeted them.

"How many?" she asked.

"Just the three of us," Kate replied.

The waitress took out three laminated menus and led them to a table close to the front of the restaurant. Kate was surprised to see it so packed. She hadn't realized that gas station restaurants were so popular. The only gas station restaurant she'd ever gone to was in Orchard Grove, and only then after midnight to sober up after a party in the woods behind Beau Trantham's house.

The waitress waited for them to sit down, and then she handed them their menus. She took out a pad of paper from her back pocket and said, "What can I get you ladies to drink?"

Genie and CiCi both said water without even looking at the menu. But Kate studied it for a few moments more. "I'll have a Dr Pepper," she said finally. "Thanks."

Genie and CiCi stared at her. CiCi had a look of abject horror on her face.

"You're ordering a soda?" she asked. "Like, a real one?"

Kate shrugged. "I'm on vacation."

Genie shook her head. "My dentist told me five years ago that if I didn't stop drinking soda, my teeth were going to dissolve in my mouth."

"I don't think that's true," Kate said. "I mean, I'm sure he was just trying to scare you. But don't worry. I don't usually drink soda. Just once in a while, on very special occasions. And I think this counts."

CiCi lifted her hand in the air and said to the waitress, "Excuse me? Could I change my drink order to Dr Pepper, please?"

"Me too!" Genie seconded with gusto. "Don't tell my dentist."

"Remember how we used to have one at every break?" Kate asked. "And even at lunch sometimes."

"I tried to drink Diet Coke as much as I could," Genie said. "But Dr Pepper was always my favorite. They took the machines out of the schools a few years ago and replaced them with water and other unsweetened drinks."

"Really?" Kate asked. "That sucks, but it's probably that way at the boys' school too. I've just never noticed."

"There was a push from the PTA," Genie said, looking pointedly at CiCi. "*Some* of the mothers felt that the soda-and-snack machines created an unhealthy environment for the children."

CiCi shrugged. "Well, do you let your boys have soda?" she asked Kate.

"Of course not," Kate replied. She kept quiet about how, after the divorce, she'd become much laxer about what her kids ate. CiCi and Genie didn't need to know about how the Pizza Hut delivery guy no longer needed her address.

"Kate, I once watched your father fill up your nephew's bottle with Mountain Dew," Genie said, taking a big sip of her drink.

"And now Riley has ADHD," Kate replied.

"That's not what causes ADHD."

"Sure doesn't help any, though, does it?"

"We had donut sticks and Dr Pepper every morning, and we turned out all right," Genie replied.

CiCi rolled her eyes. "I hate it when people say that. Just because we've always done something one way, doesn't mean we don't need to change sometimes."

"Right," Kate replied. "That's why I never spanked the boys. My dad used his belt. I can't imagine doing that today."

With this, Genie seemed to agree. "You know we can still paddle at school?" she asked, leaning in and whispering. "We don't even have to ask permission."

Kate sat back, folding her arms across her chest. "That seems like a lawsuit waiting to happen."

"Oh, it was a big deal when some of the parents found out," CiCi replied. "Some of the PTA moms started a petition, but as it turns out, people around Orchard Grove are pretty much okay with corporal punishment."

"And conceal and carry for the teachers and administration," Genie added. "Can you imagine? Me, carrying a gun at eye level with a kindergartener?"

"That's ridiculous," Kate agreed. "I can't . . . just . . . wow. I'm so glad I got out of that cesspool."

Across from her, CiCi and Genie shared a glance.

"No, I'm sorry," Kate said. "I didn't mean it *like that*. I just meant that I don't think I'd fit in there very well anymore. It's just different."

"Well, your brothers both pushed for conceal and carry in the school," Genie replied.

"My brothers are both idiots," Kate replied.

"Either way, you're related to that cesspool," CiCi said, smirking. "You can take the girl out of Orchard Grove, but you can't take the Orchard Grove out of the girl."

"You can with Botox," Kate replied, and they all laughed.

CiCi picked up her menu in time for the waitress to come back to the table for their orders. In keeping with their vacation vibe, they all three ordered fried chicken with country gravy and biscuits.

In front of them and to the left, a man sat reading a newspaper. Every time the waitress bustled past him, he lowered the paper to get an eyeful. About the third time the waitress passed by, the man stuck out his hand and brushed her bottom. She visibly bristled at this interaction, but she ignored it and hurried away.

The man went back to reading his paper, but he repeated the grab three more times. The waitress, for her part, couldn't help but go past him as she delivered drinks and food. She would have had to go all the way around two large tables full of people, and there was no way she could squeeze through the narrow opening carrying a tray. The man seemed to know this and take delight in it.

"Hey," Kate said, inclining her head toward the man. "Watch that guy behind you. . . . Don't turn around at once! Wait until the waitress goes by, and then look."

A few minutes later, the waitress came back through, carrying two trays, one in each hand, and attempted to get past the man unnoticed. This time, he reached out and full-on slapped her ass so hard that Kate nearly came up out of her chair.

"Oh my God," CiCi said, turning back around to face Kate. "Do you think that guy is her boyfriend or something?"

Kate squinted at the man. He was probably about fifty, and he was wearing a camo jacket and Carhartt overalls. He was bald in the way only babies and middle-aged men could be— with a fringe of limp hair hanging around the bottom part of his head and ears in a crescent shape. Even from where she was sitting, Kate could see the dirt underneath his fingernails. By contrast, the waitress couldn't have been more than about eighteen, with a fresh face and rounded features.

"There is no way that guy is her boyfriend," Kate finally replied. "He's old enough to be her dad, and did you see how she tenses up when she walks past him? It's like she *knows* he's going to do it, and there's nothing she can do about it."

"Gross," Genie replied. "What a creep."

When the waitress came back around the next time, she had their food with her. She twirled the tray down to hip level and began to hand them steaming plates full of glorious fried food.

Kate accepted her plate and resisted the urge to put her whole face into the chicken and start chewing at it like a starved and wild animal. Instead, she looked up at the waitress and said, "Who is that man over there? The one in the camo, reading the newspaper?"

The waitress grimaced. She didn't even have to look over her shoulder to know who Kate meant. "Oh, that's Jeff Prichard," she said. "Why? Is he botherin' you?"

"It looks more like he's bothering you," Kate replied. "I can't help but notice that he can't keep his hands to himself."

The waitress flushed. "His brother is the manager."

"So?" CiCi asked. "What's that got to do with anything?"

The waitress looked at CiCi and shrugged. Suddenly, she looked much older than she had before the conversation began. "That's just the way it is," she replied. "He grabs all our asses. Well, except for Ms. Reba. He says she's too old."

"And the manager is okay with this, just because that guy is his brother?" Genie asked, a mix of horror and confusion playing on her features.

Again, the waitress shrugged. "Can I get y'all anything else?"

The three women shook their heads and watched her walk away.

"I can't believe that," Genie said, angrily stabbing at her mashed potatoes with her fork. "That's ridiculous."

CiCi nodded in agreement through a mouthful of fried chicken.

"Really?" Kate asked, tilting her chin up slightly in question. "You can't believe that some middle-aged man feels entitled to grab a teenage waitress's ass, knowing full well his brother is the manager of this place and isn't going to do a damn thing about it? That's *surprising* to you?"

"Well, when you put it like that . . ." CiCi said, trailing off.

"Did you know that one out of every six women has been a

victim of rape or attempted rape in her lifetime?" Kate pressed. *"One out of six!!"*

"Calm down, Gloria Steinem," Genie replied, glancing around the restaurant. "We're on your side."

"It's just so infuriating," Kate said, lowering her voice. "Did you see the way our waitress just shrugged? Like it's a part of life or something? That's not okay."

"Clearly, it *is* a part of her life," Genie pointed out. "And there really isn't much you can do about it."

CiCi elbowed Genie in the ribs. "Shut up," she hissed.

Genie was so busy rubbing her sore side that she didn't notice Kate had gotten up out of her seat and was now sauntering over to where the man was sitting. Kate sat down across from him and waited patiently until he realized he was being watched and lowered his newspaper.

"Well, hello," he said, a lazy grin spreading across his face. "To what do I owe the pleasure?"

Kate gave him her sexiest smile and said, "I was just eating lunch over there with my girlfriends, and I couldn't help but notice you."

"Oh really?" Jeff sat back in his chair, running his hands down his chest to his ample belly. "See anything ya like?"

"But I also couldn't help but notice that you and that waitress seem to be pretty close," Kate continued.

"Nah," Jeff replied. "She ain't anything."

"Are you sure?"

Jeff sat up a little straighter. "Why do you care?"

"Well, it's just that I couldn't help but notice that every time she walks by, you can't seem to keep your hands to yourself," Kate said. "To be quite honest, it puts me off my chicken."

Jeff sniffed. "You jealous?"

"Very," Kate replied, leaning forward and placing her elbows on the greasy table. "So jealous, in fact, that I want to make it very clear that you better not touch her—or any waitress—in this restaurant, or any other, again. In fact, it's a good idea not to touch a woman at all without being given express permission to do so, which probably means you're going to be very, very lonely from now on."

"Huh?" Jeff furrowed his brow as if he didn't quite understand what Kate had just said.

"Keep your hands to yourself," Kate said, enunciating each word as if it were a singular sentence.

Jeff let out a laugh that turned into a cough and then lifted the newspaper back up to his face. "I don't have time for this shit," he said from behind the paper.

Kate stood up and let one of her hands fall down onto the middle of the paper, pulling it out of Jeff's hands and onto the tabletop.

"Hey!"

"Listen," Kate said, her voice sugary sweet. "You're going to keep your hands to yourself, and if you need legal help to do it, well, I can sure provide that, because I'm going to leave my card with every single waitress here, and they're going to call me if you so much as look in their direction. I will take their cases pro bono, because did I mention that I'm a lawyer?"

Jeff pulled himself up to his full height and said, "You can't harass me like this. I have rights!"

"Oh, please," Kate said. "I deal with scumbags like you on a daily basis. In fact, my last client blew her husband to smithereens with a homemade pipe bomb. They found his dick in the neighbor's begonias."

"You're crazy." Jeff backed away from Kate, his hands raised up in surrender.

"So do we have a deal?" Kate asked. "You keep your filthy hands to yourself, and I won't have to sue you for sexual harassment."

Jeff spluttered something unintelligible and pushed past her toward the exit.

Kate waited until he was gone and then sauntered back over to her table, where Genie and CiCi were staring at her, wide-eyed.

"He sure lit out of here in a hurry," CiCi said.

"What did you say to him?" Genie asked.

"Enough that we should probably pay and leave," Kate replied, reaching for her purse. She pulled out a fifty-dollar bill and a stack of her business cards. "I'll meet you two back at the car."

"Please don't kill anybody," Genie said. "I really don't want to have to drive off a cliff Thelma and Louise–style."

Kate waited until the waitress was back behind the counter and approached her. The poor woman looked half-scared of Kate, but her eyes lit up when she saw the fifty-dollar bill Kate was holding.

"Here," Kate said. "Keep the change, and I'm sorry if I caused you any trouble." She handed over the money and her cards. "This is my card. You call me if that asshole bothers you again—you or anyone else who works here, okay? I'm a lawyer in St. Louis."

The waitress smiled broadly and nodded. "Thanks a lot," she said. "Jeff is gonna be shitting his pants for a week."

"Good," Kate replied, winking at her. She glanced over her shoulder to see the Lincoln roll to a stop in front of the entrance doors. She waved at them and then turned back to the waitress and said, "Hey, do you think I could also get three Dr Peppers to go?"

Chapter 11

Genie

Genie navigated the boat-sized car through rush-hour Oklahoma City traffic and prayed she could switch lanes and get onto the exit ramp without sideswiping or rear-ending anyone.

To say that she was exhausted would have been putting it mildly. Genie felt like her limbs might detach from her at any moment and float away. It had been at least twenty years—the spring the Orchard Grove High School quiz-bowl team went to the national championships in Nashville—that she'd been in a car so long, and she'd *never* driven this far. Her father hadn't believed in vacations. He thought they were a frivolous waste of money, and even after Genie had a teaching salary and money of her own to do whatever she pleased with, she never considered actually going anywhere.

Besides . . . who would she go with? She knew that had she expressed interest, either CiCi or Kate would have invited her on their family vacations, but it wasn't much of a comfort. She didn't want to feel like an outsider on a vacation, and besides, they already seemed annoyed by her—by her lack of experience and lack of knowledge. She didn't tell them that she'd had to enlist a travel agent to help her book the accommodations; well, if a person could call a massage therapist who also operated a travel agency out of her salon an actual travel agent. She'd hoped, stupidly, that her itinerary would impress them—that they'd see she could still be a valuable part of the group without Laurie. Laurie, who always had to carry her own weight as well as Genie's. Laurie, who always had a way of making Genie feel at ease, and Laurie, who Genie missed right this very second more than ever.

"You need to take a left off this ramp," Kate said, pointing vaguely out the window. "The hotel should just be a couple miles from here."

"I'm sure Oklahoma City has a lot to offer, but the only thing I can think of is the Unabomber," CiCi said, looking down at her phone.

"What?" Genie asked, careening onto the narrow side street. "The Unabomber didn't have anything to do with Oklahoma."

"Yes, he did," CiCi replied. "He bombed that building in downtown Oklahoma City."

"You're thinking of Timothy McVeigh," Kate said. "He's the Oklahoma City bomber."

"Right," CiCi agreed. "The Unabomber."

"The Unabomber was Theodore Kaczynski," Genie said. "Two totally different people."

"Are you sure?" CiCi replied. "I thought they were the same person."

"I'm sure," Kate said. "Oh, there it is! There's our hotel!"

Genie had to do a double take. Surely Kate wasn't talking about what lay in front of them. The neon vacancy sign was missing nearly every letter, so that it just read, "van." Looking at this place, Genie thought that maybe she'd rather sleep in a van.

"*This* is the hotel you booked for us?" Kate asked as Genie rolled to a stop in front of a sign that read, "The Wigwam Motel." "You booked us tepees?"

"Wigwams," Genie corrected. "But I actually didn't book us wigwams. There was supposed to be a Budget Inn right here."

"This is not a Budget Inn," Kate replied.

"Yes, it is," CiCi said. She pointed to a sign just above them. "It says so right there."

"So . . . it's a Wigwam Budget Inn?" Kate asked. "Isn't this racist? Or cultural appropriation or something?"

"Well, I didn't *know* they were wigwams," Genie replied.

"How could you not know they were wigwams?" Kate asked. "There's a picture right here on the website." She held the phone out accusingly. "How did you make a reservation for Wigwam Budget Inn *without* seeing the *wigwams*?"

Genie pushed open the car door and got out, CiCi and Kate

following suit. "I didn't actually book the rooms myself," she admitted.

"What?" Kate asked. "Who booked the rooms? Your dad? I know he's senile, but Genie, he's not blind."

A look of understanding dawned on CiCi's face, and she said, "Oh, Genie. Please tell me you didn't let Hazel book the rooms for you."

"So what if I did?" Genie replied. "She's a travel agent. That's her job."

"Hazel from the massage place?" Kate asked. "Hazel from the massage place, with no pinkie finger on her right hand? Hazel from the massage place who lost her license to actually *be* a masseuse when the health department found out she was running an illegal cockfighting ring in her basement? *That* Hazel?"

"Yeah," Genie said, trying to sound as if none of the disturbing facts Kate just spouted mattered whatsoever. "That Hazel."

"I can't believe this," Kate replied.

"I'm sure it's fine," CiCi said. She smiled encouragingly at Genie. "Hazel booked a cruise for my parents last summer, and they said it was great."

"Minus the food poisoning," Kate snapped. "My brother told me."

"Which brother?" CiCi asked. "Didn't you say they were both idiots?"

"They're apparently not the only idiots."

"That's a little dramatic, don't you think?" CiCi asked Kate.

"I don't care if they're built out of cow dung," Genie retorted. "I'm exhausted, and I'm going inside."

"Fine," Kate sighed. "But I'm staying under protest."

"Everything you do is under protest," CiCi replied, rolling her eyes. "Not everything is a fight for social justice."

"Not for *you* it isn't," Kate said.

Genie ignored them, following CiCi to what appeared to be the front office but in reality was just a concrete building with two squat windows and a door.

Genie pulled the door open, and it let out a groan as if it hadn't been opened in a very long time. There was a man behind the desk watching an old television set, and he didn't even turn around when they entered. Genie had to ring the rusty bell twice before the man turned to acknowledge them.

"Got a reservation?" he asked.

He had a face like a chewed-up piece of leather, and Genie couldn't stop staring at the way his thick black eyebrows met in the middle.

Genie nodded at him. "Yes," she said. "Should be three rooms . . . uh, wigwams. It's under Eugenia Walker."

The man's eyebrows furrowed even further into one another as he pecked away with two fingers at an ancient Dell desktop. "I see yer name here, but I ain't got but one a them wigwams."

Now it was Genie's turn to knit her eyebrows together. "Well, I reserved three," she said. "I think the reservation was made online."

"Probably my half-wit nephew," the man replied. "He's in charge a tha computer, but it says here . . . let's see . . . yep . . . three guests, one wigwam."

"Three guests, *three wigwams*," Genie said.

"We're booked up for the night," the man said. "There are two beds in this room, though. Should be enough room for you ladies."

"I find it hard to believe you're booked for the night," Kate said under her breath.

The man looked up. "Nevertheless," he said. He grinned a wide, toothless grin at them. "Three guests. One wigwam."

Genie extended her Mastercard to the clerk and said, "Just give us the key."

They unpacked their bags from the car wordlessly, and despite the crumbling exterior, inside the wigwam was surprisingly spacious, and Genie cast her bags to the side and flopped down, face-first, onto the bed. "It's not so bad," she said.

"It could be worse," Kate admitted.

"It's clean," CiCi said.

Genie called the nursing home to check on her father while Kate and CiCi called their children. Kate's call was relatively short, after only one of the twins agreed to speak to her, but CiCi spent a considerable amount of time arguing with Lily about something Genie didn't understand but was almost certain had to do with the fire video circulating around social media.

She knew that if she checked her phone, she'd have a message from Lily making some sarcastic remark about CiCi, and Genie knew she'd have to figure out a way to both defend CiCi and placate Lily, and she wished there was a handbook somewhere she could read about dealing with the teenage daughters of lifelong friends who were going through marital trauma. She firmly believed that if more things came with a handbook, there would be much less confusion in the world.

Kate sat down beside Genie and nudged her with her elbow. "What do you think she's saying?" She nodded her head toward the window, where CiCi stood outside and appeared to be screaming into her phone.

"I don't think I want to know," Genie replied.

"Did you know that Brent was cheating on her before she lit his clothes on fire in the backyard?" Kate asked.

Genie bit her lip, hedging what she wanted to say.

"Oh, come on," Kate said. "I'm not going to tell her you knew if you did."

"Everybody knew," Genie replied, unable to stop herself. "Brent's been cheating on her since the girls were little, and everybody, including CiCi, knew it."

"That's kind of what I figured," Kate said. "Nobody's life is as perfect as CiCi makes it look on social media without big problems in real life."

"Really?" Genie asked. "Nobody?"

"Nobody," Kate replied.

"Not even you?"

Kate laughed. "Especially not me."

Genie opened her mouth to reply, but Kate shushed her and nodded her head toward the door. CiCi was coming inside in a huff.

"That fucking asshole," she said, plopping down on the bed beside Kate. "That motherfucking, two-timing *asshole*."

Genie and Kate shared a look. It wasn't like CiCi to talk like that. Kate and Laurie had always been the potty-mouthed friends of the group. It was strange, even though they were no longer teenagers, to hear their friend use that kind of language, even in private.

"Are you all right?" Kate asked, slipping her arm around CiCi's shoulders. "What's going on?"

CiCi took a deep breath in through her nose, releasing it slowly through her mouth, before she said, "Lily told me that when Brent picked her and Sophie up from my parents' house today . . . he had a *woman* in the car with him."

"The same woman from Laurie's funeral?" Genie asked.

"Yes," CiCi replied. "That's who it has to be."

"Do you know who she is?" Kate asked.

"I've seen her before," CiCi said. "But I can't figure out where besides the dealership."

Genie stared down at her hands. She knew exactly who the woman was, and she knew that if Kate or CiCi looked over at her, they'd know that she knew.

"Do you know her, Genie?" CiCi asked, nudging her lightly. "Why are you so quiet?"

"You know her too," Genie replied, looking up. There was no use in hiding it now. CiCi was going to figure it out anyway. "She's a third-grade teacher at the elementary school—Chrissy Long."

"Oh my *GOD*," Kate hissed.

CiCi sat up straight and brushed away Kate's hand. "It's fine," she said, sniffing.

"I don't want to talk about it anymore," CiCi said, standing up and heading for the bathroom. "I'm going to go freshen up, and when I come back out, I want this conversation to be over."

Kate put up her hands. "Fine with me," she said. "Genie, let's go out to the car—I think I left my makeup bag in the trunk." She motioned for Genie to follow her.

Genie sighed and got up, following her outside. "I could have given you the keys," she said.

"Don't you think CiCi is being *ridiculous*?" Kate asked. "I mean, she's acting like she wants Brent back. How could she want him back after this?"

"I don't know," Genie replied. "She didn't say she wanted him back."

"Oh, come on," Kate said. "She always takes him back."

"I feel like it's different this time," Genie said. "And did you see her with Wade at the funeral? I swear, the way he was looking at her . . . Didn't you notice it?"

Kate nodded. "Yeah, I did. Do you think they were having an affair too?"

Kate grabbed at her wrist and pointed to the front of the office, where little puffs of smoke were coming out from the alleyway.

"Is something on fire?" Genie asked, panicked.

"What?" Kate asked, turning to stare at her. "No, can't you smell it?"

Genie shrugged. "Smells like someone ran over a skunk."

"Jesus Christ, Genie," Kate replied, a smile lifting one side of her mouth. "It's *pot*."

"Oh, well, excuse me if I wasn't expecting to smell pot in broad daylight in a public place," Genie replied. "Sorry my nose for drugs isn't as keen as yours."

Kate pulled Genie along with her toward the cloud of smoke. Genie tried to twist herself away from Kate as they moved forward, and it took her a minute to realize that there was someone standing in the alleyway behind the smoke.

"Kate," Genie said. "Kate, what are you doing?"

"Shhhh," Kate replied. "Just let me do the talking."

The kid standing in the alley couldn't have been more than about seventeen, at the most, and the confused expression on his face when Genie and Kate approached was almost comical. He immediately hid the joint he was smoking behind his back and narrowed his eyes at them.

"It's okay," Kate said, as if she were talking to a wounded animal. "We're friendly."

"What do you want?" he asked.

The boy was tall, with gangly arms and legs that appeared to be hard to control as he shifted from one foot to the other. He was wearing a black T-shirt with "The Wigwam Motel" embossed across it and a name tag that read, "Brian."

"Are you the manager's nephew?" Kate asked.

"Maybe."

"Look," Kate continued. "We've been in the car all day driving here from Missouri, and we're wiped out. Do you think you might share with a couple of weary travelers?"

"Wait," Brian said, a laugh catching in his throat. "You two want to smoke with me?"

"I was hoping you might have some available for purchase," Kate replied.

"You two cops?"

Kate rolled her eyes. "Do we look like cops?"

Brian narrowed his eyes further and then pulled the joint out from behind his back, took a long drag, and after a few moments blew the smoke out and right into their faces. "Sorry. This is the last of it."

"Okay," Kate said. "Well, how about I give you fifty bucks, and you give me the joint?"

"That's a lot for some shit like this," Brian said, his eyes still narrow.

"Whatever," Kate said. "You want the money or not?"

"Kate," Genie hissed, tugging on her friend's arm. "What are you doing?"

Kate ignored her, reaching into her pocket and handing over a crisp fifty-dollar bill. Brian took it and held out the joint, only to think better of it and recoil away from them.

"I wanna see your tits too," he said. "Then you can have it."

"Are you kidding me?" Kate asked.

Brian seemed to think about it, and then he replied, "No. Show me your tits." Then, his glance sliding to Genie for the first time in the conversation, he said, "Yours too."

Genie turned her back to Brian. "Okay, I'm done now," she said. "Time to go."

"Give me my money back," Kate said to Brian. "I'm not showing you anything. You don't even look old enough to say that word."

"TITS," Brian replied, indignant. "I'm nineteen."

"I'm going back inside," Genie said.

"You have two choices here," Kate said to Brian, grabbing onto Genie's arm so she couldn't escape. "You can give me that joint or you can give me my money."

"Or?"

Kate sighed. "I breastfed twins for nearly two years. Trust me, kiddo, you don't want to see that."

"Gross," Brian said. "Here, just take it." He shoved the joint into Kate's hand and pushed past them, mumbling to himself.

"It was a pleasure doing business with you!" Kate called after him.

Genie stood there for a moment and then began to laugh.

"Oh my God," she said. "I thought he was going to throw up right there."

"Joke's on him," Kate said. "I had a lift two years ago, and my boobs are fanfuckingtastic."

HALF AN HOUR later, Kate returned with three bottles of Boone's Farm wine, a lighter, and five-dollar pizzas from Little Caesars. "Pizza! Pizza!" she declared when she burst through the door. "Who's hungry?"

CiCi's face brightened. "Did you get bread sticks?"

"Of course."

"And the garlic-butter dipping sauce?"

Kate threw a bag that smelled like a garlic farm onto the bed between CiCi and Genie. "Do you really think I'd forget?"

"It's just like being back in high school," CiCi replied, ripping into the bag. "Now all we need is a VCR and that Disney concert with Boyz United playing in the background."

"Oh, and those little mini cupcakes," Genie replied, licking her lips.

"Man, the cupcakes!" Kate exclaimed, unscrewing a bottle of Boone's Farm. She took a swig and passed it around to Genie and CiCi. "I totally forgot about those."

"It's no wonder we didn't have boyfriends," CiCi said.

"Cupcakes trump boyfriends," Kate replied.

Genie wiped at the drops of wine that rolled down her chin

before she said, "You two always had boyfriends. It was me and Laurie who ended up in her room on Friday nights while the two of you went on dates."

CiCi rolled her eyes. "Yeah, like four times the entire time we were in high school," she said. "I always picked Boyz United and cupcakes and friends over dates with boys."

"Until Brent," Kate pointed out.

"And what a fucking mistake that turned out to be," CiCi muttered.

"And on that note . . ." Kate held up the lighter and pointed to the half a joint sitting next to the television. "Shall we?"

"I don't know," CiCi replied, shifting. "I haven't smoked pot in years."

Genie clapped a hand over her mouth to keep from laughing, but Kate couldn't stop herself and got a pillow in the face for her effort.

"Shut up!" CiCi cried. "Shut up! I don't want to talk about it!"

"Well, *you* brought it up!" Kate replied, taking great gulps of air. "Oh my God, I forgot all about that night!"

Genie gave in and began to laugh, and by the time CiCi was out of pillows to throw, they were all three dissolved into a fit of giggles.

It had been spring break of their senior year in high school, and they'd been invited to a party out in the Mark Twain National Forest with a bunch of college freshmen. Brent was one of them, home for the holiday to help his father during the busy tax-return season at the car lot. Most of the time, Genie opted to stay home when her friends went to parties. Parties made her uncomfortable, and she knew that if word got around to her father that she'd been out at one, she'd be grounded for the rest of her life.

But it was spring break of her senior year, and Genie wanted to have *something* to remember it by. So she told her father that she was spending the night with Laurie, and since it was the season finale of one of his favorite detective shows, Genie's father didn't ask too many questions. As long as she was home to cook dinner, she was free to go anywhere she wanted after.

The problem was that Brent thought CiCi understood that she was supposed to bring her older brother with her—not only to buy the beer, but to also provide pot for the entire football team. CiCi, of course, hadn't gotten the memo and was upset to find out that she'd been invited only for her drug connection. Despite Genie's suggestion that they tell the football players to shove off and find their own illegal substances, CiCi was desperate to impress Brent, so they all grudgingly agreed to go with CiCi to, at the very least, collect the goods from her brother. Convincing the girls to ride anywhere with CiCi wasn't a problem, most of the time. She was the *only* one of them with a new car, and it was the dream car of teenage girls everywhere—a 1999 celery-colored Volkswagen Beetle. Laurie and Genie didn't even have cars, and Kate drove an old pickup that sometimes stalled and died at stoplights. So it was never a difficult decision to figure out whose vehicle to take.

CiCi's brother Chris had been living at home ever since he

flunked out of his first semester of college nearly three years ago. CiCi's parents liked to call him an entrepreneur, but the reality was that Chris was a loser who wasn't particularly interested in anything he had to work for. He sold the kind of marijuana only teenagers would smoke and would occasionally buy beer for underage kids, as long as he got a twelve-pack out of the deal.

When the girls got to the house, Chris's little Ford Ranger wasn't in the driveway, but there were cars everywhere, all up and down the street.

"Are your parents having a party?" Kate asked.

CiCi shrugged. "They didn't say anything to me. I told them I was staying with you tonight, and all they said was to call them before I came home tomorrow morning."

"Where's your brother?" Genie asked. "He's always home."

"Maybe he parked around back," CiCi said, throwing the car into park. "Sometimes he does that when Mom and Dad have people over. I guess he could be over at a friend's house. I'll have to ask Mom where he went."

"He has friends?" Laurie asked.

"A couple," CiCi said, getting out of the car. "You guys want to come in?"

"I have to pee," Kate replied. "And I'd prefer not to go in the woods, where I know half the senior boys are waiting with cameras for that specific purpose."

"Ew," Genie and Laurie said in unison.

"The door is locked," CiCi grunted, pushing against the handle. "Let me run back to the car and get my keys."

Laurie, who'd chosen to stay in the car, dangled the keys out the window, while Genie and Kate stood on the front porch and waited. There was clearly a party going on inside, and Genie was curious about it. Her own father never went to parties and never hosted parties of his own. In general, he thought himself too good for most of the townspeople, and he had few friends except for the ones he'd known before Genie's mother died. Genie couldn't even begin to imagine him at CiCi's parents' house.

She peered in the window to get a better look. There were a few people that she could see and knew right off—there were CiCi's parents, of course, and standing by them was Mrs. Osborne, the family-and-consumer-science teacher at the high school. Up until this year, the courses Mrs. Osborne taught had been called home economics, but because that term was deemed no longer politically correct, the courses had been changed to family and consumer science. Genie knew this only because Mrs. Osborne, who was young and pretty but set in her ways, blamed feminism for the change, and Kate had rolled her eyes so hard that Mrs. Osborne sent her to the office.

While Genie thought about this, Mrs. Osborne reached out and took the hand of CiCi's father, dropped a pair of keys into a bowl in the center of the room, and led him upstairs. Confused, Genie looked to CiCi's mother, who was watching this all take place calmly, until a man with close-cropped hair and a light gray suit leaned over and planted a kiss on her lips.

Genie stumbled back so far that she lost her footing and tumbled down the stairs, landing in a heap in the grass.

CiCi rushed over to her and said, "Oh my God, Genie! Are you okay? What happened?"

"Don't look in the window," Genie managed to croak, but of course it was too late. Kate was already looking, and her horrified shrieks were likely to wake up the neighborhood. Well, the part of the neighborhood *not* at CiCi's parents' very obvious swingers party.

By the time Kate came to her senses, CiCi was screaming in horror as well. Genie picked herself up off the ground and grabbed both of their arms, leading them down the stairs and to the car. They drove in silence back to the party, with the exception of Laurie asking them what she'd missed, and they'd never talked about it since.

Now, more than twenty years later, Genie was laughing so hard that she thought her sides might burst. Even CiCi, the same horrified expression on her face, eventually broke down into a fit of giggles.

"I will *never* be able to get those images out of my head," Kate said, gasping. "Did I ever tell you guys the man in the suit actually worked with my dad? I don't even know where he would have *gotten* a suit like that!"

"No!" Genie said. "You never told us that."

"At least you two didn't have to go home to my parents the next day," CiCi replied, wiping at her eyes. "Oh my God, I couldn't look at them for weeks!"

"I still can't look at them," Genie said. "Every time your parents came to a school event for your daughters, I had to look at their feet when I talked to them."

Kate lit the joint and then passed it over to CiCi. "I can't believe Laurie missed it," she said. "We should have told her, at least."

"I would have killed you both if you'd said anything to anyone," CiCi replied.

"I'm pretty sure half the town was in on it," Genie said. "I was so glad when Mrs. Osborne left the year I got my first teaching contract."

"She moved to Texas," CiCi said, giving Genie the joint. "She divorced her first husband and married some guy *my parents introduced her to.*"

Genie took a hit and passed it back to Kate. "I don't want to hear any more," she said. "Change the subject, please."

Chapter 12

CiCi

CiCi lounged around every pillow in the room, her bare legs dangling off the side of the bed. She shoved a slice of pizza into her mouth, took a bite, and chewed thoughtfully. They'd been silent, eating pizza and recovering from the day, with the exception of Kate telling her about how she'd been propositioned to show her breasts to a teenager. She eyed both Genie's and Kate's chests with envy. Kate's had always been small, and so at nearly forty, they were still perky. Genie's were by far the biggest, but they weren't saggy the way CiCi thought her own were. She figured that was because Genie had never breastfed.

She'd been afraid to let Brent see her without a bra after breastfeeding two babies. She didn't even like to see herself without a bra. Her breasts looked . . . deflated, saggy. As a teenager and when she was in her early twenties, CiCi's breasts had been a source of pride. She knew it was stupid to be proud of a body part, but God, she loved her breasts, and Brent had too. But after having their younger daughter, she noticed that Brent didn't seem as interested in her physically as he had before, and he once made a crack about her breasts looking like the nose of his best friend's basset hound. Well, she resorted to wearing a bra all the time—even during lovemaking. It was uncomfortable, and the straps left divots in her shoulders, but at least she wasn't flashing her dog-nosed tits all over the place.

Now, if she were being honest with herself—which she rarely ever was, but if she were being completely honest—she knew that Brent wasn't coming back, and she knew it wasn't because of her breasts. She knew that when she got home from this trip, what was left of his belongings would be gone, and she'd be in their big house alone with her daughters. The thought made her want to cry and rejoice at the same time. She didn't even know how that was possible, but she guessed it would be a lot more comfortable to cry in bed without wearing a bra. What would it be like, she wondered, to be comfortable in her own house . . . in her own skin?

"If I eat another piece, I'm going to be sick," Genie said, breaking up CiCi's thoughts. "Okay, maybe just one more. If I don't eat the crust, it should be all right."

CiCi leaned over the side of the bed and realized that Genie was on the floor, in between the two beds, wrapped in one of the bed's comforters like a burrito. "What are you doing down there?" she asked. "That can't be comfortable."

Genie sat up. "I don't know," she said, glancing around. "Have I always been down here?"

"Wow. You're so high right now," Kate said, laughing.

Genie blinked. "Am I high?"

Kate and CiCi exchanged amused glances. "This is why we never invited you to parties," CiCi said. "You're too extra."

"I don't even know what that means," Genie said, flopping back down onto the carpet. "Because I'm old."

"It means you're over-the-top, right?" Kate asked. "My kids use it sometimes, and there's another word. Yeet? What is that? How is that even a word?"

"We used stupid made-up words when we were teenagers too," CiCi replied. "Don't you remember we actually said *gettin' jiggy with it*?"

"Will Smith said it, so it was okay," Genie protested.

"And *crunk*," CiCi continued.

"Justin Timberlake said it, so it was okay," Genie said. "I mean, I'm sure someone said it before him, but the first time I heard it was on some Disney concert special with *NSYNC."

"Oh, I remember that concert!" Kate exclaimed. "Remember we had it on tape? We used to watch it all the time."

"In Laurie's room!" Genie finished. "She had that big TV that she won in some foster-kid Christmas drawing."

"She took it to college with her too," Genie said. "We had it in our dorm room freshman year."

"I remember that," Kate said. "Because when I came to visit

you two at Mizzou, every kid in your hallway was in your room watching *The Real World* on a giant TV."

"I hated that show," Genie grumbled.

"I never did get to come visit," CiCi said. "I was planning my wedding at that point, and I thought that was *the* most important thing in the world."

"I know," Kate said. "Because I was your maid of honor, and you didn't speak to me for almost a month after I told you I was too busy with finals to throw you a bridal shower."

"I was an idiot," CiCi replied. "Hell, what did you know about bridal showers? You were just a kid. *I* was just a kid."

"We were all kids, and we were all idiots," Genie said. "Sometimes I think *teenager* is synonymous with *idiot*."

"Eloquent," Kate said.

"Shut up," Gene replied. "It's true, and you know it."

"Lily has a group of friends like us," CiCi said after a few moments. "One of the girls has a new boyfriend, and she's stopped spending time with the group. Lily is angry at this other girl, and they aren't speaking right now, except of course to write snarky posts on Twitter about it. She asked me what she should do, because she's devastated about losing her friend."

"What did you tell her?" Kate asked.

CiCi shrugged. "I told her that 'best friends forever' doesn't always mean forever when you're a teenager."

A silence settled over them, until finally Kate said, "Sometimes it doesn't matter how old you are. Things change, and we don't really have any control over it."

"We stayed friends," Genie replied.

"But not like we were friends in high school," CiCi said.

"Well, no," Kate said. "Because we grew up."

"Growing up sucks," CiCi replied. "It sucks hard."

On the other bed, Kate sat up, pieces of her auburn hair sticking up and her mascara smeared underneath her eyes. "I think I have to go to sleep now," she said.

CiCi turned to the clock on the nightstand. "It's only ten o'clock."

"And we have a full day of driving ahead of us, don't we?" Kate asked.

"Where are we headed tomorrow?" Genie asked, her voice muffled from inside the comforter on the floor.

"You're the driver!" CiCi exclaimed. "Aren't you supposed to know?"

"Humphflump," came the response.

CiCi leaned over the bed so that her head was nearly touching Genie's. "I wanna see your boobs."

"No way," Genie said, sitting up and nearly bumping heads with CiCi. "Once this decade was enough."

"Oh, come on! I've *never* seen them."

"I've seen yours enough for both of us," Genie muttered.

"You haven't seen them in a long time," CiCi replied. "Trust me, you don't want to see them now."

"I didn't want to see them *then*!" Genie said.

"You've never seen mine," Kate threw out. "Neither one of you have."

"Are you sure about that?" CiCi wanted to know. "I swear there was that one time in eighth grade . . ."

"Eighth grade doesn't count," Kate replied, indignant. "I didn't even get my first period until I was a freshman in high school."

Suddenly, Genie stood up, a broad grin stretched across her face. "Okay," she said. "I'll show you mine if you two show me yours."

"Not fair," Kate replied. "I don't want to."

"Then you owe me one," Genie said.

"I don't want to," CiCi replied. "Mine are ugly."

Kate shrugged. "So are mine. We've both had two kids."

"Did you breastfeed yours until they were two years old?" CiCi asked.

"I did," Kate replied. "That's why I got a breast lift."

Genie rolled her eyes at Kate and said to CiCi, "Your boobs are fine. I can see them through your sleep shirt, anyway."

CiCi crossed her arms over her chest, but she relaxed slightly. "Okay," she said. "But you two have to promise not to laugh."

Kate rolled her eyes. "Fine." She stood up and motioned for CiCi to do the same. "On the count of three, okay?"

CiCi and Genie nodded.

"One," Kate said, grabbing the bottom of her Willie Nelson concert T-shirt. "Two . . . THREE!"

As if in some kind of breast-related standoff, all three women lifted their shirts at the same time and stood there, staring at each other for what felt like the longest moment ever. Then, just as quickly as it happened, they covered themselves up again and fell back down onto the beds, laughing.

"We can't ever tell anyone about this," Kate said, checking to make sure she'd pulled her shirt down all the way over her stomach. "They'll think we're insane."

"I'm pretty sure I already have the monopoly on crazy in Orchard Grove," CiCi replied. "After my stunning display of pyromania last week."

"I don't know why you were so worried about showing us," Genie said, propping herself up on one elbow. "Your boobs still look great."

"You can be honest," CiCi said. "It's okay. You won't hurt my feelings. I know they look like dog noses."

"What?" Kate screwed up her nose. "Seriously, CiCi, they're still amazing. I don't know where you got this idea that they aren't, but you're wrong."

For a minute CiCi thought she might cry. She collected herself and said, "I think we should call it a night, especially if we're going to get on the road early tomorrow."

Kate made her way over to slide underneath the covers next to CiCi.

"I guess I'll just sleep by myself," Genie muttered.

"You absolutely will," Kate replied. "You snore."

"I do not!" Genie replied. "Besides, so does CiCi."

"Not since they fixed my deviated septum," CiCi protested.

"Is that what we're calling a nose job now?" Genie asked, her eyes halfway closed. "Huh, could have fooled me."

Chapter 13

Kate

In Laurie's most recent murder-mystery novel, released just a few months before she died, the murderer was a middle-aged woman named Minnie who lived in a little town in Kansas and raised goats and rabbits. The lead detective on the case discovered several decapitated heads in the rabbit hutches. Kate remembered that Laurie's foster home before she moved to Orchard Grove had been at a farm that had rabbits. She wondered if that had anything to do with her choice of setting for this book.

It wasn't a question that Kate would ever get an answer to. Not now.

Kate knew, realistically, she never would have asked, because Laurie would have told her the complete and unabridged truth about it, and Kate didn't always know if she wanted the truth. Laurie had always been that way, though—telling the truth even when it wasn't necessary. As an adult, Kate appreciated the truth (most of the time), but as a child, she'd never understood why Laurie didn't just *lie* about some things, especially about the things that hurt, like why she was in foster care or why her mother was in prison. That's what Kate would have done; in fact, that's what she did do for a little while in elementary school.

Since the fifth grade, she'd attended a math camp in Columbia, Missouri, on the University of Missouri campus. Most of the kids she went with were well-off, with the exception of a few scholarship kids like her. Kate had never wanted anyone to know where she came from or the fact that her family had next to nothing. Every summer, she borrowed a week's worth of clothing from CiCi, spent the money she'd saved all year on makeup and highlights at the beauty shop, and lied to every single person at camp about her family. For one week, she got to be someone else—someone other than poor runt of the family Katherine. She was Katy, an only child with lawyer parents who doted on her. It was a fantasy she looked forward to all year.

"Are you asleep back there?" CiCi turned around from her position in the front passenger seat to look at Kate. "You're being awful quiet."

"I'm fine," Kate replied. She held up Laurie's book. "I have a headache from trying to read in the car."

"Wanna trade me places?"

Kate shook her head. "No."

"Come on," CiCi insisted. "I want to take a nap, anyway."

"What are you doing?" Genie asked, swerving slightly as CiCi threw one leg into the back seat.

"Just keep your eyes on the road," CiCi said.

"Uh, that's kind of hard to do when you've got your ass in my face," Genie replied. "Jesus, CiCi."

Kate flattened herself against the door as CiCi came tumbling into the back seat in a heap. "Really," she said. "This could have waited."

CiCi settled in next to her and plucked the book from Kate's hands. "Is this any good?"

"Yeah," Kate replied. "It's a lot like the others, but it's good."

"I've never read any of her books."

"Not any?" Genie asked from the front seat. "I always try to read them, but they freak me out."

"Yeah, there are no happy endings in these books," Kate said. "It's not really your style."

"You know I don't really like to read," CiCi replied. "It's not that I don't *want* to read; it just takes me so damn long to finish anything."

"Do you guys remember Laurie's very first book signing in St. Louis?" Genie asked. "How long has it been? Fifteen years?"

"I remember," CiCi said. "There were, like, five people there, including the three of us."

"I think Kitty and Dan were the other two," Kate said.

"But we went to the Cheesecake Factory afterward," Genie continued. "That was a lot of fun."

"That book went on to be a *New York Times* bestseller," Kate replied. "There was a line out the door at her last signing about a week before she died."

"I didn't get to go," Genie said. "That was the last week of school, but I called her and told her how proud I was of her. I got her voice mail."

"I didn't even call," CiCi admitted. "I should have."

"None of us could have known what was going to happen," Kate said, willing herself to believe it. She'd gone to the signing, but she hadn't stayed. There'd been so many people, and Laurie looked so busy and important. She'd gone instead to the bar around the corner from Barnes & Noble and had a drink before heading home.

"Well, I want to read that book when you're done," CiCi said. "It's the least I can do, right?"

Kate nodded in mock agreement. "Of course. Absolutely."

CiCi reached over and pinched her arm.

"Hey, ow!"

They both burst into giggles, and then Kate said, "I still can't believe we're doing this."

"Doing what?" CiCi asked.

"*This*," Kate said, waving her arms around the back seat of the car. "Driving halfway across the country to go to a concert like we're teenagers."

"To be fair," Genie said, "we never did this as teenagers."

"We should have, though," Kate replied.

"Well, we're doing it now," CiCi said. "And I think it makes us awesome. Nobody in my cul-de-sac would ever do this."

"Oh God, mine either," Kate replied.

"Everybody in my cul-de-sac is like ninety years old," Genie said. "The only place my neighbors ever go is to the morgue."

"Wow," CiCi whispered. "That got dark."

"Do you think it's weird we all live in cul-de-sacs?" Kate asked.

"I think the plural form of the word is *culs*-de-sac," Genie replied.

"Are you sad that you know that?" CiCi asked. "Because I'm sad that you know it."

"I actually think it's weird that anybody lives in a cul-de-sac," Kate continued. "I mean, it's basically just a fancy way of saying you live on a dead-end street."

"I like it," CiCi said. "It's safer, and there's not any through traffic."

"I know," Kate replied. "That's why when Austin and I moved from Florissant, our new house was on a cul-de-sac. But I still think cul-de-sacs are stupid."

"*Culs*-de-sac," Genie said.

"Oh my God, can we please stop talking about sacs of any kind?" CiCi asked, rolling her eyes.

"My neighbors two houses over are going to Napa Valley later this month," Kate said, ignoring CiCi. "They invited me to go with them."

"Just you?" CiCi asked. "They didn't ask Austin?"

"Us," Kate said quickly. She could have kicked herself. "They asked us. But you know, we've just been so busy lately . . . anyway, we couldn't make it work."

"Brent and I took the girls to the beach every summer," CiCi said. "Then a few years ago, Brent stopped going because he said he needed to work." She shrugged. "I knew better, but I like the beach."

Kate reached over and took CiCi's hand. "It's going to be okay," she said. "I know it doesn't seem like it now, but it will, I promise."

CiCi snatched her hand away and said, "How do you know? Your husband would never cheat on you."

"No," Kate agreed. "He wouldn't."

"See?"

The car was silent for a few minutes, and Kate knew that she should take this opportunity to tell Genie and CiCi. CiCi, at least, would probably be grateful. But she didn't have the emotional energy at the moment to go through the whole thing—to talk about it in detail the way she'd need to talk about it so they could understand that while she was sorry for the way things had turned out, she wasn't sorry she loved being a lawyer more than she loved being a wife. During her weakest moments, she told herself that she was just like her own mother, who'd left when Kate was in elementary school, and that she didn't deserve to be a mother either.

"Hey, there's a gas station at this exit," Genie said, breaking the silence. "Do you guys want to stop? I need some caffeine."

"That sounds good to me," Kate replied.

"We're going to need gas soon, anyway," Genie continued. "Taking this car has really messed up the schedule. We shouldn't need to stop for another fifty miles."

"What if we'd needed to stop before fifty miles?" Kate asked.

"I would've told you to hold it," Genie replied. She steered the car off the interstate. To the left there was a small gas station, with old crank pumps.

"This place looks like a horror movie waiting to happen," CiCi said.

"I'm sure it's fine," Kate replied. "Let's at least go in and see if they have a bathroom."

They went inside, and Kate asked the bored-looking cashier if there was a bathroom. She turned around and grabbed a key attached to a wooden board that had the word *women's* burned onto it in crude writing.

"Here," the cashier said. "Bathroom's around back."

"It's outside?" CiCi asked.

The cashier blew a bubble with her gum and then said, "Yup."

"Where are we?" CiCi whispered to Kate as they left Genie inside to find the bathroom.

Kate shrugged. "I think we're still in Oklahoma somewhere." She handed the key to CiCi and waited outside the door, arms crossed over her chest as she scanned the parking lot. She hadn't spent much time in Oklahoma. She didn't know anything about it other than the fact that it bordered Missouri and was prone to tornadoes. Glancing around the empty and litter-covered gas station lot, she figured that was probably adequate information to have.

At the far end of the parking lot, by a giant dumpster, an older SUV was parked with its hatch open. There was a cardboard sign that when Kate squinted, she could see read, "Free Puppies."

Unable to stop herself, Kate walked across the lot to check it out. There was a little old woman standing beside the SUV, and she hardly looked tall enough to climb up into it, let alone drive it. She smiled as Kate came nearer to her, and Kate noticed that in the back of the SUV was a white laundry basket with a blanket shoved down inside. Coming from the blanket were several soft, small whimpers.

"Afternoon," the woman said. "You just passin' through?"

Kate furrowed her eyebrows. "How could you tell?"

"Your plates, for one." The woman pointed toward the Lincoln. "Plus, ain't no local gonna use that bathroom."

"Well, that make sense," Kate replied. She peered into the SUV at the puppies. They were cute and small—maybe some kind of long-haired Chihuahua mix.

"You interested in a puppy?" the woman asked. "They're free an' been wormed."

Kate shook her head. "Oh, no, thank you. They're cute, though." She peered further into the laundry basket and saw a bigger puppy off to one side. It was looking at her with its little bulgy eyes. Maybe Kate was losing it, but she could have sworn it was using its underbite to smile at her. "What's with that one?" she asked.

"He's from the last litter," the woman replied. "He's sweet, but he's got a wonky leg. I keep bringin' him, though, in case someone wants him."

Without asking, Kate reached into the basket and picked up the dog. He was bigger than the others but still small. When she nestled him into the crook of her arm and leaned down to get a better look at him, he licked her nose, and that was it. She wasn't going to put him back down in that basket.

By the time she got back to the car, both Genie and CiCi were staring at her with their arms crossed over their chests.

"What is *that*?" CiCi asked. "Looks like some kind of long-haired rat."

"It's a dog!" Kate replied.

"But why do you have it?" Genie wanted to know. "You're not getting in the car with that thing."

"It's a dog, not a velociraptor," Kate replied. "It's fine. I'm going to take care of him." She stroked the dog's head, and he nuzzled further into her.

"He could be rabid for all we know," Genie said.

"I'll find an ER vet at our next stop," Kate said, trying not to sound as annoyed as she was. She knew they were right, but she was already attached, and there was no changing it now. "Please, you guys. Look at him! He's so cute, and he's got a busted leg." Kate held the dog out for them to see, including the dog's left back leg and the small, twisted paw attached to it.

CiCi's face softened, but Genie only glared. "Fine," Genie

said finally. "But if it shits in the car, you're both walking to Vegas."

"I think I saw a sign for a grocery store," Kate said, ignoring Genie. "Can we just run down there and get some food and food bowls and stuff?"

Genie sighed. "We're going to be so much later getting to the hotel," she said.

"If the hotel even lets us stay," CiCi replied, and Kate shot her a withering look. "Who knows if they're dog friendly."

"I didn't even think about that!" Genie said. "What will we do if we can't stay because of that dog? You better take it back to that lady over there right now."

"No," Kate said, pulling away from Genie and sliding into the back seat of the car. "I'm not doing that."

CiCi got in beside Kate, leaving Genie alone in the front seat, muttering to herself. "He's so cute," CiCi said. "What are you going to name him?"

"I don't know," Kate replied. "I'll probably just have to let him choose."

Genie pulled out of the gas station and drove down the road to a small grocery store. When they got inside, they saw it was more of a catchall than anything else—there were groceries, but there were also souvenirs in the shape of Oklahoma and barrels of saltwater taffy. It was the kind of place where people on family vacations stopped. There was a little something for everyone. She looked in her rearview mirror and said to Kate, "You'll just have to *let him choose*?"

"Yeah," Kate replied. She opened up her purse and put the little dog down into it. He didn't seem to mind in the least and was, in fact, sound asleep by the time they got inside.

"You're the reason the health department has to make rules about sanitation," Genie whispered to her as they passed through the double doors.

"Shit," CiCi said. "I forgot to give the cashier back the key."

"We'll return it after we leave," Genie replied. "I doubt the cashier will even notice. She hardly looked up the whole time I was in there."

"Oh my God," CiCi said. "Oh my God."

"What's wrong?" Kate asked, turning around to face her. "We'll take the key back."

"No," CiCi said. "Look at this." She thrust her phone into Kate's hands. "Just *look* at this."

Kate looked down and saw a picture of a woman she vaguely recognized from high school, bending down and hugging a little girl about ten years old. The caption read, "This girl done so well today at the track meet! Her daddy and I are so proud!"

"So?" Kate looked up at CiCi and handed her the phone. "I mean, her grammar is terrible, but I don't think that's a new development."

"Not that," CiCi said. "Not them. . . . See the couple *behind* them?" She handed the phone back to Kate. "Look who it is."

Kate squinted and finally had to enlarge the picture to see what CiCi was talking about. They were fuzzy and pretty far in the background, but Kate was able to make out Brent and his apparent new girlfriend, holding hands and sitting on the bleachers at the track field. "Ooooh," Kate said.

CiCi looked close to tears. "It's like she's moved right in and taken my place," she said. "I haven't even been gone two days!"

"She could never take your place," Kate said, even though she knew just exactly how CiCi felt. "I bet nobody else sees it, anyway."

"Are you kidding me?" CiCi asked. "That's why Miranda took that picture to begin with! She knew I'd see it! She knew everyone would see it."

Kate picked up a set of metal pet bowls and tried not to eye CiCi too skeptically as she said, "There is no way Miranda did that on purpose. She doesn't even know when to use *did* instead of *done*."

"She stood in front of them on purpose. I'm humiliated. Everyone is going to see it," CiCi said. "Everyone."

"You set his clothes on fire in your backyard," Kate reminded her. "I think everyone knows that you two are over."

"I can't believe she would do this to me," CiCi continued. "I drove her daughter to every single junior-high cheerleading practice last year, when she was working at the Gas 'n' Go after Trevor left."

"Why do you even care what these people think?" Kate asked. "Seriously, CiCi, you're better than all of them."

"When we get back from this 'trip' . . ." CiCi said.

CiCi used air quotes around the word *trip*, as if it were alleged, and they weren't standing there in the middle of BFE with a bunch of . . . Kate looked around . . . male models? She couldn't tell. Why were there so many hot guys in this place?

"Kate? Are you listening to me?"

"Hmm?"

"Kate!" CiCi exclaimed. "I'm in the middle of a CRISIS."

Kate sighed. "If you really want to stick it to Miranda or Brent or whoever, then you've got to make it look like you're having a better time than they are." She took the phone out of CiCi's hands. "I mean, really, CiCi. I thought you, of all people, would know that by now. It doesn't really matter if you're miserable, as long as you pretend like you aren't."

"I mean, I'm not *miserable*," CiCi said, the beginnings of a pout forming on her lips.

"Just shut up," Kate replied, pulling her over to a man inspecting a case of strawberries at the far end of the store. He was wearing a white tank top that made his tan and toned arms look almost cartoonish in size.

When he saw them barreling toward him, he held the strawberries out in defense. "Here," he said. "You can have them. I don't need them."

"Hi," Kate said to him, flashing her most charming lawyer smile. It was the smile she used when there was an older male judge sitting on the bench that she needed to win over. It was a smile that said, *I'm too pretty to lie to you, and even though I'd never consider touching your old, wrinkled ass, it'll be fun for you to pretend I might.*

"Hi . . ." the man replied. He brushed an errant strand of long, golden hair off his shoulder.

Kate resisted the urge to call him Thor. He really did look like Chris Hemsworth's twin. "Listen," she said to him. "This is my friend CiCi, and she really needs to impress her Podunk friends back in Missouri, because she recently caught her husband cheating on her with a woman half her age."

CiCi smacked Kate's arm and said, "Hey!"

"But as you can see," Kate continued, "she's clearly in her prime. She's gorgeous, isn't she?"

The man nodded, a small smile playing at his lips.

"And you're gorgeous," Kate went on. "I mean, seriously, where did you even come from?"

"Texas," the man replied.

"Well," Kate said. "I do hear everything is bigger in Texas."

The man laughed, revealing very white and perfectly straight teeth. "What can I help you ladies with?"

"Okay, then, Mr. Toned Texas, can you stand here and act like my friend is the most amazing woman you've ever seen while I take your picture?"

"I can do that." He popped open the carton of strawberries, took one out, and offered it to CiCi. "Like this?" he asked.

Kate stepped away from them and opened the camera on CiCi's phone. "Perfect," she replied. "Okay, CiCi, open your mouth like he's going to feed it to you."

CiCi hesitated but eventually did as she was told, and a giggle managed to escape from her mouth as she took a bite of the strawberry and a bit of red juice trickled down her chin.

"Got it!" Kate said. "Perfect. This will send them into a frenzy."

"The pleasure was all mine," he replied. "This was the best time I've had all day."

Genie, who'd wandered off to look at something on the other end of the store, walked toward them, eyebrows raised. "What's going on here?" she asked.

"Oh, you know," Kate replied airily. "Just making new friends."

"I'm Troy," the man said, sticking his hand out to Genie. He was giving her a good once-over with his eyes.

Genie realized she was doing the same thing to him and said, "I'm Genie."

"Do you want a picture too?"

"Oh, no," Genie said. "I'm good."

"Are you sure?" Troy asked. "I've got plenty of strawberries."

Before Genie could answer, the door to the store flew open, and everyone turned around to see the sweating and rather annoyed store clerk from the gas station up the road marching toward them, her hand outstretched.

"You stole my key," the woman said.

"What?" Kate asked.

"The. Key. To. The. Bathroom," the woman, whose name tag read "Kelly," replied. "Do you know how much that key costs?"

"No," Kate replied. "This is our first bathroom key theft."

"Cute," Kelly said. "Real cute, lady. Listen, that key costs fifteen dollars, and they'll take it out of my check if I don't get it back. Where is it?"

"I'm sorry." CiCi stepped in, handing over the key. "Really, I didn't mean to take it."

The clerk snatched it out of CiCi's hand. "You're lucky I didn't call the cops," she said. "This is the third key this month."

"It was an accident," Kate said.

"It was stealing," the clerk replied.

"Why don't I just give you fifteen dollars, and we can call it a day?" Kate asked.

"Make it fifty," the clerk said. She gave Kate a grin that was most certainly not white and not perfect. "For my trouble."

Kate contemplated this while at the same time wishing she were licensed to practice law in the state of Oklahoma. This woman had probably needed a lawyer or two in her lifetime. As she jammed her hand down into her purse to search for cash, she accidentally woke the dog, who gave a little yelp at being disturbed. He poked his little apple-shaped head out and looked around.

The cashier took a step forward and smoothed her grease-stained polo shirt. "You take one of Ms. Rita's dogs?"

Kate scratched the top of the dog's head. "I don't know her name, but she was in your parking lot giving away puppies, and I took one."

"Aw," the cashier said, peering into Kate's purse. "You took the bigger one. Nobody ever wants him."

"I do," Kate said, already feeling protective. She held out a wad of bills to the woman. "Here."

The woman shook her head. "Naw, never mind. Ms. Rita's good people. Sorry I came at ya so hard about the key."

"It's okay," Kate said. "We're sorry we took it."

Kate watched the cashier named Kelly walk away, and when she turned around and back to her friends, they were standing there, one on each side of Troy, all three of them looking down at CiCi's phone.

"It already has fifty likes!" CiCi gushed. "I bet half the town has sent it to Brent." Then she got a worried look on her face and said softly, "I wonder if I should delete it."

"Why?" Kate asked.

"Well, other people might see it too."

"Like your parents?" Kate asked. "Or someone else?"

Kate thought she might have a pretty good idea about who CiCi was worried about seeing the photo, and she wondered if she should say out loud that it was Wade, the hottest undertaker to ever live, when she felt CiCi's elbow in her rib cage.

"Look," CiCi said.

Genie, it seemed, was having her very own conversation with Troy, the obliging Thor clone, who was pointing down at the book Genie was holding. Kate recognized the cover as Laurie's.

"Whatcha got there?" Troy asked her.

"Huh?" Genie looked up at Troy. "Oh, um, a book."

"I know that much," Troy replied. "Can I see it?"

Reluctantly, Genie handed it over.

"It looks good," Troy said after a minute. "Where did you find it? I've got a long day ahead of me. A book might help."

Genie turned and pointed to the opposite end of the store. "All the way down there on that endcap," she said.

"Would you mind showing me?"

Kate mouthed the word, "Go," to Genie, and then she said, "We'll meet you out front."

Kate and CiCi wandered the aisles until Kate found a suitable collar and leash for the dog, as well as a small carrier and food. It wasn't the same brand she fed Pat Sajak, but she didn't figure she'd be able to find that brand anywhere but a pet-specific store. It was expensive.

Later, in the car, CiCi leaned over the back seat to show Kate her phone. "Look," CiCi said. "The picture has a hundred likes already."

"Great," Kate replied. "I guess you can't delete it now."

"No," CiCi said thoughtfully. "But that's okay. It doesn't mean anything, anyway. It's just a picture."

Kate squinted at the picture. "That guy was pretty hot, though, wasn't he? What did he say his name was?"

"Troy," Genie said.

Kate and CiCi turned to stare at Genie, whose neck had begun to turn red, and the color was creeping up toward her face.

"I bet he remembers your name too," Kate said.

"Shut up," Genie replied. "He looked like Thor's long-lost brother."

"Chris Hemsworth!" CiCi exclaimed. "That's who I was thinking of."

"Well, the only way Chris Hemsworth is remembering my

name is if we're the last two people left on earth," Genie said. "And there are no goats."

"I don't know about that," Kate replied, pulling on Genie's ponytail from the back seat. "You're certainly the cutest goat I've ever seen."

"He wouldn't be interested," Genie continued. "Besides, I'm never going to see him again, anyway."

"Okay, first of all, there can't be that many Troys out there who look like him," CiCi replied. "I'm sure we could find him if we really wanted to."

"If that's his real name," Kate pointed out.

"Whose side are you on?" CiCi asked. "And secondly, I don't see any reason why he *wouldn't* be interested."

"I've got at least two hundred pounds, uh, reasons why he wouldn't," Genie snarked. "You two are gorgeous. You don't understand."

"Fuck that," Kate said. "That's ridiculous. You are gorgeous, and it pisses me off you refuse to see it."

"I see it every day," Genie replied. "Naked. Trust me. Nobody wants it."

Kate picked the little dog up and put him up to Genie's face, and he promptly licked her. "See," Kate said. "He thinks you're cute."

"He's a dog," Genie replied.

Kate shrugged, giving the dog a pet on his head. "Well," she said. "I hate to break it to you, but so are most men."

Chapter 14

Kate

There had been a time in Kate's life when, like CiCi and Genie, she cared very much what other people, especially people on social media, thought of her. Extra weight had to be hidden. Wrinkles had to be smoothed. Images had to be maintained. In fact, the unhappier she became in her marriage to Austin, the harder she tried to make her life look happy from the outside—the more pictures she took, the more posts she made with *#blessed,* and the more she threw herself into the dizzying stratosphere of make-believe family life.

It was this desire that prompted Kate to prod Austin until he agreed to make an offer in the gated subdivision with the designer tennis courts and absolutely *insane* HOA fees. She posted pictures of their move-in, so everyone would know they'd been accepted into such an exclusive and expensive area. She bought tennis gear, even though she'd never played a day in her life, and she made the boys wear matching clothes on their first day in their new school, just so she could snap them standing in front of her BMW station wagon and post it with a caption that read, "Sending these two cuties off to their first day at Primrose Academy!"

A few months after they moved in, Kate and Austin started receiving violation notices from the HOA board. The basketball hoop they'd put up for the boys was an eyesore. The fence they were building wasn't up to standard; the new siding they'd chosen, although it had once been an approved color, was somehow inappropriate. Nothing they did seemed to be in keeping with the rest of the neighborhood, and the added stress of it all fueled the nightly fights the two of them had about everything else in their lives.

Austin, who was a tiger in the courtroom, was passive everywhere else, and Kate was tired of always being the one to push for things. Austin, to put it simply, was tired of being pushed. He wanted to live a quiet life. He wanted to come home from work and have a beer. He didn't want to go places. He didn't want to be seen. He didn't want to talk to his wife about anything, unless it was about the kids. Kate knew he didn't love her, not like he used to, and she tried to ignore that and the fact that she didn't blame him, for the sake of the life she thought she'd built—for the sake of all of the hashtags she'd cultivated over the years to make others jealous.

Then one evening, after a long day of work, she went outside to retrieve the trash cans after the pickup. As she lugged the cans up the driveway, the golf cart of the HOA president pulled up, carrying the president of the HOA. Kate *hated* that stupid golf cart.

"Your trash cans are looking a little worse for the wear, Kate," she said.

"They're *trash cans*, Bobby Sue," Kate replied. "Aren't they supposed to look a little worse for the wear?"

"I'd suggest giving them a good coat of black spray paint," Bobby Sue continued, as if Kate hadn't spoken at all. "Or better yet, get a couple of new cans."

"Okay," Kate replied, trying not to roll her eyes.

"Today would be great," Bobby Sue said. "Before the next trash pickup at the latest."

"I'll get to it when I can," Kate said, fully aware that Austin was watching the interaction from the window. "Have a great day, Bobby Sue."

"I don't want to have to send you another citation," Bobby Sue said. "Two more, and we'll have to call you and your husband in front of the board."

Kate closed her eyes, willing herself not to cry. She was out of tears. She was out of words. At this moment, she was also entirely out of fucks. When Kate opened her eyes again, Bobby Sue was still sitting there in her stupid golf cart, waiting for a response.

"I said I'll get to it when I can," Kate said through gritted teeth.

Bobby Sue, who absolutely had one of those *may I speak to your manager* haircuts, gave Kate a thin-lipped smile and replied, "I'll just give Austin a call."

Unable to stop herself, Kate picked up one of the trash cans and held it over her head as Bobby Sue watched in horror, her mouth hanging wide open. "You know what, Bobby Sue?" Kate asked. "Why don't you take this trash can right now and do it yourself?"

"Don't you throw that at me!" Bobby Sue screeched. "Oh my God! You're *insane!*"

Kate followed after her as the golf cart skittered off, hurtling the trash can down the street as far as she could before Austin came out and pulled her back inside, demanding to know what in the holy hell had gotten into her.

"I can't do this anymore," Austin said. It was the same mantra he'd been repeating since he came home from work earlier that day. It's why she'd gone outside in the first place—to clear her head. Stupid fucking Bobby Sue.

"Do what?" Kate asked. "Deal with the HOA?"

"No," Austin replied. "This. Us. You. I can't do this anymore. I'm moving out."

At that moment, Kate wished she'd brought the sole surviving trash can inside so she could throw it at Austin too. Instead, she sat down next to him, took him by the arm, and said, "I know. Please don't tell the boys without me."

Two weeks later, Austin moved out and into a small apartment not far from the house. The boys, appropriately devastated, blamed Kate, and to be perfectly honest, she blamed herself as well. The kindly, bespectacled family psychiatrist in the city they'd hired more for the boys than anyone else suggested Kate was being too hard on herself, but singularly refused to convince Austin the divorce was a bad idea, and eventually, people began to find out.

First it was the couple friends she shared with Austin, and Kate knew that he would keep them all. She didn't have the personality for friends on her own—she'd always known that. CiCi had been her shield before Austin. Nobody in their right mind would choose her over Austin. When she'd finally told Laurie, she'd nearly been convinced to call Genie and CiCi and tell them as well, but she simply couldn't and swore Laurie to secrecy. It was one thing for all of St. Louis County to know, and it was quite another for all of Orchard Grove to know.

Still, on more than one occasion, Kate considered picking up and moving home to Orchard Grove, but she knew she couldn't leave her children, regardless of how angry they were at her. As a lawyer, she knew picking up and moving would mean that she'd likely lose custody, and she just couldn't risk it. If she'd known at the time what CiCi was going through, her decision, at least to tell them, might have been different. She wondered how, after all these years, they still called themselves best friends when they clearly kept secrets from each other.

Now all Kate had was Facebook, and Lord only knew she couldn't be honest on there. So she did the only thing she knew to do—she deleted her Facebook. If anyone noticed, they didn't say so. Kate figured they were all talking about it behind her back, but it didn't matter much now that her life had fallen apart.

Chapter 15

Genie

The accommodations in Albuquerque, New Mexico, were much better than in Oklahoma, and it was once again difficult for Genie not to fall, exhausted, this time with relief, into bed as soon as they'd opened the door to the hotel room. They'd had to pay nearly one hundred dollars in a pet deposit, which Kate happily forked over.

Now, however, there was the task of finding a veterinarian open late enough in the evening to see the dog Kate had taken at a gas station, of all places, and Genie wanted to scream about it. Not because she disliked dogs. Quite the opposite, in fact, but it was completely irresponsible to take a dog none of them knew anything about on a cross-country road trip.

"Aren't you two tired?" Genie asked.

"Exhausted," Kate said. She scrolled through her phone, calling out numbers of veterinary clinics for CiCi to dial.

"There are restaurant suggestions on the itinerary," Genie said.

"We have to find a vet clinic," Kate replied.

"Is that really necessary?" Genie asked. "He looks fine."

The dog, after eating and drinking his fill, had fallen asleep in the little kennel Kate bought for him, on top of a pillow that belonged to the hotel and that Genie was sure she'd have to pay for before it was all said and done.

"I'm sure he is fine," Kate replied. "Even his leg isn't as bad as I thought it was, but he still needs to be checked over and have vaccinations before we get to Las Vegas."

"I know you're right," Genie said. "You two keep calling. I'm going to call and check on my dad."

Genie pulled the hotel door open and stepped out into the hallway. She pulled her phone from her pocket and pressed the call button. Ugh. Seriously. A dog. Now, instead of a nap and dinner, she was going to spend her evening at a veterinary clinic.

"Hey, Leah," Genie said when she heard the calm, smooth voice on the other end. "It's Genie. How's my dad today?"

"Oh, honey, you know," Leah said. "Today was a bit of a rough one."

"What's wrong?" Genie asked. "Do I need to come home?"

"Oh, I don't think it's as bad as all that," Leah replied. "He's just not eaten much the last couple of days, and he's got a bit of chest congestion."

"Okay," Genie said. "Has he noticed I haven't come by?"

There was a pause on Leah's end. "Which answer would make you feel better?" she asked.

"The truth," Genie replied.

"Genie, the truth is that he wouldn't remember even if you had come. It's nice you come, and don't think it doesn't matter when you visit, but no, I don't think he's noticed that you've been gone," Leah said.

"Thanks, Leah," Genie replied. "I'll talk to you tomorrow."

"Bye, Genie," Leah said. "Oh, and Genie?"

"Yeah?"

"Have a good time. You deserve it."

Genie closed her eyes but couldn't get rid of the overwhelming guilt she felt for not being there for her father. At the same time, she was also glad he didn't know where she was, because if he had known, he wouldn't have approved. Still, it was hard for her to feel okay about leaving him, about being so far away.

She wondered if this was what it was like having children—feeling guilty for no apparent reason. She'd been told there was such a thing as "mom guilt" by some of the mothers of her students.

She'd always thought she'd have children, thought she'd get married. The closest she'd ever come to getting married, and thus having children, was with her college boyfriend, Harry. He'd been her first real boyfriend, her first everything, basically. He'd wanted to be a computer engineer, and all those years ago, that profession had sounded a little silly to her. Still, they'd supported each other, and after graduation, they'd talked about getting married. It was around that time that Genie's father started talking about her coming home, to Orchard Grove, to stay. He was close to retirement, and he'd never been very good at taking care of himself. He'd paid for her education, after all, and she owed it to him. Laurie was angry when Genie told her she was moving home.

What about her career?

What about her boyfriend?

What about her *life*?

The condescension with which Laurie said those things had hurt. They'd been living together in an apartment off campus, and they'd spent the better part of their senior year discussing what life might be like after graduation, much like they'd done in high school. This time, though, the future was less decided, less finite.

Laurie was so full of ambition. She'd been working on a memoir for her senior project—a personal story telling the facts of the case against her mother. Her talent was evident, and Laurie's friends in the MU journalism department were blown away not only by her ability to tell a story but that her life had actually *been* a story. This newfound admiration gave Laurie the push she needed to start talking about her life, instead of hiding it. Genie could admit now that she'd been jealous of Laurie's success, of her freedom. Laurie loved Kitty and Dan, but she wasn't tied to them the same way Genie was tied to her own father. They wanted Laurie to live her own life, and in turn, Laurie wanted Genie to live hers as well.

Their fight about graduation and the future came the night

before Laurie's senior project was presented. Genie hadn't intended to go, but she couldn't stand sitting in their apartment knowing she was missing something so important, and so she'd shown up at intermission, with flowers, and they'd apologized to each other and cried, and everything was back to normal before the show was over. It'd always been like that with Laurie.

Easy forgiveness.

Genie thought for a while that she might meet someone, might fall in love and get married, but it was difficult to meet someone when her time was divided between work and her father, and eventually, somewhere along the way, she gave up. She'd heard through mutual friends when Harry got married, and now she was friends with him on social media and saw pictures of him and his wife and their three children—all the first-day-of-school pictures and beach vacations. She was happy for him—Harry deserved it—but it was like a little needle through her heart. Somewhere, in those hard-to-reach places of her mind, she couldn't help but wonder if that could have been her.

She wished now it was so easy to forgive herself.

"Genie!" Kate called through the door. "What are you doing out there?"

"Yeah, hurry up!" CiCi shouted. "We found a vet!"

"Coming!" Genie said, wiping at her face. She hadn't realized she'd been crying. She hadn't realized how much life she'd missed and just how very much she missed her friend.

Chapter 16

CiCi

When Genie came back inside, CiCi and Kate were sitting on the edge of her bed, looking at her expectantly.

"Well?" Genie asked. "You found a vet?"

CiCi nodded. "Yeah. We got lucky. I guess they stay open late two nights a week, and tonight is one of them."

"Great," Genie said, walking to the dresser and pulling her hairbrush out of her toiletries bag. "Ugh, my hair is such a wreck. It still hasn't recovered from putting the top down on the car yesterday."

"Want me to French braid it?" CiCi asked.

"Do we have time?"

Kate looked down at her phone. "We've got about an hour, and Google says it's just about ten minutes away, so we should."

"Okay." Genie handed CiCi the brush and then plopped down beneath her on the floor by the bed. "Thanks. I haven't had my hair braided in . . . well, you were probably the last one to do it, and it was in high school."

"The girls won't let me do it anymore," CiCi replied, busying herself with the rat's nest that was Genie's hair. She'd always had thick, dark, curly hair, and CiCi had always been jealous of it. She had thin hair, always had, and she used to fantasize about what she'd do with a mane like Genie's.

"Hey, ow," Genie said. "You're brushing too hard."

"Sorry," CiCi replied. "You've got lots of tangles back here."

"I know," Genie said, reaching back to feel her hair, only to be smacked in the hand with the brush by CiCi. "I use detangler, but it's just a mess."

"When was the last time you saw Tammy down at the salon?" CiCi asked.

CiCi couldn't see it, but she knew that Genie was scrunching up her face in thought. "I don't know," Genie said. "A couple years."

CiCi stopped brushing. "Genie."

"I know, I know," Genie replied. "It's just so expensive."

CiCi looped her fingers around strands of Genie's hair and began to braid. "I can tell you color it yourself. You do a pretty good job, but Tammy could help you with the split ends and tangles."

Genie sighed. "Or you could just do it."

"I'm not qualified," CiCi said. She almost added, *and you're not dead,* to the end of that, but held back. Right now probably wasn't the right time to tell her friends about her job at the funeral home . . . or about the fact that she'd quietly deleted the picture of her and that hot guy they'd met at the supermarket, because she'd been afraid it would get back to Wade. Technically, Wade shouldn't care, and technically, she shouldn't care that Wade shouldn't care. But technical or not, the reality was that she *very much* cared about what Wade might think.

"You're pulling again," Genie said, jerking her head forward, causing strands of braid to come loose.

"Sorry!" CiCi said. "Sorry."

On the bed next to them, Kate sat flipping through the channels on the television, while simultaneously checking her phone. "My children are ignoring me," she said. "I just want to know how their games went."

"Welcome to the club," CiCi said dryly. More dryly than she meant. Her oldest was a senior in high school. She was probably supposed to hate her mother. But boys, CiCi had always heard, loved their mothers unconditionally. She wondered why Kate had had such little contact with her sons over the last few days. She wondered why Austin hadn't come down for Laurie's funeral. These were questions CiCi would wonder, but she would never ask. Kate would only give her a lawyer answer.

As Kate clicked through the channels, she stopped on a re-run of *Ellen*, as a grinning and suave Justin Timberlake graced the audience dressed as Frank Sinatra, plugging his newest album, which was all covers of Sinatra's music. When the cheering ended and Ellen began to tell the audience they'd all go home with a copy of the album, the sleeping dog beside Kate began to bark. It was an absurd bark—both raspy and high-pitched, and as he barked, he spun around in circles, dragging his injured paw.

"Is that dog having a stroke?" Genie asked.

"Shhh!!" Kate said, turning up the volume on the TV.

CiCi and Genie stared at Kate as Kate stared at the barking dog. This went on for nearly five minutes before, finally, CiCi couldn't take it anymore and said, "What are you *doing*?"

"I think he just chose his name!" Kate exclaimed, picking the dog up.

"What? Justin Timberlake?" Genie asked.

"No," Kate replied, sounding insulted. "Frank Sinatra."

"Your dog wants his name to be Frank Sinatra?" Genie turned around to look at CiCi, who could only shrug. "How is that a thing you even know?"

"I don't make the rules," Kate said.

"Seems like maybe you should," Genie replied. "Since, you know, you're the human."

"Have you told Austin about your new family pet?" CiCi asked. "I can't even imagine how Brent would have reacted if I brought home a dog."

Kate stood up and switched off the television, waving off CiCi's question. "He doesn't care," she said. "We better get going, though. Just in case there's traffic."

Genie and CiCi stood up, and Genie looked into the mirror, patting at her hair and grinning. "I love it," Genie said. "Thanks, CiCi. I forgot how good I look in a French braid."

"Keep it in tonight," CiCi said. "Then your hair will be extra wavy in the morning."

"Come on," Kate said, impatient. "I don't want to be late."

"You said we had plenty of time not even fifteen minutes ago," Genie said, grabbing the keys. "Calm down."

"Hey," CiCi said to Kate as they walked out the door. "I'll braid Frank Sinatra's hair too, if he wants. All he's got to do is say the word."

Chapter 17

Kate

The Lawton Veterinary Clinic wasn't anything like Kate expected. Instead of a small, sterile facility, it was located in a gorgeous stucco building that glowed pink in the waning daylight. The inside was as serene as the outside, so instead of feeling nervous about taking her new dog in to see a vet she didn't know, she felt calm looking at the scene before her.

"Ah," the receptionist said when the door chime went off and the women stepped inside. "You must be our seven o'clock."

"Yes," Kate said. "Thank you for seeing us on such short notice."

"No problem," the woman replied. "Here are a couple of forms to fill out. I know you mentioned this little guy is a rescue, but give us as much information as you can."

Kate handed the dog off to CiCi and began to fill out the paperwork. She couldn't answer most of the questions. She didn't know how old he was or his medical history. She knew he wasn't neutered, and she knew he was *probably* less than a year old. She knew that he appeared to be in good health, but really, that was it. She also knew she wasn't supposed to cross state lines with a dog without a health certificate, a little tidbit she'd learned from Laurie and her animal rescue contacts. So she made a mental note to ask the vet about providing one for her as long as Frank was healthy and his leg wasn't too bad off.

By the time Kate was finished with the paperwork and had handed it back to the receptionist, the lobby was empty except for them. An elderly woman with an elderly calico had left with a treatment for ringworm, and a harried-looking woman with two young daughters picked up a chocolate lab from a spay surgery. Just when Kate was starting to feel restless, she heard her name being called from the back corner of the clinic.

"Katherine Farmer and . . . Frank Sinatra?"

Kate stood up and was greeted by two of the greenest eyes she'd ever seen in her entire life.

"Hello," the owner of the green eyes said. "I'm Dr. Benjamin Lawton. But you can call me Ben." He stuck out his hand to her.

Kate tucked Frank in the crook of one arm and stuck out the other hand to shake Dr. Ben's. "Hi," she replied, trying to pretend she hadn't just been completely disarmed by him. "You can call me Kate."

"Come on back, Kate," Dr. Ben said. "And bring . . . Frank, is it?"

"Yes," Kate replied.

"That's an interesting name for a dog," Dr. Ben said as they made their way back into the examination room. "Maggie, my receptionist, tells me he's a rescue and that you don't know much about him?"

"*Rescue* is a term I'd use loosely," Kate replied, handing the dog over to the vet so that Dr. Ben could place him on a metal scale to weigh him. "My friends and I are on a road trip, and I got him in a gas station parking lot in Oklahoma. A lady was giving away puppies. He was older than the rest, and he has a bum leg."

"Hmmm," Dr. Ben said, bending over to examine Frank's back left leg. "It looks like a luxating patella to me."

"A what?"

Dr. Ben moved the dog's leg just a bit, bending it slightly back and forth. "It's when the kneecap slides in and out of place," he replied. "We see it most in smaller breeds, and although it can come from trauma, it's usually a congenital defect. In other words, most dogs are born that way, and it usually becomes evident after about four or five months, and I'd say your dog is about six months old."

"Is he going to be okay?" Kate asked. "Is he in pain?"

"He'll be fine, and he's likely not in pain," Dr. Ben said. "There are several grades of patellar luxation, and unfortunately, I'd say his is a grade three or four. He will likely need surgery to fix it, but it's not an emergency."

Kate let out a breath she hadn't known she'd been holding.

"Okay," she said. "I'll call my regular vet when I get home and schedule a consultation."

Dr. Ben looked up from Frank to her. "Where are you from?" he asked.

"St. Louis," Kate replied. "Well, technically, I'm from a small town south of there, but I've lived in St. Louis for the last two decades."

Dr. Ben broke into a wide grin. "I went to veterinary school at Mizzou," he said.

"Really?" Kate asked, surprised. "Are you from St. Louis?"

Dr. Ben shook his head. "No, but Mizzou is a great school, and I got a scholarship. I loved living in St. Louis. I would have stayed there indefinitely, but my wife, er, ex-wife, wanted to settle down here, where we're from."

Kate cringed when the veterinarian took a blood sample from one of Frank's legs. "That's how I ended up in St. Louis," she said. "My ex-husband is from there, and that's where we started our practice."

Dr. Ben looked up at her. "Practice?" he asked.

"Lawyer." Kate pointed to herself. "We were in private practice until about a year ago. Now he has the private practice, and I work for another firm in St. Louis County. Mostly defending victims of domestic assault who finally fought back."

"That must've been fun," he replied. "Two lawyers getting a divorce."

"It was mostly amicable," Kate said, grinning. "We share the kids, and he got the house and a girlfriend, and I rent a town house and adopted a dog . . . well, two dogs, now, I guess."

Kate wasn't sure why she was telling him all of this. Her divorce wasn't something she ever talked about, especially not with strangers. It was his damn spectacular eyes, she told herself, and the way his body leaned inward toward her every time she spoke. His body was, she mused, pretty spectacular as well. He must be a total ogre, she thought, for a woman to want to divorce him.

"What brings you to Albuquerque?" Dr. Ben asked. "Just passing through?"

"We, my friends and I, are on our way to Las Vegas," Kate said. "They're not exactly thrilled I picked up a hitchhiker." She scratched Frank's head.

"I'm guessing those are your friends out in the lobby?"

"Yes," Kate replied. "We've been friends since junior high."

"My receptionist is going to Vegas in a few days to see some boy band that was really popular when she was in high school," Dr. Ben said. "I was about five years too old for them, so I can't say that I remember who they are." He eyed Kate. "Would that have anything to do with your road trip?"

Kate felt her cheeks pinken. "That would have everything to do with it," she admitted.

"I should've been in a boy band," Dr. Ben said with a grin.

"I'm sure you do just fine," Kate said, before she could stop herself.

Dr. Ben handed her the dog and held up the vial of blood he'd taken. "I'm going to go run a few tests. Sit tight."

When he returned a few minutes later, he was smiling. "All clear," he said. "Let's get him vaccinated and started on flea and heartworm preventative."

"That's a relief," Kate replied. "My other dog, Pat Sajak, tested light heartworm positive just before I adopted him. We had to do a slow kill with Heartgard, and it was pretty scary worrying about him."

"Your dogs have interesting names," Dr. Ben said.

"They pick them," Kate said, fully aware of how that sounded. "When I first got Pat, his name at the rescue had been Jingle. I guess because they'd gotten him around Christmastime. We both thought that was a stupid name."

Dr. Ben laughed. "Well, I can't disagree there."

"My friend Laurie told me I should keep it because he answered to it, but it turned out he wasn't answering to the call of his name . . . he was answering to a cheese wrapper," Kate said. "So it wasn't hard to change it."

"Most dogs do love cheese," Dr. Ben replied. "In moderate amounts, of course."

"Pat was five pounds overweight when I got him," Kate said. "Laurie had been giving him several slices a day under the nose of the shelter staff. He still goes wild when he hears the crinkle of cellophane."

"Is Laurie out there?" Dr. Ben asked, pointing toward the lobby. "Because if she is, I should probably have a talk with her about canine obesity."

Kate's smile faded, and she looked down at her hands. Her

nail polish was chipped, and for some reason, this embarrassed her. "No," she said finally. "Laurie passed away unexpectedly two weeks ago."

Dr. Ben stopped what he was doing and looked up at Kate, startled. "I'm so sorry for your loss," he said. "Truly."

"Oh, thank you," Kate replied. "It's okay, really."

Dr. Ben reached across the metal examination table and covered her hand with his and said, "It's a hard thing, I know, to lose a friend."

Kate was so startled by the sudden intimacy, by the warmth of his touch and the tone of his voice, that she had to fight back tears and an urge she'd never had before in her entire life—to collapse into the arms of a man and let him tell her it would all be okay.

Before she had the opportunity, however, Kate heard the receptionist's voice call, "Dr. Lawton, your eight o'clock is here."

Ben removed his hand from Kate's and cleared his throat. "I guess that's my cue," he said. He turned around to the cabinet behind him where the scale and vaccinations were kept, and he opened a drawer, pulled out a small, white card, and taking the pen from his scrub shirt pocket, scrawled something on the back. "Here's my card," he continued. "I get over to St. Louis now and then to see some vet school buddies. I'd love to hear from you sometime . . . you know, just to see how your little fella is doing."

"I'd like that," Kate said, taking the card. "Oh, before I forget—won't I need a health certificate before I can take him across any state lines? I mean, you know, minus the crime I clearly committed today by taking him from Oklahoma to New Mexico."

Ben laughed. "Besides that," he said. "Sure. I'll ask Maggie up front to print one out for you."

"Thanks again for getting us in tonight. It's a relief to know that Frank is healthy."

"The pleasure was all mine," Dr. Ben said as Kate left the examination room. "Absolutely all mine."

Chapter 18

Genie

The outside air was cooler when they stepped out of the vet clinic, and so they decided to walk down the street a bit to see what there was to offer by way of New Mexican nightlife. Kate was in an unusually good mood, and Genie guessed it was because the little dog was healthy as a horse. She figured the attractive vet hadn't hurt anything either.

"I can't believe so many of the shops are still open at nine o'clock at night," CiCi said, marveling. "Of course, I guess we're not in Missouri anymore."

"That's Orchard Grove," Kate replied. "Plenty of places stay open late in St. Louis."

"It's all little towns," Genie said. "It's not just us."

"Well, I could get used to this," CiCi said, stopping to admire a storefront with long, flowing dresses in the window. "Can we go in here?"

The inside of the shop was busy, with patrons milling around. The women broke off from each other, drawn to clothing and trinkets that caught their eye. Genie couldn't really see herself wearing anything inside the shop, and that was mostly because the jewelry and clothing both were bright colors. She tried to stick to gray and black most of the time. Black, of course, was the most slimming color. It was one of the few things she remembered her mother saying to her. In Genie's mind, her mother had been a shimmering goddess, with her glossy, curly hair and pale skin. She couldn't remember that her mother needed to wear slimming colors, but years of being raised by her father led Genie to realize that her mother probably wanted to look slender for him. He was nearly obsessed with appearances. Once, when she was very young, they'd taken a trip to the Gulf Shores for a week, and while her father spent most of his time in the condominium reading, he'd come down to the beach one day while Genie and her mother were building sand castles, stood there over them with his arms crossed over his chest, and marveled that he had the "best-looking family on the beach." Her mother had been pleased with that, and so Genie had been pleased with that.

Now, standing in front of a full-length mirror, holding a purple tie-dyed dress up to her chin, Genie figured she'd been trying to recapture that moment for the last three decades.

"Do you like this?" Genie asked CiCi, who was standing beside her. "I can't decide."

"I think it would look nice," CiCi said. "You should try it on."

"It would probably be too tight," Genie said. "I feel like I'd look like a sausage in a casing."

"It's huge," CiCi said. "I mean, it's supposed to be huge. It's like a hippie dress or something, but there is no way it'll be tight."

"I would never wear it," Genie said. "I would feel self-conscious the whole time."

CiCi rolled her eyes. "I don't know why you say that kind of stuff," she said. "You do know that your dad would never even know if you wore it. He doesn't even know who you are half the time."

"CiCi!" Kate gasped, overhearing their conversation and walking over to them. "Don't say that."

"What?" CiCi asked. "I'm just stating facts."

"I'm going to go try this on," Genie said, backing away from both of them. She didn't want to hear any more, but their conversation continued as she hurried down the hallway to the dressing room.

"Don't remind her that her dad is sick," Kate said. "You know that upsets her."

"I wasn't trying to upset her," CiCi protested. "But she spends all her time worrying about what her father is going to think, and his brain is mush. She should be celebrating, and instead she's hiding like we're still in high school."

"CiCi!"

Genie pulled back the curtain to the dressing room, went inside, and sat down. CiCi was right. She knew she was, but it still hurt to hear. She knew CiCi, and probably Kate, thought her life was small. It was small. But it was her life. *And besides,* she thought, *it's not like CiCi has any room to talk about what I should be doing with my life. Her life is a shit show.*

She shook her head. That was a hateful thought. CiCi's life might be a shit show, but she'd always been good to Genie. She'd always tried her best to make sure Genie was included in that shit show of a life, and Genie knew she should be grateful. Right now, though, all she felt was hurt and angry.

"I don't care about your feelings," Kate continued outside the dressing room. "And don't give me a guilt trip just because you never managed to get any further away than next door to your parents. You're not winning any friendship awards either."

"I can't help it if I care about my parents," CiCi said. "I'm not going to leave them to rot in a house that ought to be condemned, unlike some people I know."

Genie hadn't heard the part leading up to the comments about their parents, but she emerged from the dressing room without even trying the dress on. "I'm going to buy it," she said. "It's cute."

"Show it to us," Kate replied.

"It's getting late," Genie said. "I'll show you later. I just want to pay and go back to the hotel."

"Okay," Kate agreed, turning her back on CiCi. "Frank is probably ready for a potty break, anyway."

Genie followed behind Kate toward the registers and almost

crashed right into her back when Kate stopped, because Genie had been looking out the window at the waning shadow of a man who looked incredibly familiar.

"Did you see that?" Genie asked Kate. *"Did you see that?"*

"See what?" Kate asked, brow furrowed. "I don't see anything except a couple of elderly tourists on the other side of the street with an upside-down map."

"It was him," Genie said, breathless. "It was him—that guy from the store earlier today . . . remember?"

"I don't know who you're talking about," Kate said. "What guy?"

"From the store!" Genie exclaimed, nearly jumping up and down. "Troy! Remember? The hot guy from the store!"

"Oh my God, really?" Kate stepped forward. "Where?"

"Well, he's gone now," Genie replied. "But I swear he just walked by. I swear it was him."

"Are you sure?"

"I thought he was going to come inside," Genie continued. "But he was wearing this weird costume—he looked like he was dressed as a caveman."

Kate scrunched up her face. "Okay, now I know you're seeing things."

"Seeing what?" CiCi asked from behind them.

Kate turned around to face CiCi. The anger had drained out of CiCi's face, but she was clearly making a concentrated effort not to look at Kate.

"Oh," Kate said, turning back to the window. "Genie thought

she saw that hot guy we met at the store earlier today. Trevor or something."

"Troy," Genie replied, still staring out the window.

"Whatever," Kate said. "But she said he was dressed like a caveman, and now I think we should probably take Genie home for a nap."

"I saw him," Genie said.

"I'm sure you did," CiCi replied, rubbing Genie's arm and glaring at Kate.

Genie wanted to shrug away from her, but she didn't want to cause any more trouble than she already had. So she stood there and endured it while paying for her dress.

"This dress is so totally cute," the twenty-something clerk said. "I bought one in every color last week."

"I hope I can pull it off," Genie said nervously.

The clerk eyed Genie up and down. She was wearing glitter eye shadow and had butterfly clips in her hair, and Genie was tempted to ask her if she had somehow commandeered an old Delia's catalog from 1998 and managed to order from it.

"You can pull it off," the clerk said finally, handing Genie back her credit card. "You've got the perfect skin tone for it."

"Thanks," Genie replied, pleased.

Genie carried her bag, rather triumphantly, as they exited the building and strolled into the now deserted streets. As they left, there was a click of the lock behind them, and the shop went dark. None of them said anything as they walked to the car, and Genie wondered how long Kate and CiCi would stay mad at each other this time. Their longest streak had been nearly a month their senior year in high school, when Kate wanted all of them to go to the prom together, rent a limo, and have their pictures taken as each other's dates. Both Laurie and Genie had been relieved at the request, since neither of them had dates, but CiCi had refused, because she'd been invited by Brent.

Genie understood why CiCi would say no. After all, if anyone had invited *her* to the prom, she would have jumped at the chance. That year, she'd saved enough money from tutoring other students in math and English to buy a dress in St. Louis at a department store instead of an ill-fitting and too-small dress locally. Her father, unsympathetic to what he deemed her "weight problem," saw no need to spend the extra money buying a dress in her size in the city. He told her if she cared enough about her appearance, she'd lose enough weight by prom to fit into a *regular* dress.

CiCi drove them all, including Kate, who was going under protest, into St. Louis to buy dresses. They'd had a great time, despite the tension between Kate and CiCi, and by the end of it, they were sort of talking again. All of that ended when CiCi and Brent were chosen as prom king and queen and danced to "Angel of Mine" by Monica, which had been the theme that year. Kate angrily stormed out of the building and then got her pickup stuck in a ditch outside the gymnasium. Brent and his buddies had to come pull her out, and Kate was forced to concede that maybe Brent was good for *something*.

Still, Genie thought Brent had caused a rift that time hadn't yet healed, and at the time, she hadn't understood why Kate was so upset. It was logical that they'd have boyfriends and experiences that would cause them to drift apart, but she also always believed they'd come back together in the end. Now, twenty years later, Genie understood that "the end" meant something very different, and as she slid into the driver's seat of her father's old Lincoln, she was incredibly, painfully aware that one of the seats was empty.

Chapter 19

Genie

The next morning, Genie woke up to an empty room, with a note on the dresser telling her that CiCi had gone down to the lobby to take advantage of the continental breakfast and Kate had gone out to walk the dog. She resisted the urge to wear her new dress, and pulled on the least wrinkled thing she could find in her suitcase. She hadn't thought to hang up her clothes the night before, and she inwardly chastised herself when she realized that Kate and CiCi had both made use of the hotel room closet.

She was desperately craving coffee and wishing she'd looked in the mirror at her leftover French braid when she entered the dining area a few minutes later. She saw Kate and CiCi at one corner of the room, waving at her in a cartoonish and ridiculous way that Genie didn't understand until she saw that they were pointing to the opposite side of the room, where a group of men all sat, talking loudly and eating what looked like mountains of biscuits and gravy.

"Is the dog allowed to be down here?" Genie asked, pointing to Frank the dog, who was busily lapping up gravy from a paper juice cup. "I swear if we get kicked out . . ."

"Shhh!" Kate hissed. "Sit down, but don't turn around and look at those guys over there."

Naturally, Genie did the opposite.

One of the men had his head bent back and was laughing. When he finally righted himself and reached out to grab a glass of orange juice, Genie caught his eye, and she realized with a jolt that she *knew him*. Well, she didn't exactly know him, but she knew him—it was Troy, the guy from the store in Oklahoma, the guy she thought she'd seen downtown last night. She knew she hadn't been seeing things!

"I told you guys I saw him last night," Genie hissed, feeling the back of her neck turn red.

"I stand corrected," Kate said. "I'm sorry I ever doubted you."

"He's coming over here," CiCi whispered. "Genie! Look up!"

Genie lifted her head to see Troy sauntering over to their table, a wide grin on his face. She considered for a moment that maybe it wasn't Troy. After all, Troy was someone she'd met once for a few minutes, and maybe this person walking toward them wasn't Troy at all, but just some handsome look-alike heading for the orange juice dispenser behind them. Yeah, that was it.

But now the Troy look-alike was standing in front of their table, his tan skin seemingly illuminated by the plain white

T-shirt he was wearing. "Hey," he said. "I get the feeling I've seen you ladies somewhere before."

Genie felt a wave of relief wash over her when Kate started to speak.

"You're that guy from that store, right?" Kate asked.

"And you're those women who stole a bathroom key from a poor, unsuspecting gas station attendant, right?" Troy replied. "Wait, it was just one of you. . . ." He trailed off and stared directly at Genie.

"We didn't mean to steal it," Genie blurted. She clamped her mouth shut when she felt CiCi stomp on her foot underneath the table.

"So," CiCi said. "What are you doing here? Are you following us?"

"I was going to ask y'all the same question."

Genie noticed a slight Southern drawl in his voice that she hadn't caught the first time they'd spoken. Of course, they'd hardly spoken at all, and she was entirely too busy looking at him the first time to pay attention to the way he talked.

"My buddies and I are headed to Flagstaff today," Troy said. "But the ultimate goal is Las Vegas."

"That's where we're headed too," Genie said. She felt Kate kick her under the table, and Genie knew it was because she'd revealed their destination to a virtual stranger. She resisted the urge to roll her eyes—she was pretty sure she'd overheard Kate telling that hunky veterinarian where they were going the night before.

When none of the women offered more explanation, Troy asked, "Girls' trip?"

Genie nodded, still ignoring Kate. "Uh, yeah. Basically."

"In that case"—Troy held up a finger—"I'll be right back."

He jogged over to the front desk, just a few feet away from the dining area, and picked up a flyer that was sitting in a stack on the desk. The woman behind the counter visibly blushed when Troy spoke to her. A few seconds later, he jogged back over and planted the flyer on the table.

"If you're going to be in Vegas for a few days, you should come check out our show. We leave flyers at every hotel. Some people come from states away to see us," Troy said. "We travel every few months, but our home base is Vegas."

All three women looked down at the flyer. There were several shirtless men staring back at them, their chest muscles flexed and oiled. Troy, in all his bronzed wonder, was one of them. The flyer had a black background with glossy, hot-pink text that read: "Girls' Night Out: Featuring the One and Only Bad Boyz of Las Vegas!" Beneath that were tour dates for the year, all of them ending with a two-week-long run in Las Vegas.

Genie bit down on her bottom lip to keep from . . . what? She didn't know—laughing or gasping or both. All she knew for certain was that she was absolutely not equipped to deal with this at 8 A.M. on a weekday.

"Well," Kate said under her breath. "This explains the cave-man costume."

"It's a pretty sweet flyer, right?" Troy asked. "My buddy Jax designed it." He turned around to where he'd been sitting with the table of other men and shouted, "Hey, Jax, man—they like your flyer!"

A bulked-up redhead with a sprinkle of freckles across the bridge of his nose and a full beard made a whooping sound and then went back to the stack of pancakes he was obliterating.

"He's our lumberjack," Troy said, leaning in conspiratorially. "He'd rather be the cowboy, but he looks like a lumberjack."

"So you're a traveling Chippendales group?" Kate asked.

"We're not technically Chippendales, but yeah, pretty much," Troy replied.

"I saw a show like this once in Branson," CiCi said, still eyeing the flyer and, Genie suspected, trying to keep the drool off her chin. "It was for Mindy Metcalf's bachelorette party."

"I knew I should have come down for that," Kate said.

"You both got invited?" Genie asked, turning her attention away from Troy to her friends. "I didn't even get invited to the wedding, and we were neighbors our whole lives."

"She's a bitch, anyway," CiCi said, waving one of her hands.

"Well," Troy said. "You're invited to this. I'd love it if you came."

Genie felt a deep blush creeping up her chest. He was looking at her. Really looking at her, and she wasn't used to anyone, especially an attractive man, paying her that much attention. "Uh, okay," she said. "I mean, maybe. We'll see, I guess."

"We'll see," CiCi echoed. She gave a small wink that made

Genie more than a little envious. How did she do that? Genie could hardly even blink at the moment.

"Good enough," Troy said, beaming. "It was nice to see y'all again."

Genie watched him saunter back over to his table. When he sat down, he caught her eye and gave her a broad smile. She tried to smile back, but she wasn't sure her mouth moved at all. She felt embarrassed. It wasn't a good kind of embarrassment, like she'd felt yesterday when he'd spoken to her at the market.

"Can you believe that?" CiCi whispered. "I mean, I guess we should have known. Look at him."

"We should have known he was a stripper?" Genie asked. "How could we possibly have known that he makes his money by . . ." She trailed off and then whispered, *"Doing that."*

"You make him sound like a hooker," Kate said. She turned to Genie. "He's not a sex worker; he's an exotic male dancer." She held up a finger. "Although there is nothing wrong with sex work as long as nobody is coerced into it."

Genie couldn't help but roll her eyes this time. She wasn't sure that she saw much of a difference. "Either way, I guess I *should* have known that a guy who looks like that wouldn't talk to a girl who looks like me unless he thought there was a possibility that money would be involved."

"That's ridiculous," Kate replied. "He's being nice to you. He's not soliciting you for a payday loan."

"And anyway," CiCi said. "He wasn't just talking to you, was he? He was talking to all of us, and I for one would love to go see that show."

"We can decide later," Kate said. "Right now we should go upstairs and pack up. If we get on the road now, we can probably beat traffic."

"I haven't even eaten breakfast," Genie said.

"Grab a muffin or something."

"Or," CiCi said. "You could stay down here with the sexy stripper and his friends."

Genie stood up, nearly knocking the table over onto its side. "That's okay," she said. "I'm not even that hungry."

Kate and CiCi shared a look and began giggling. Genie wanted to be angry, but she couldn't be, and despite herself, she began to laugh with them. She was laughing so hard that she didn't even feel the buzz of her phone in her pocket until they were halfway down the hallway to their room. When she pulled it out, she saw she had a text from CiCi's oldest, Lily.

I need to talk to you, was all it said.

What's wrong? Genie texted back.

Can I call you?

She looked at CiCi and Kate in front of her. Kate was baby talking to the dog, and CiCi was telling her she sounded ridiculous. Neither of them was paying attention to her. They probably wouldn't notice if she trailed behind a little bit further.

Before she could even make a decision, Genie's phone was

ringing, and as they were all three about to round a corner to the final hallway to their room, she stayed behind and answered.

"Hello?"

There were a few seconds of unintelligible sobbing, and then Lily managed, in between gasps, to say, "Micah . . . broke . . . up . . . with . . . me."

"Oh, Lil," Genie replied. "I'm so sorry."

"I . . . don't . . . know . . . what . . . to . . . do . . ." Lily said, gasping for air and then hiccupping. "He's . . . the . . . love . . . of . . . my . . . life."

"I know it feels that way," Genie said in the same voice she used when one of her kindergarteners was having a meltdown. "But if he just broke up with you, then he's probably not the love of your life, and he doesn't deserve you."

"You don't understand!" Lily wailed.

And in truth, Genie didn't understand. She really had no basis for comparison, especially when it came to high school love. "You know," Genie replied. "You really ought to call your mom. I know she'd love to hear from you, and I think she could answer the question better. . . ."

"NO!" Lily said. "This is *all* her fault!"

"That can't be true."

"It is!" Lily continued. "*Everybody* is talking about her and my dad. A couple of Micah's stupid friends told him . . ." A sob escaped her throat. "They told him that if my mom is crazy, it's only a matter of time before I am too. *Like mother like daughter!*"

"That's ridiculous!" Genie exclaimed, a little louder than she'd meant to. "Your mother isn't crazy! If Micah is foolish enough to listen to his friends, then he's not as smart as he thinks he is. And listen, I love all of my students, but I had Micah in school just like I had you, and he was never the brightest crayon in the box."

At that, Lily gave a hoarse little laugh. "I just don't know what to do. Everything here is so messed up, and then Mom just *leaves*. Dad is practically living with that lady, and yesterday, Grandpa Joe had Dad's car towed from the Walmart parking lot, because it was double-parked!"

"Call your mom," Genie said again. "Please. I know she has a lot of things she wants to say to you."

"I'll think about it," Lily replied. "Thanks for talking to me."

Genie said her goodbyes just as CiCi came around the corner looking for her. "Where have you been?" CiCi asked. "Did you get lost?"

"No," Genie replied, shoving her phone back down into her pocket. "No, sorry."

"What were you doing?"

"Nothing," Genie said.

CiCi eyed her skeptically. "Were you hoping Mr. Sexy Stripper was going to come and be your private dancer?"

"Shut up!" Genie said. "Oh my God."

"Come on," CiCi replied, putting her arm around Genie's waist. "Let's get back to the room before Kate starts putting our clothes on that damn dog."

Chapter 20

Kate

Kate stretched out luxuriously in the back seat of the Lincoln. The car was old and got terrible gas mileage, and more than once she'd felt a rattle or two on the freeway, but the car truly couldn't be beaten when it came to spacious back seats. At first she'd thought sitting up front would be better, so her gazelle-like legs wouldn't be cramped, but she'd been wrong. And now she was glad to let CiCi sit in front and entertain Genie for a while.

From the front seat, CiCi chirped on about Brent, browsing social media every few seconds to angrily show Genie a picture that Genie couldn't see because she was driving.

Kate smiled to herself. This was nice. This had been nice. True, they weren't eighteen anymore (thank *God*), but many elements of their young friendship fell right into place as the trip progressed. What was happening in front of her was no exception. She only wished that Laurie were there with them to see it. If Laurie were here, she told herself, she'd be braver about telling CiCi and Genie about her divorce. She'd have been braver about telling CiCi she *ought* to get a divorce. Laurie wouldn't have hesitated—about any of it. Kate worried that as angry and hurt and defiant as CiCi was now, all of that would melt away when she got home and reality set in—starting all over again at nearly forty. It was scary and difficult, and for lots of women she knew, it was just a whole lot more appealing to forgive, forget, and move on . . . together. She'd seen it before with friends in St. Louis, and those friends had all been shocked that she and Austin actually went through with their divorce. *Who does that?* they'd wanted to know. *So unsophisticated. What about the children?* But, she had to admit to herself, her children were doing pretty well, all things considered, and she didn't regret ending her marriage.

From the front seat, Kate saw one side of Genie's mouth tick up at something CiCi said. It was funny watching them interact. They were both wound so tight, but in completely different ways. Of course, Kate knew she was wound pretty tightly too. When she stopped to think about it, nearly every woman she knew her age was wound tighter than an eight-day clock.

Had they always been this way? Kate wasn't sure, but she didn't really think so. Sure, her life had been stressful nearly every step of the way, but that feeling of being on edge hadn't started until just before her divorce. There was just so much pressure—sure, the boys were older. She was no longer a frazzled mother of toddlers or elementary-school-aged children. She wasn't new to her job or profession. She wasn't a newlywed. Still, being nearly forty felt an awful lot like being eighteen. Who was she, really? Where was her life going? What was her plan? Where would she be in five years? These were all questions she'd asked herself nearly twenty years ago.

All of those questions made her sleepy, and just as she was drifting off to sleep, the car hit a huge bump, and Kate nearly bounced from the seat onto the floor. By the time she got herself upright, the car was zigging and zagging all over the road, and Genie was gripping the steering wheel in a futile attempt to keep them from swerving into the other lane and into oncoming traffic. Kate saw the truck up ahead and she closed her eyes and braced herself for the impact. The whole event took maybe ten seconds, but to Kate, it felt like an entire lifetime.

When she opened her eyes again, she was safe and alive and not smashed, and she realized they were on the right side of the road, halfway onto the median and halfway onto the dirt bank just beyond the median.

Nobody said anything at first, all three of them breathing in and out, in and out, trying to process what just happened.

"Is everyone okay?" asked Genie finally. "Nobody's hurt?"

"I'm okay," Kate said, her voice sounding a bit tinny. "What just happened?"

"Did we hit something?" CiCi asked. She still had both of

her hands pushed up against the roof of the car. "Was there an animal in the road?"

"I don't think so," Genie said. "I didn't see anything."

"Well, there has to be a reason you almost killed us," CiCi said, pushing open the passenger-side door. "I told you that you should have let one of us drive."

"I didn't do anything!" Genie said, following CiCi out. "I was just driving, and then . . ."

Kate opened the door nearest to the road and stepped out. Sure enough, staring all three of them in the face was the back left tire, completely blown out. "Maybe we drove over a nail or something," she said. "It looks pretty well shot."

Genie began to work her way around the car, going over every inch meticulously, muttering about how her father would kill her if he found out.

"Relax," Kate replied. "It's just a flat tire."

"Do you know how to change a tire?" Genie asked. "Because I don't."

Kate shrugged. "I'm sure I can figure it out."

"Neither one of you knows how to change a tire?" CiCi demanded, crossing her arms over her chest. "Kate, aren't you supposed to be some kind of feminist or something? What feminist doesn't know how to change a tire?"

"Sorry, that wasn't on the feminist test," Kate replied dryly.

"Where's the spare?" CiCi asked.

"I figured it was in the trunk," Genie replied.

"Well, it's not," CiCi said after a few minutes of rummaging past the luggage. "There isn't anything back here. I don't think there's a spare at all."

Genie sighed and leaned up against the car. "Great. Now what are we going to do?"

"Why didn't you check that before we left?" CiCi asked.

"I didn't even know we were taking this car until then," Genie replied, the tips of her ears turning red. "In fact, I didn't even *want* to take this car. You two"—she pointed her finger back and forth between CiCi and Kate—"demanded we take it. Remember?"

"Well, I figured you knew a thing or two about it," CiCi replied. "Since it's your car."

"It's *not* my car!" Genie said. Her voice was registering at least one octave above hysterical.

"Right," CiCi said. "It's your dad's car. Whatever."

"Let's just all calm down," Kate replied, holding her hands up. "Surely we can call someone to help. Genie, you have AAA, right?"

Genie shook her head. "No. My dad always thought it was too expensive."

"I have roadside assistance through my insurance," CiCi said. "I think it'll even work on someone else's car."

"Why didn't you say that before?" Kate asked.

CiCi shrugged. "I forgot about it until just now. Hang on, I'll grab my phone. I think I have the number saved."

CiCi reached into the front seat of the car. When she'd still not emerged with her phone a minute later, Kate said, "Hey, what are you doing in there? Did you get lost?"

There was a muffled reply, and then CiCi reappeared, holding two phones. One of them was Genie's. CiCi was gripping it so tightly that her knuckles were turning white. She marched over to Genie and held the phone in front of Genie's face.

"Can you explain to me," CiCi said, in a voice so controlled it threatened a whisper, "why *my daughter* is texting you about *me*?"

Genie's look of confusion gave way to sheer terror. "You know she texts me sometimes," Genie mumbled.

"I thought she was texting you about books and college applications, not about how her mother is a psychopath and she wishes she belonged to you instead of me!"

"She never said that!" Genie protested.

"She might as well have!" CiCi replied, throwing the phone at Genie so hard that it bounced off Genie's chest and fell to the ground.

They all three heard the screen shatter.

Genie bent down to pick it up and then said, "I've been defending you *this whole time*! I have never encouraged her to say anything bad about you! She's confused and scared and angry. I was just trying to help!"

"YOU AREN'T HER MOTHER!" CiCi exploded. "You aren't *anybody's mother*. How could you do this behind my back?

You should have come to me and told me she was talking to you about this stuff."

"Why?" Genie asked, finally angry. "So she could lose faith in both of us?"

"That's not fair," CiCi replied. "That's not fair and you know it."

"What I know is that I was trying to do the right thing by both of you," Genie said. "I told her over and over she should talk to you, but she didn't want to. What was I supposed to say to her? Did you want me to ignore her?"

"No," CiCi said. "I wanted you to come and tell me, because we're supposed to be best friends, and best friends don't keep secrets like that from each other."

"Oh really?" Genie quipped. "You want to talk to *me* about keeping secrets? You never *once* confided in me about your marriage trouble with Brent. I had to find out about it at a teacher's conference from your neighbor! Any time I'd ask, you'd tell me everything was fine, even though it clearly wasn't."

"Who was it?" CiCi asked. "Alice Reid? She's a busybody, and marriage trouble is private! That isn't the same thing!"

"Fine," Genie replied. "Then why didn't you tell me about your top-secret job at the funeral home with Wade Collins? Surely that's information a best friend should know, right? Suuuuuurely it's vital information for someone to know when her best friend is on the verge of an affair with *the owner of the local funeral home.*"

CiCi gasped, and for a moment, Kate actually thought CiCi might slap Genie right across the face. She felt like an outsider watching the drama unfold. She hadn't known about any of it—the texts between Lily and Genie, the marital troubles with Brent, at least not until recently, and she absolutely hadn't known anything about CiCi and Wade Collins.

"I am *not* cheating on Brent with Wade Collins!" CiCi screamed, making fists with both of her hands. "I'm not cheating on Brent with anyone!"

"Well, I wouldn't know, would I?" Genie retorted. "Since you didn't even bother to *tell me*."

"I cannot believe I *ever* thought you were my friend!" CiCi continued. "You are nothing but a backstabbing, lying . . ."

Kate couldn't take it anymore. CiCi looked like she was ready to pounce on Genie, and Genie looked like she was ready to burst into tears, and if Kate didn't do something fast, they'd need a whole lot more emergency roadside service than a tire change.

"HEY!" Kate yelled. "HEY!"

Genie looked over at Kate for a split second and then back to CiCi, who was still ignoring Kate completely.

"HEY!" Kate yelled again, and this time, when neither one of them looked in her direction, she continued, "HEY, AUSTIN AND I GOT A DIVORCE SIX MONTHS AGO!"

That got their attention.

Now they were both staring at her, openmouthed, waiting for the kind of explanation Kate had been practicing since she signed the papers, and right now she couldn't find the words to say it.

"Six months?" Genie said finally.

"How come you didn't tell us?" CiCi asked.

Suddenly feeling very hot and overwhelmed, Kate sat down on the ground. "I don't know," she said, thankful for the glaring sun so she didn't have to look directly at either of them. "I was embarrassed, I guess. I feel like a fucking failure."

"You aren't a failure," Genie replied. "We would never think that about you."

"Genie's right," CiCi said. "I'm pissed at her right now, but she's right."

"Does your family know?" Genie asked. "Your dad and brothers?"

Kate nodded. "I asked them not to say anything. I'm actually really surprised they listened."

"We could have helped," CiCi said. "At least I could have commiserated a little."

"Yeah," Genie replied. "We're supposed to be your friends."

"Are we?" Kate asked. "Friends? Apparently, we've all been keeping secrets. I've spent months worrying about keeping this from you two, and literally the only reason I told you is because I thought you were about to get into a fistfight, and I can't be lawyer to both of you."

"Did Laurie know?" Genie asked.

"Yes," Kate admitted. "I couldn't have gotten through it without her."

Genie ran her hand across the cracked screen of her phone and then said, "I don't know if we can get through this without her."

They all three sat there for a moment, silent, unsure about what to say or do next, when they heard a squealing of brakes so loud that they turned to see where the noise was coming from.

Pulled over on the side of the road, across from where the car was pulled over, was a giant bus. In fact, it was a tour bus, and it took Kate just a few seconds to realize exactly who the bus belonged to.

The flyer they'd seen earlier in the hotel, given to them by Troy, was now larger-than-life on the side of the bus. Kate was, quite literally, blinded by pecs. Beside her, Genie audibly gasped and began to frantically wipe at her cheeks.

The bus door opened, and out came two men, one of them Troy. He grinned and waved at them. However, when he got closer he frowned.

"Are y'all okay?" Troy asked. "What happened? Will here"—he pointed to a man with a buzz cut and a small scar above his eye standing next to him—"recognized you standing here on the side of the road. Thought you had a flat tire or something."

"We had a blowout," Kate said, drawing herself up to her full height. "I guess we're lucky it wasn't worse."

"But everybody's okay?" Troy asked again. He was looking at Genie, even though she hadn't spoken a word. Her face was red and splotchy and she was wiping at her eyes furiously.

"We're fine," Kate said when it was obvious Genie couldn't or wouldn't respond. "We're just a little shaken."

"You have a spare?" Troy asked. "We could change it for you."

Kate wanted to roll her eyes at his offer, because even though she knew he was just trying to be nice, the underlying sentiment was that he assumed none of them knew how. He wouldn't have asked three men that question. It would have been an insult. But she didn't have it in her to protest, especially because it wouldn't matter. They didn't have a spare, and she *didn't* know how to change it. God, she was such a hypocrite.

"No," CiCi said. "There's no spare." She gave a sidelong glance to Genie, who didn't return it. "I guess we'll have to call AAA or something."

"No need," Troy replied. He looked to Will, and when Will said nothing, he jabbed him slightly in his ribs.

"Oh yeah," Will said. "Sorry, I hate this goddamn heat. My uncle's got a shop in Flagstaff. We aren't that far off. I'll give him a call, and he'll send Leroy out with a tow."

"Oh, that's all right," Genie said, finding her voice. "Thanks, but we can take care of it."

Both Will's and Troy's eyebrows knitted together. "But why would you need to take care of it?" Troy asked. "Will's uncle will fix you right up, and likely, if you called a tow, that's where they'd take you anyway."

"I don't know if anyone will have a tire to fit," Genie said.

"If anybody in Flagstaff does, it'll be him," Will replied.

"Come on," Troy said. "You can wait in the bus while we call."

Without saying a word, CiCi began to stalk off toward the bus, followed by Will and Troy. Only Kate and Genie hesitated.

"I have to get Frank!" Kate said, nearly panicked. "I almost forgot about him. Oh God, I hope he didn't get too hot."

"I left the car running," Genie said, following Kate back over to the car.

"Oh, that's right," Kate said, sighing. "Okay."

She reached inside and picked up a sleeping Frank, who nuzzled into her arm. She immediately felt better. She'd had this dog only two days, and she was already unsure about how she lived without him before. Dogs were the best; they truly were.

"You think they're going to cut us up into little pieces?" Genie asked as they walked toward the bus.

"Nah," Kate replied. "It's much more likely they'd make a skin suit to wear onstage."

With this, Genie laughed. "I mean, I guess we don't have much choice. We can get on the bus with the air-conditioning and a bunch of attractive men, or we can sit in the sun and bake."

"I prefer hot men to hot deserts," Kate replied.

"I'm sorry about the divorce," Genie said. "I'm even sorrier you didn't think you could tell us."

"It's not your fault," Kate replied. "Any of it, but thank you. I'm just . . . you know, everything is so messed up right now."

Once inside the bus, Kate let out a sigh of relief when the cool air hit her across her face. She was *so hot*. Really, they hadn't been outside long before Troy and his magical bus of men showed up. She always wondered idly if being this hot for almost no reason meant she was about to hit menopause, but surely that was a ridiculous thought. Most women didn't go through menopause at not even *forty*, did they? But Kate stopped thinking about all of that the minute she got up the bus's steps and saw what was awaiting her.

Men.

Lots and lots of men.

Even CiCi, who'd stomped up to the bus without the two of them in a rather pointed mood, seemed to be in awe. Behind CiCi, Will was talking into a phone, and Troy pushed past the both of them to offer Kate and Genie each a bottle of water and Frank a pet on the head.

"That's a cool-ass car," he said, inclining his head in the direction of outside. "Not one I'd take on a road trip, probably, but still cool."

"It's mine," Genie replied.

"Oh yeah?" Troy asked. "You know a lot about cars?"

"Oh, God, no," Genie said. She laughed. "Absolutely not. My dad did, though. Or, does, rather . . ." Her face grew warm. "Anyway, it was a stupid idea to bring it."

"Good news," Will yelled. "My uncle is on his way. Said he'd pick it up himself. Said he's never seen a car like that out here. Said he can find you a new tire by tomorrow morning."

"Oh, thank you," Genie yelled back, relief evident in her voice. Kate wasn't sure if it was because the car would be fixed or because Will's interruption had stopped her blathering to Troy.

"Looks like you'll be spending the night in Flagstaff," Troy said. "I guess now you'll have to come to our show."

"My uncle says you don't have to wait on it," Will said, coming toward them. "Here, give me the keys, and I'll put 'em somewhere only my uncle can find 'em."

Genie hesitated. "I thought we'd wait on him," she said.

"No need for that," Will replied, waving her off. "Can't all of you fit in that truck, anyway."

"We'll take you into Flagstaff," Troy said. "Bert said he didn't mind a few beautiful ladies for a change."

"Who's Bert?" Genie asked.

"I'm Bert," came a voice up front. "I'm the driver of this device for debauchery. We've got to get a move on it, though, boys. We'll be late if we don't scoot."

Will extended his hand, but still Genie didn't hand over the keys.

"You can stay," CiCi called from where she'd positioned herself in between two men with baby faces. "I'm going."

Kate knew she ought to say or do something that would make Genie feel like she had a choice, but the reality was that she didn't *want* to get back off the bus full of beautiful men and wait for a tow truck, even if, statistically speaking, it was probably safer. She wanted to stay here, in the air-conditioning, and enjoy the view. So she just looked at Genie and shrugged.

"Fine." Genie sighed and handed the keys over to Will. "But I don't even know where you're taking my car!"

"To my uncle's!" Will said over his shoulder as he bounded back down the bus steps and outside.

"I'll get you the address," Troy said to Genie. "Come on. We better sit down before Bert tries to drive off. He thinks it's a big joke to pretend to leave us, and Will is going to be chasing the bus for at least a mile."

Genie followed Troy, muttering some reply, and Kate strained to hear the rest of their conversation but couldn't. Instead, she sat down next to the man she recognized as the architect of the illustrious flyer Troy gave them at the hotel.

"Hi," Kate said, smiling at him. "Okay if I sit here?"

He nodded. "Oh, sure. I'm Jax. Nice to meet you."

"Nice to meet you too," Kate replied, a little shocked at his politeness.

"I hope your car's gonna be okay," he said. "And that dog sure is cute."

"It just needs a tire, and thanks. His name is Frank." Kate adjusted herself in the seat so she could see out the window without getting too close to him, but just as Kate saw Will walking toward the bus, it lurched forward, and she practically fell into Jax's lap. "Sorry," she said. "I didn't know we were getting ready to move."

Jax watched out the window with amusement, scarcely noticing her on top of him. "Aw, man, he's gonna be so pissed when he finally catches up." He looked over at her. "I think I'm the one who's supposed to be giving the lap dances."

"I'm so sorry."

He laughed. It was a rich, deep laugh. "I'm just kidding," he said. "I don't do the lap dances. I'm just backup."

Frank, now fully awake and alert, crawled onto Jax's lap and settled in. Kate was about to take him back when she realized Jax was petting him, almost absently, as he continued to stare out the window.

"Who does the, uh, lap dances?" Kate asked, interested. "Troy?"

"Sometimes," Jax said. "Sometimes it's Will. They're always the crowd favorites."

"Is he a good guy?" Kate asked. "Troy?"

Jax shrugged. "I guess. I mean, he doesn't take advantage of the ladies, if you're worried about that," he said. "None of us do. We don't ever take advantage of the ladies."

Kate smiled. "Well, that's nice."

"I'm not saying we don't want to sometimes," he continued. "You know, take advantage when they're practically begging for it. They wait for us after the show, ya know? Ask to take us home. But if we do, we're out. That's the rule."

Kate tried to picture the kind of woman who would wait outside a Chippendales show in the hopes of taking home one of the dancers. She thought they must be the same women who, over a decade ago, despite being middle-aged, proclaimed to be

Team Edward or Team Jacob. The same women who had *can I speak to your manager* haircuts and argued with cashiers at CVS over the price of laundry soap. On the internet, these women were called Karens, or at least she thought that was what they were called. She hoped she wasn't one of them.

"So you like him or something?" Jax asked.

"What?" Kate pulled herself away from her thoughts. "No, I don't like him. But I think my friend might."

Jax turned around to look at Troy and Genie. Kate did too. Troy was sitting on the outside of a seat, and Genie was on the inside. She was laughing at something Troy said. When Genie looked up and caught Kate's eye, she smiled.

"He's always the favorite," Jax said.

"I'm sure they like you too," Kate replied. She couldn't help but feel a little sorry for him. He couldn't be any more than twenty. He had big brown eyes and a strong jawline, but he also had a smattering of pimples across his forehead and chin, and he had a full beard that he seemed to be quite proud of. He reminded her of her younger brother—a boy who'd woken up one morning in the body of a man and wasn't quite sure how to navigate the world or himself.

Jax shrugged and pulled out his phone to record Will, still outside and now in a full sprint, chasing the bus alongside the highway. He was waving his arms and, it looked to Kate, cursing profusely. She didn't blame him. He had to be pissed off and hot.

"This is the fourth time this week." Jax laughed, still recording. "What a dumbass."

Kate sat back, closed her eyes, and tried not to think too hard about how she, an educated and professional lawyer from Missouri, had ended up in Arizona, riding on a bus filled with male strippers bound for Las Vegas.

Chapter 21

CiCi

CiCi sat in the back of the bus, trying not to be mad at Genie and trying not to be hurt that Kate hadn't told her about her divorce. They could have helped each other *so much*. All throughout the trip, Kate had so many opportunities to speak up, and yet she'd stayed silent, knowing how CiCi was agonizing over Brent and her own looming split.

She wondered if Kate hadn't told her because she thought CiCi would judge her. She wouldn't have, but she guessed she could see how Kate would think that, considering how CiCi always acted like everything was so perfect even when it wasn't. Now, of course, it was no secret that her marriage wasn't perfect. It probably never had been.

Their marriage was over. It had been over since their younger daughter was born, maybe even before that. She'd been the last to know about it, though. Even when she'd been postpartum, carrying a toddler on one hip and an infant on the other, Brent hadn't cared one bit about her feelings. In fact, it was like he'd cared less. How *that* was even possible, she'd never know.

It just felt like everything was wrong, and she'd hoped the trip would fix the way she felt. It was a Band-Aid, and she knew it. But sometimes Band-Aids help.

"Are you still pissed off?"

CiCi looked up to see Kate standing in the aisle as the bus bumped along. She was holding on to the bus seat for balance; otherwise, CiCi knew, she'd have both arms crossed over her chest.

"I'm fine," CiCi replied.

"Shut up and scoot over," Kate said. She heaved herself down next to CiCi.

"Why didn't you tell me?" CiCi asked. "About you and Austin."

"I don't know," Kate said. "It sounds like a cop-out, but it's true. I wanted to tell you, and Genie too, but I just didn't know how."

"After you saw that video of me burning Brent's clothes would have been a good time," CiCi replied. "It would have helped me so much, you know, if you'd told me I wasn't alone."

"I know."

"Nobody ever told me it would be like this," CiCi continued. "I mean, I'm not an idiot. I always knew Brent wasn't perfect.

I always knew he had a wandering eye. But I loved him. I love him, I guess."

"He doesn't deserve you," Kate replied. "He never did."

"That doesn't make me feel any less shitty."

"It's going to feel really shitty for a while," Kate said.

"How long?"

"I'll let you know."

"Was Austin cheating on you?" CiCi asked.

"No," Kate replied. "He wasn't."

"Were you—"

"No!" Kate said, cutting her off. "We weren't cheating on each other. It was just . . . over. We'd been fighting for a long time. It wasn't getting any better."

"What were you fighting about?" CiCi asked. She knew she was asking a lot of personal questions, but she wanted to know. She wanted to know *why*. Maybe if she knew why Kate's marriage hadn't worked out, she'd understand more about why hers hadn't.

"It was a lot of little things that turned out to be big things," Kate replied. "Austin wanted me to be home more. He wanted more family time, but it always had to be on his time. I couldn't . . ." She paused. "I *wouldn't* sacrifice my work for him. I love Austin, and I love my children, but I'm not cut out for domesticity. I messed up. I messed our marriage up. It was my fault. That's why I couldn't tell you. It was all my fault, and I just couldn't say the words out loud."

CiCi looked at her friend. "It wasn't all your fault," she said. "It's never all anybody's fault, is it?"

"I'm pretty sure it's all Brent's fault," Kate said, wiping away a tear and attempting a smile. "You're a great wife."

"I am a good wife," CiCi said.

"I was a terrible wife," Kate admitted. "Good lawyer, terrible wife."

"Does it have to be one or the other?" CiCi asked.

"For me it did," Kate said. "Having it all is bullshit. At best it's bullshit; at worst it's sadistic. Who decided women needed to have it all or wanted to have it all? And what is *all*, anyway?"

CiCi shrugged. "I thought you had it all."

"What I had was anxiety and sleep deprivation," Kate replied. "What I had was a home that looked perfect on the outside but was dying a slow, painful death on the inside."

"So it's impossible to have it all?" CiCi asked.

"No," Kate said. "What I'm saying is that there's no such thing as having it all. It's a lie some asshole made up to make women feel even more guilty for existing."

"I didn't think it would be this hard," CiCi said.

"Me either."

"Do you miss being married to Austin?" CiCi asked.

Kate thought about it for a minute. "No," she said at last. "Sometimes I miss Austin, and sometimes I miss being married, but I don't miss being married to Austin. I miss having a partner. I miss coming home to a full house. I miss my children."

"I've been miserable for so long, but it's familiar, you know?" CiCi said. "I'm afraid that whatever it is I'll feel once I'm divorced will be worse."

"It might feel worse at first," Kate admitted. "I'm not going to lie to you. It feels really fucking shitty at first."

"I won't know how to act."

"You'll make it work," Kate said. "Lots of people make life work, even if it's not how they thought it was going to be."

"I guess everybody is just trying to make it work," CiCi said, leaning back into the bus seat. "I tried to make it work for a long time."

Kate put her hand on CiCi's and said, "It's not your fault that you couldn't."

"Will you be my lawyer?" CiCi asked.

"I can be your lawyer or your friend," Kate replied. "But I can't be both. Besides, that's not the kind of law I practice." She bumped her shoulder into CiCi's and continued, "That doesn't mean I can't give you some friendly advice, though."

"What's your friendly advice?" CiCi wanted to know. "Stop whining and enjoy the ride?"

"Well, yeah," Kate replied. "But also, don't post anything on social media that would be disparaging about him, and don't send him any hateful text messages."

"You mean, aside from the video going around of me burning his clothes in my backyard?" CiCi asked.

"Aside from that," Kate said, laughing. "Not much we can do about that now."

"I'm sorry I've been so hard to deal with," CiCi said. "I know you don't deserve it."

"Neither does Genie," Kate said. "She's just trying to help you."

"I know," CiCi replied. "I'm not really mad. I'm just hurt that my kid would go to her instead of me."

"Would you have gone to your mother about . . . anything at Lily's age?" Kate asked.

"No way," CiCi said. "I didn't realize my mother was a saint until I was at least thirty."

"Then there you have it," Kate said. "If anything, be glad it's Genie and not someone else. At least you know Genie won't steer her wrong."

"That's true," CiCi replied. "I know they're close, and I'm honestly grateful for that. It's just hard. I'm either angry or sad or both, and I just want to hit someone . . . or throw something."

"Once right after my divorce, I threw a bag of peas at a woman at the grocery store," Kate said with a laugh. "Actually, I feel like I was throwing a lot of things around that time. So, at least you aren't resorting to actual physical violence—only thinking about it."

"You threw a bag of peas? Why?"

"She cut in front of me in line at the deli, and then when I told her I was already in line, she completely ignored me," Kate said. "So I took out a bag of frozen peas from my cart and threw them at her head."

"You did not," CiCi gasped. "How did you not get arrested?"

"I missed her," Kate replied. "They sailed right into the deli. Landed on some guy's feet. Nobody saw me do it. I just pretended like I had no idea what happened."

"I'd like to throw a bag of peas at Brent's head," CiCi muttered.

"I never did like him," Kate said. "I feel like a bag of peas to the head might fix a lot."

Chapter 22

Genie

Genie watched the road signs for Flagstaff fly past them, and she was both eager and reluctant to get off the bus. She'd been having a fantastic discussion with Troy about travel—her admitting she hadn't done much or gone anywhere, and him admitting he'd begun to tire of life on the road—and now there was a lull in the conversation, and Genie didn't know what to do. Troy, for his part, didn't seem perturbed by the quiet. He was staring out the window, every once in a while glancing over to smile at her. It was as if he wanted to remind her that he hadn't forgotten she was sitting next to him.

Genie couldn't imagine forgetting she was sitting next to Troy. She felt her synapses crackle together every time he moved beside her or looked her way or—heaven help her—smiled at her. Genie knew that this wasn't just because he was attractive. There were plenty of attractive men on this bus, and she didn't feel a single thing when they looked at her. No, she knew that what was happening with Troy was *attraction*, her body's physical response to his presence, and she knew this because she'd read nearly every single romance novel the Orchard Grove Public Library had to offer.

She'd only had to wait thirty-eight years to feel it.

"What are you thinking about?" Troy asked, bumping his shoulder playfully into hers. "You've got a look on your face."

"A look?"

"Yeah," Troy said. "You know, like you're thinking about something important or maybe thinking about something you shouldn't."

There was a mischievous twinkle in his eyes, and Genie had to look away. She didn't like being asked what she was thinking about. It was a question she would *never* ask someone else. Most of the time, you didn't want to know what someone else was really thinking about, and that was a lesson she'd learned at a very young age.

Once, on the way home from school one afternoon, her father was oddly quiet in the car. Usually, he was full of chatter about his classes and quizzing her about what she'd done in school that day (her father never thought any of the elementary school teachers were worth their salt). But this day, he hadn't even asked Genie how her spelling test went, and they'd been practicing all week.

Finally, after what felt like a lifetime of fidgeting in the back seat, Genie leaned up and said to him, "What are you thinking about, Daddy?"

Her father cringed. He hated it when she called him "daddy." She forgot sometimes, though, and had to be reminded. At first he didn't answer, and Genie thought it was because of her misstep. Then, as they were pulling into the garage at their house, he said, "I'm thinking about how I ended up here, in the armpit of Missouri, raising a child I never wanted and working a job I'm too smart for."

Genie stared at him. She was afraid to blink, just in case she started crying. Crying made her father feel bad, and he didn't like to feel bad. She didn't want to make him feel bad.

Her father pushed the automatic garage door button on the car's sun visor, and then turned around to stare at her as the garage door eclipsed the afternoon sunlight. "I keep trying to figure out who you look like," he said to her. "You look a little like your mother, but you don't look a thing like me. I was gone quite often around the time you were conceived. I've always thought it was possible that you aren't my child at all. The milkman, perhaps? The trash collector? Dogcatcher? Who knows. Before I met your mother, she could be quite . . . indiscriminate."

Genie had to look up *indiscriminate* in her dictionary when she got inside, but she still wasn't sure what her father meant. Now, of course, she knew, and it was precisely the reason she would never, ever ask someone again what they were thinking.

They bus veered right, and it exited past signage that boasted three Waffle Houses and more than a dozen hotels.

"I'm thinking about where we're going to stay tonight," Genie said. "We hadn't planned for this stop."

"The Holiday Inn, of course. It has a convention center," Troy said as they pulled into the parking lot of a large hotel. "We've been performing there for about four years. It's one of our biggest shows of the year, not counting Vegas, since this is Will's hometown."

"Do you really think his uncle can get my car fixed?" Genie asked.

Troy nodded. "Yeah, but you're stuck here for the night, right?"

"I guess," Genie replied. "I'll need to ask Kate and CiCi what they want to do. I think we've had a lot of togetherness over the last few days. Maybe too much."

"So there was something more than the tire going on," Troy said. "I thought so."

"It's my fault," Genie said.

The bus came to a stop, and Troy pushed past Genie and walked to the back, to where Kate and CiCi sat together. "I hope you two are planning to come to the show tonight," he said, grinning down at them. "You're on the VIP list."

Kate and CiCi looked at each other. Finally CiCi said, "Well, it's not like we have anything else to do tonight."

"Great!" Troy replied, rubbing his hands together. "Let's get off this bus. I'm sure we'll be able to get you a room on our floor."

"Genie staying with you?" CiCi asked.

Genie slid down in her seat and covered her face with her hands.

"No," Troy replied. "Not that I'm opposed to it, but I'm pretty sure she's more concerned with the fact that one of you—and I'm guessing you—hates her right now than anything else."

"Nobody hates her," Kate said.

"Good," Troy replied. "I'll have our manager pay for your room, and I'll make sure all three of your names are on the list for tonight."

Genie smiled weakly up at Troy as he walked back past her. "Thanks," she whispered.

"I'll see you tonight," he said.

"Nice job getting your boyfriend to talk to us for you," CiCi said from the back of the bus. "He's too hot to be rude to."

"CiCi," Genie began. "I'm sorry. Please, you have to know that I didn't mean to hurt you. You know that, right?"

"I know that," CiCi relented. "But I'm still angry."

Kate stood up. "I move we call a recess on our deep-seated psychological traumas until tomorrow," she said. "Let's all just . . . chill out for the rest of the day, all right? No more talk about divorce or death or anything like that."

"I second the motion," CiCi replied. "It seems stupid to keep arguing about it when our other option is a room full of male strippers."

"Exotic dancers," Kate and Genie said at the same time. "Whatever."

AN HOUR LATER in the hotel room, Genie sat down on the bed and tried not to listen to the intermingling conversations of CiCi and Kate checking in with their children. She'd already called and spoken with the nurses at the nursing home. Her father'd had a rough night, and he'd still been asleep when she called. Since the dementia diagnosis, he'd had a habit of getting up in the middle of the night and wandering around. It was one of the reasons Genie made the decision to move him from the house to the nursing home in the first place—she was terrified she'd wake up one morning to discover he'd taken to wandering the streets of town in a state of undress. She'd tried, through it all, to keep his dignity intact. The Alzheimer's and dementia unit at the nursing home was more equipped than she was for nighttime wandering.

But the nurse said that her father hadn't gotten out of bed—it was just that he'd been restless all night, and every time they'd come by to check on him, he'd been tossing and turning and mumbling in his sleep. Eventually they'd given him a Benadryl, and that seemed to work. When Genie asked if she needed to cut her trip short and come home, the nurse said, not unkindly, that her being there wouldn't really make much of a difference. After all, he didn't even know who she was. In fact, sometimes her presence agitated him, because he sensed he was supposed to recognize her, but he didn't, and it angered him. More than once, he'd stormed out of his room or thrown something at her, which despite his outward disdain for her, he never would have done before he got sick. Genie's father maintained control in all situations, and this loss of control, loss of his faculties, made Genie wonder if this was how he'd always wished he could behave.

"Well, Lily still refuses to speak to me," CiCi said, throwing her phone down on one of the beds. "I'm ruining her life, apparently."

"There are a thousand reasons," Genie replied. "Maybe if you ask her, you'll get an answer."

"Nope," Kate said, holding up one of her hands. "None of that."

"Fine," CiCi replied. "Fine, she's just so frustrating. Children are so frustrating!"

"Kids are assholes," Kate said. "That's why they make them so cute when they're little. The boys don't even want me at their lacrosse matches, because they don't like having to explain to their friends that their parents are divorced."

"That's pretty common, though," Genie said. "To have divorced parents."

"It is," Kate agreed. "But I yell a lot at the referees, and it embarrasses them."

"Everything we do embarrasses them," CiCi said. "When the girls were little, I was their best friend. Now my mere existence is a personal affront to theirs. I'm going to end up alone with a bunch of cats. I'll be like that lady whose pets ate her face after she died, because they were hungry, and nobody cared enough about the lady to go check on her."

"You will not," Kate said.

"Nobody will even notice until I start to smell," CiCi continued. "And all my cats will have to be euthanized because they ate my face!"

Genie had to bite the insides of her cheeks to keep from giggling, because honestly, the image was at least a *little bit* funny. When she looked over at Kate, she realized she was doing the same thing. When a little sob emitted from CiCi, they sat down on either side of her and pressed themselves against her.

"That isn't going to happen," Genie said. "I promise. I'll check on you, okay?"

"But you'll be a cat lady too!" CiCi wailed.

"I don't even like cats," Genie replied. "I can guarantee you that my face will never be eaten by a pack of hungry cats, which means I can make sure yours isn't either."

"I overfeed the dog," Kate said, her voice almost a whisper.

"What?" CiCi sniffed.

"The last time I took him to the vet, they said he needed to lose three pounds," Kate continued. She looked over momentarily at Frank, who for the moment wasn't even the least bit overweight. "Which is a lot for a little dog like him, but I figure if he's not hungry . . . well . . ."

"He can't eat your face off," CiCi replied, her tone serious.

"Exactly," Kate said.

Genie couldn't hold it in anymore. It was too much. She began to laugh, silently at first, but when the tears began to roll down her cheeks, Kate and CiCi noticed and, after a few moments, were laughing as well.

"You two are lucky to have your kids," Genie said in earnest when they'd stopped laughing. "They'll grow up and stop being jerks and take care of you when you're getting older."

"Not all kids do what you do, Genie," Kate said.

"Maybe not," Genie agreed. "But I know for a fact you've paid to make repairs to your dad's house over the years, and I know you do it because he refuses to move. And CiCi, I know that living next door to your parents has its advantages for you, but don't you think it also has its advantages for your parents? They know that if they need help, you're literally right there."

"I could do more," Kate admitted. "But I don't, because I don't know what to do most of the time. Caring for older parents is just as baffling as caring for teenagers."

Genie nodded, even though she didn't really know what it was like to care for teenagers. All she knew was that her kindergarteners loved her, and by the time they were in junior high, they pretended like they didn't know who she was at the supermarket. She figured the way they treated their parents was probably similar, and most days, she was glad she didn't have to take a surly, pubescent child home with her.

There was a knock at the door, and Genie jumped up to answer it as CiCi made a vain attempt to wipe away the mascara smeared underneath her eyes.

It was Will, all smiles. "Hey," he said. "My uncle found you a tire in Phoenix. It'll be here tomorrow before ten A.M."

"Oh, that's great," Genie replied. "I can't thank you enough for all your help."

The tips of Will's ears turned pink. "It wasn't anything," he said. "Besides, it won't be cheap. I don't know that I did ya any favors."

"It's a tremendous favor," Genie said.

"Well, I gotta get going. We're starting rehearsal in a few. I reckon I'll see you ladies tonight." He tipped an imaginary hat and was gone.

"It looks like we're going to make the concert," Genie said, closing the door. "A few hours on the road tomorrow, and we'll be there. We should have time to get checked into our hotel if we get to Will's uncle's place by ten A.M."

"I guess we'll just have to make the most of tonight," Kate said, winking. "I wish I'd brought something sluttier to wear."

"Your legs are so long, everything you wear looks slutty," CiCi replied.

"You're one to talk, Tits McGee," Kate shot back.

"You both always look great," Genie said. "I'm the one who needs help."

Kate and CiCi turned to look at her appraisingly. "Yeah, you've got to be cute for *Troy*, don't you?" CiCi asked. "He's so damn yummy. I'd be jealous, but I don't think it's probably appropriate for me to be jealous of another woman's man yet."

"Okay, first of all," Genie began, "he's not my man. I don't even know if he's my friend."

"Is there a second of all?" Kate asked.

"Second of all," Genie continued, "he is pretty yummy."

"So you're the one who needs something slutty to wear," Kate said. "All right, then. Show us what you packed."

Genie shrugged. "I didn't pack anything that would be considered slutty," she said. "Besides, aren't you morally opposed to using that word?"

"No," Kate said. "Not when I'm using it to describe myself or someone else I know in an empowering way."

CiCi rolled her eyes. "Can I still call someone a skank?"

"I guess you can call yourself a skank," Kate replied, beginning to root through Genie's unzipped suitcase. "It would be pretty accurate."

CiCi threw a pillow at her, but Kate ducked, and it hit Genie instead. "Watch it, skank!" Genie chirped.

"Oh, just because I wasn't a virgin until college like *you two*," CiCi said.

"I wasn't a virgin when I went to college," Kate said. She held up the dress Genie bought the night before in New Mexico. "This will be cute."

"Wait," CiCi said. "When did you have sex in high school? *Who* did you have sex with in high school?"

"Richard McHenry, junior year," Kate said. She handed Genie the dress. "I'm sorry. I thought you two knew already."

"You hated Richie McHenry!" CiCi exclaimed. "You used to talk all the time about how obnoxious he was."

"I didn't hate him," Kate replied. "He was obnoxious, but he was also convenient. He was at my house all the time hanging out with my brothers." She sat down on the bed. "You remember that movie *Cruel Intentions*? I think Reese Witherspoon is in it."

"I love that movie," Genie said.

"Well, one night, Richie was over, spending the night with one of my idiot brothers, I can't remember which one, and they'd all fallen asleep. We were watching *Cruel Intentions*," Kate said. "The whole movie is basically about sex and who's having it and who's not. We'd been into my dad's whiskey, and well, you know, one thing led to another."

"One thing led to another with *Richie McHenry*?" CiCi squeaked.

"We were both virgins," Kate said with a shrug. "We thought if we practiced on each other, we might get pretty good at it, and you know what? We were right."

"Oh my God," Genie said. "He's married to the first-grade teacher. I share a hallway with her."

Kate laughed. "She should write me a thank-you card."

"I'll never be able to look at her the same way ever again," Genie replied.

"Oh, don't feel too bad for her," Kate said. "I wish someone had practiced with Austin before we met. Good Lord, I practically had to write him a manual and draw him a map."

"I always thought you were saving yourself for a member of Boyz United," Genie replied. "Like me and Laurie."

"Oh, Laurie was so serious about that," CiCi said.

"Do you guys remember what happened when one of my brothers tore Laurie's Boyz United poster out from the inside of her locker senior year?" Kate asked.

"She kneed him right in the groin," Genie said, a giggle escaping. "I thought Robert might pass out right there in the hallway."

"Well, he did ask her to prom the next week, so I guess it worked out okay for both of them," CiCi replied. "Robert was pretty cute, Kate."

"Ew," Kate replied, wrinkling her nose. "I'm going to tell him you said that."

"Don't you dare!" CiCi gasped. "Besides, I don't want Laurie's sloppy seconds. Everybody knows they went all the way after prom."

"'Went all the way'?" Kate asked. "What are you, ninety?"

"Wait," Genie said, pulling on her dress. "Are you two telling me I was the *only* virgin?"

"We didn't want you to feel left out," Kate replied. "So we thought it was better not to tell you."

"I can't believe you guys!" Genie exclaimed. "I expected this from CiCi, but you, Kate?"

Kate shot a glance at CiCi before she said, "See? I told you that you were a skank."

Chapter 23

Genie

Genie wanted out of her clothes, and it wasn't in a fun or sexy way. She couldn't *believe* she'd let Kate and CiCi talk her into wearing what she had on. As if her hair and makeup weren't enough to make her feel ridiculous, she was also wearing a pair of CiCi's pants—jeggings, rather—that looked like they'd been painted on by Bob Ross.

"Stop pulling on your dress," Kate scolded. "You're going to stretch it out."

"I know," Genie grumbled. "That's what I'm trying to do."

"Well, quit," Kate replied. "It's just going to make you look sloppy."

"Sloppy covers my ass, at least," Genie said.

"You don't want to cover your ass tonight," CiCi said. "You want someone to slap it."

"I do not," Genie replied.

"Yes, you do," Kate replied. "I left poor Frank in his kennel to come tonight, and you're going to enjoy yourself or it won't be worth it."

"I do feel bad for Frank," Genie replied in earnest, "but I do not want anyone slapping my ass, at least not without my permission. Not even to appease Frank."

"Yes, you do," CiCi said. "Everybody who comes to this show wants that."

Genie looked around the already packed lobby of the hotel. The doors to the event weren't open yet, but women milled around everywhere, primped and primed for an entertaining evening. Most of them looked like they did—huddled in an excited group, talking and laughing.

"I think we may be the youngest people here," Kate whispered.

"There's a bachelorette party happening in the corner," CiCi replied. "But otherwise, I think you're right."

"I can't decide if this is empowering or predatory," Kate continued.

"Oh, could you take off your feminist hat for just one night?" CiCi asked. "Could you not take offense to anything for just a couple hours?"

"Fine," Kate replied. "Because I've been dying to tell you two to look over by the entrance—see that group to the left? Look at the woman in the middle of the crowd. Do you see what she's wearing?"

Genie and CiCi turned around to look. It didn't take them long to spot the woman wearing a leather catsuit—complete with a mask and a whip. She stood at least five inches above everyone else in her stilettos.

"I know it's wrong to disparage other women," Kate said. "But yikes."

"I don't know," CiCi said, turning back to Kate. "I can't decide if it's empowering or predatory."

WHEN THE DOOR finally opened, Genie, CiCi, and Kate were near the back of the line. When they got up to the front, a man wearing an earpiece and carrying a clipboard asked for their tickets.

"We don't have tickets," Genie said.

The man looked up from his clipboard and said, "Show's sold-out. Unless you got will-call tickets, you're outta luck."

Genie leaned in closer to the man and said, "Uh, I think we're on . . . on a list?"

The man eyed her skeptically, and Genie pulled at her dress. "Name?" he asked.

"Genie Walker," she said. "I have ID if you need it."

The man waved away her offer. "Nope, I've got ya. Says it right here. Hang on a sec." He pulled a walkie-talkie from his pocket and spoke into it. "Yo, Sal. I've got Troy's girl here. Bring me the passes."

Genie's heart skipped a beat at the mention of her being "Troy's girl," and she couldn't help but grin at the man until he gave her a questioning look.

She cleared her throat and pulled at her dress again until Kate slapped her hands away. A few seconds later, another man with a clipboard and an earpiece appeared and ushered them through the doors and down the aisle to the front of the stage. Instead of regular seating like one might find at a play or a concert, the entire floor area was full of tables with four to six chairs placed at each. Their table had only three chairs, and it was as close as it could be to the stage and off to the right. There was a little "reserved" sign sitting in the middle.

"Here we are, ladies," the man said. "Drinks are on the house tonight, but if you get drunk and act like an idiot, we'll throw you out, understand?"

Genie, Kate, and CiCi nodded.

The man handed them each a VIP lanyard. "These will get you in and out, backstage after the show, and your drinks. Sitting here means you agree to the possibility you'll be pulled onstage for a lap dance or any other activity the talent sees fit during the performance." He stopped, catching his breath. "Of course that doesn't include actual sex acts, just simulated ones. Do you agree?"

Again, they nodded.

The man smiled. "Don't give me any trouble, please. I always get trouble in Flagstaff."

"We won't," Genie said. "I promise."

The man attempted what looked to Genie like a smile, but it was awkward on him and made him look creepy more than anything else. "Enjoy the show," he said before hurrying off.

"Well, this is nice," CiCi said, sitting down. "Look how close we are to the stage!"

"And free drinks," Kate added. She motioned to a bare-chested waiter with a bow tie around his neck. "What do we want? Gin and tonic?"

"Vodka," Genie said.

Kate looked over at her and raised an eyebrow.

"And tonic, of course," Genie finished.

"I can't drink vodka anymore," CiCi said. "Not after that party, Kate, in your field senior year."

"You should've had your stomach pumped that night," Kate replied. "Instead, you threw up all over my shabby chic comforter, and I had to throw it away."

"So I did you a favor," CiCi said.

Kate ignored her and smiled at the waiter. "We'll have two gin and tonics and one vodka tonic," she said.

The waiter winked. "Be right back."

"So," CiCi said, turning her attention to Genie. "Are you ready for a lap dance?"

Genie blanched. "I'd rather not," she said.

"So you're saying if Troy pulls you onstage and gives you a lap dance, you won't enjoy it?" Kate asked. "Because I'm finding that very hard to believe."

"She wants a private lap dance." CiCi giggled. "In his hotel room later."

The waiter returned with lightning speed, and Kate tipped him five dollars. "Gotta save my singles for later," she said. She pretended to shove money down into the waistline of her jeans.

Genie took a big gulp of her drink. It tasted like courage. "I'm only putting money in Troy's G-string," she said.

Kate and CiCi laughed. "Now that's what I'm talking about," Kate replied. "You might save a couple bucks for Will, though. After all, you kind of owe him."

"Look how crowded it is," CiCi said, turning around. "Every table is full."

It was true. The room was packed with women and a few men at every single table. There were two other VIP tables down front with several women at each. Genie wondered who'd invited them. Maybe Troy had invited them all. It wasn't beyond the realm of possibility.

"Don't you bet they're all jealous?" CiCi continued. "I would be jealous of us if I were sitting back there."

"Hell, I'm jealous of us now," Kate said.

"Lean in," CiCi said, and flipped her phone screen around to take a selfie. "I want to remember this night."

"Don't post any pictures of me," Kate said, making duck lips and then thinking better of it. "Or tag me. I can't have potential clients searching my name and coming up with pictures of me, drinking, with my hand on some guy's thong."

"Or me," Genie said. "Kindergarten teachers don't touch thongs either."

"Fine," CiCi said. "But everybody already knows we're together."

"As long as there isn't photographic evidence," Kate replied.

"Your parents will have a heart attack," Genie said.

"Oh please," CiCi replied. "My parents fucked half the town. They're hypocrites, and so is everyone else in Orchard Grove. You don't need social media to know what's going on. Everybody knew about Brent and didn't say a word to me about it. If I want to put my hands down the pants of a strange man while he gyrates in my face, I ought to be able to do it. I've earned the right."

"Normally, this would be the part where I tell you that argument won't hold up in a court of law," Kate said. "But I'm not a lawyer tonight. I'm your friend, and as your friend, I encourage you to put your hands down as many pants as you can tonight."

"Aw, thanks, Kate," CiCi said, touching Kate's arm. "That's really sweet."

Genie was about to ask if they could order another round of drinks, but the lights dimmed and the crowd began to scream at an earsplitting decibel.

"It's starting!" CiCi squealed. "It's starting!"

When the music began to play, the screaming got louder, and Genie resisted the urge to cover her ears like her kindergarteners often did during assemblies. The screaming died to a dull roar when the spotlight shone on a man with a microphone off to the left side of the stage. He was standing on what looked to be another man bent over like a footstool. The first man held up his hand to quiet the audience further, and then he jumped from the footstool man to the stage floor.

Genie squinted at him. If he was the MC, he didn't look like she'd expected him to look. Of course, her only frame of reference was Matthew McConaughey's character from *Magic Mike*. This man was short and squat. He looked more like Danny DeVito than anyone else. He was wearing a leather vest open to his bare chest and a long neck tie that nearly reached his knees. Genie had to assume this was meant to be amusing.

"Welcome!" he boomed. "Welcome, ladies and"—he peered down into the crowd—"gentlemen." There was a spurt of laughter from the audience. "I'm your host, Tommy Timber. Are you ready to see me dance?"

There was a mixed reaction from the crowd, as everyone tried to figure out if Tommy Timber was being serious. There were several cheers and lots of laughter before Tommy held up his hand again and said, "I'm just kidding! You didn't pay to see me! You paid to see my boys, and they're certainly ready to see you! Get ready! Get ready for the ride of your life!"

Tommy faded into the background as the stage illuminated to show a dozen men standing in a line, all clad in matching white sailor suits. "SOS" by Rihanna began to play, causing another round of screaming from the audience. Genie couldn't make out Troy from the lineup. The men gyrated synchronously for a while as the audience whipped themselves into a frenzy, and then broke out to individual positions on the stage. Genie didn't recognize any of the dancers on their side except the slightly young and awkward (but very buff) guy Kate sat next to on the bus. It appeared as if he gave Kate a wink while thrusting in her general direction, but Genie was so taken aback by all that was going on, she couldn't be sure.

When the song was over, the men disappeared, and Tommy Timber promised they would return shortly over chants for more from the crowd. Genie was relieved when the waiter appeared with more drinks, and she sank down into her chair, feeling exhilarated and exhausted.

"You all right?" Kate yelled into her ear. "You look a little flushed."

Genie took a drink. "I'm fine! That was just really loud."

"Well, get ready," Kate replied, nodding toward the stage. "They're coming back."

This time the men had on only the sailor hats and tight white shorts. They came down off the stage and into the audience, one by one. "I Wanna Sex You Up" began to play, and at first the men stayed stationary in between a few tables. Eventually, though, they each picked a table and a woman to grind on. The women at the chosen tables went wild, and Genie felt slightly relieved that their table hadn't been picked for this go-around. Troy was on the other side of the room, and she tried not to think about him dancing in front of someone else. Then she immediately scolded herself for having that thought. This was his *job,* and she wasn't his girlfriend. He could do whatever he wanted.

The evening continued, with plenty of opportunities for Kate and CiCi to stick their money down into the nether regions of attractive men. Even Genie got in on the action when Will was on their side, and she gave him a fifty-dollar bill. He leaned in and gave her a kiss on the cheek, securing Genie ire from the tables nearest to her for the rest of the night.

It was fun. Everyone was having a good time, Genie realized. Even the few women that Genie could see who were, like her, a bit embarrassed to be there eventually loosened up and enjoyed themselves. The alcohol and the music and the men seemed to provide an insulation for women Genie suspected rarely let loose in their daily lives to have a little bit of fun, a little bit of fantasy. Then, after it was all over, they could go home to their husbands without any guilt. Where else could they do such a thing? Genie could see the merit in the relative safety of it all.

Even CiCi had stopped looking at her phone every five seconds after the show started. In fact, she'd reached over and given Genie a hug and said a little breathlessly, "Isn't this fun?"

It was fun, and toward the end of the show, when the MC came back onto the stage to announce the final number, Troy finally came over to her side of the stage. All of the men onstage were standing behind chairs and wearing black suits.

"This is our favorite part," the MC said. "You've all been amazing, and you've gotta know Flagstaff is one of our favorite cities. Now, if you've ever been to one of our shows before, you'll know what these chairs behind me mean."

There was an eruption from the crowd. Kate elbowed Genie in the side and mouthed, "It's lap dance time."

"Okay, boys," the MC continued. "Go get 'em."

The men left the stage one by one and grabbed a woman from the audience. Will picked CiCi, to her utter delight. When Troy made his way into the audience, Genie readied herself. She could feel his eyes on her, and he gave her a wide grin as he . . . walked past her?

Genie swiveled around to watch him take the hand of an older woman with a red sequined top and gray hair. The woman was so excited she burst into tears being led onto the stage, where Troy sat her down in a chair and began to move to "Please Me" by Bruno Mars and Cardi B.

Genie knew that Kate was looking at her, but she couldn't bear to check. She felt so stupid. She couldn't believe she'd thought Troy was coming to get her. Of course he wasn't going to rush down the stairs and pull her onstage. He had hordes of women at his disposal. The entire thing would have made her laugh if it wasn't so embarrassing.

After the show was over and CiCi had been returned to them, they made their way out of the emptying auditorium. "What an incredible night," CiCi said, sighing happily. "I'm so glad we had a flat tire."

"You aren't the one who has to pay for the tire," Genie grumbled.

"What's gotten into her?" CiCi asked Kate.

From the corner of her eye, Genie could see Kate giving CiCi a warning glance and run a finger across her throat.

"It was weird that Troy didn't bring you up onstage," CiCi said, ignoring Kate. "I don't know who that grandma was." She bounced up beside Genie and handed her a folded scrap of paper. "That reminds me—Will asked me to give this to you from Troy."

"What, like we're in junior high?" Kate asked as Genie took the note. "What does it say?"

"It says he'll be in the hotel bar about eleven P.M., if I want to join him," Genie said, reading it.

Kate looked down at her watch. "That's just in an hour."

"Are you going to go?" CiCi asked, looking over Genie's shoulder at the handwritten message.

Genie shrugged. "I don't know."

"Why not?" Kate wanted to know. "He's clearly into you."

"I'm tired," Genie said. "Besides, what's the point? We're leaving tomorrow morning, and it's not like I'll ever see him again."

"Maybe that is the point," Kate said. "Look, I'm not usually one to advocate for one-night stands, but you need one in the worst way."

Genie felt her cheeks redden.

"It's nothing to be embarrassed about," Kate continued when she saw Genie's face. "It's completely normal and healthy."

"I think 'normal and healthy' is pushing it," mumbled Genie.

"Why?" Kate asked. "You got a chastity belt on under there?

Is he gonna have a hard time finding your clitoris or something? I don't understand."

"He doesn't look like the kind of guy who'd have a hard time finding a clitoris," CiCi said, tilting her head to the side as if she were truly pondering the thought.

"Oh my God, you two," Genie said, lowering her voice to a whisper. "We're in public."

"Trust me, every single one of these women knows what a clitoris is," Kate said, gesturing to the women who were still streaming out of the building. One woman walking past them overheard and gave Kate a high five.

"Please stop saying *clitoris*," Genie said.

"I'll stop saying *clitoris* when you walk your ass over to the bar, sit down, order a drink, and wait for Troy," Kate replied. She crossed her arms over her chest.

"You're going to feel bad if he's a secret serial killer," Genie said. "Really, really bad."

"You're giving me way too much credit," Kate replied dryly. "Now go."

Genie opened her mouth to protest but realized that she really didn't want to. Instead, she turned on her heel and marched through the lobby to the bar at the other end. It was fairly busy, she assumed left over from the show.

She found an empty table toward the back of the bar and sat down. She watched the comings and goings of the people at the bar, as the crowd slowly died down and it was obvious that the only people left having a drink were guests of the hotel. It was an odd turn this day had taken, that was for sure. She'd thought they'd be, and planned to be, in Las Vegas by tonight. She'd envisioned some sort of elegant meal before hitting a casino and, for her at least, spending exactly twenty dollars before calling it a night. She would've gone to bed thinking about their fun evening, and she would've finally had something to talk about with the rest of the teachers after summer break was over. It would be her go-to story for years, she'd already known it.

Now, though, she wasn't even sure what she'd say. This wasn't the kind of day she'd planned for, and it threw her off balance. Sure, there had been days when not everything had gone according to plan—the day she found out about Laurie's death, for example. That entire night had been one surprise after another. If anyone had told her that morning that she was going to end up in CiCi's backyard watching Brent's clothes burn up, well, she'd have laughed. Still, it was the first time in a long time that she could remember an entire day blowing up like this day had blown up, and she tried to quell the anxiety building up inside her. She wished she'd taken that prescription for Xanax when the doctor recommended it.

"Excuse me? Is this seat taken?"

Genie looked up to see Troy standing in front of her. She'd been so lost in thought that she hadn't noticed him walking toward her. "Sure," she said. "Sorry, I wasn't paying attention."

"What were you thinking about?"

There was that question again. Genie shrugged. "Oh, just about how this day has been weird."

Troy sat down on the bar stool beside her. "How so?"

"Well," Genie began, "it's not every day I end up on a bus full of male, uh, dancers."

"You can call me a stripper," Troy replied. He signaled the bartender. "Can I get you a drink?"

Genie wished he'd sat down across from her instead of right beside her. It was hard to think with him so close. "I wasn't trying to insult you," she said.

"I'm not insulted," Troy said. "I *am* a stripper. An exotic dancer. A Chippendale knockoff. Whatever you want to call it. It doesn't offend me."

"Does anything bother you?" Genie asked.

Troy appeared to think about it. "I don't know," he said. He leaned in to her. "Attractive women who seem to be uncomfortable sitting next to me, maybe?"

His breath was hot on her ear. Genie turned her head to look at him, and they almost knocked into each other. "Look," she said. "I'm going to save you some time. I'm bad at this. Astoundingly bad at this. You're going to have to tell me what it is that you want, because this is a game that I can't play."

Troy leaned back and looked at her. If he was offended or irritated, he didn't show it. The bartender came and went, and Troy took a drink of his beer. "I thought," he said at last, "that I was pretty obvious about what I wanted."

"I just don't understand why you want it from me."

Troy reached into his pocket and placed a ten-dollar bill on the table before standing up and extending his hand to her. "Come on," he said.

Genie knew she had a decision to make. She could excuse herself and run up to her room. She already knew that he wouldn't try to follow her. Or she could take his hand and go with him, risking a night of the unexpected. She felt a little bit like she'd finally stopped at an oasis after being in the desert for so long. A dying man shouldn't be given too much to drink all at once, but she was so, so thirsty.

She took his hand.

Chapter 24

Genie

Troy's room was on the same floor as the one Genie shared with Kate and CiCi but at the opposite end. Genie looked over her shoulder until she was safely inside. She sat down on the king-sized bed and put her hands underneath her legs, because she didn't know what else to do with them. She already felt out of control enough as it was. She didn't need her hands getting away from her, touching things all willy-nilly.

"I wish you could see my apartment in Phoenix," Troy said. "I think you'd like it."

"Is that where you're from?" Genie asked. She realized how very little she knew about him . . . how very little they knew about each other.

"Phoenix by way of Texas," Troy replied. "I've lived in Arizona for about a decade. My apartment is my favorite place in the whole world. It's cozy. Everything is comfortable."

"That does sound nice," Genie admitted. "My house is . . . well, it's more sterile."

"Sterile?"

"It's not my house," Genie said. "It's my father's house. He lives in a nursing home now, but it's still his house."

"You could make it your house, couldn't you?"

Genie thought about it. "I guess I could," she said. "But it'll always be his house. Even when it's my house, it'll be his, you know?"

Troy sat down next to her on the bed. "Then you need to find your own place to be. A place to feel safe."

Genie let out a little snort. She couldn't help it. "I can't remember the last time I felt safe," she said.

Troy brushed a piece of stray hair away from her face and said, "Everybody deserves to feel safe."

"I'm working on it," Genie said.

"Do you want to know why I want to be here with you, right now?" Troy asked. "Is that what you wanted to know downstairs at the bar? Why I'd want to be with you?"

"You didn't pick me," Genie said. It sounded ridiculous, but it was all she could think of to say in the moment. "You didn't pick me to come up onstage, and I thought . . ."

Troy leaned in and kissed her before she could finish her thought. It was a soft kiss, lighter than she would have expected, and when he finally pulled away from her, he was grinning.

"If I had picked you," he said, "it would have been a clear sign that I wasn't interested. I never pick a woman from the crowd that I'm attracted to, and I'd for sure never pick a woman like you."

Genie resisted the urge to touch her lips where they were tingling.

"When I bring a woman onstage," Troy continued, "it's part of an act, part of my job. I love my job; don't get me wrong. I'm good at it, and I love making women happy. But it's not real. When the show's over, it's over. I would never bring you onstage. I don't want anyone else to see what I want to do with you . . . to you. That's not for anyone else to see but us."

If there had been an option for Genie to be out of her clothes and under the sheets with a snap of her fingers, she would have done it. For once in her life, she wasn't going to analyze anything about this moment. She wasn't going to be rational. She wasn't going to worry about whether he was telling her the truth or whether she was one of many women, or the pros and cons of the decision she was about to make.

Instead, she let one of his hands wander lazily underneath her dress until he found the small of her back. She let him unclasp her bra, and when she giggled nervously, he whispered, "Is this okay?"

Genie tilted her head back as his fingers rolled around one of her nipples. "Yes," she said. "Yes, it's okay."

With that response, Troy guided her down onto the bed and helped her undress. Only when she was completely naked did he undress himself and descend upon her, first kissing her mouth and then kissing her all the way down to the parts of her body that were alive with desire for the first time in what felt like forever.

There was a moment when, just after his tongue had finished exploring, he nipped at the inside of her thigh playfully with his teeth, and Genie felt sure that she could smell, see, and taste colors all around her popping and fizzling—a moment where the bliss of being in her own skin was so acute that she nearly burst into tears.

Troy slid up next to her and nestled her into the crook of his arm. "We're not done yet," he said. "Show me what you want."

Genie lifted her head to look at him. She took him in, all of him, his hair matted with sweat, his square jaw muscle, and his lean, naked body next to her—every part of him aroused. It was all for her; he was all for her, and she was hesitating.

When Troy sat up to kiss her again, she put her palms flat against his chest and pushed him down onto the bed, straddling him. The look of surprise and then excitement on his face nearly made her giggle, but when she felt him at last, at long last, thrust himself inside of her she was lost again to a multitude of colors.

Chapter 25

Kate

Kate stretched her legs out under the hotel comforter and lazily stuck a foot out of one side. It was barely daylight outside, but she'd been awake ever since Genie sneaked in at about 4 A.M. and sidled into bed next to her. The agreement had been for Genie to sleep with CiCi, since Kate believed that being four inches taller than the both of them entitled her to her own bed. But she guessed that Genie (rightly) assumed getting into bed with CiCi would wake her and signal the third degree about what she'd been doing with Troy all night. Kate had gotten up very briefly to take Frank out, and then she'd gotten right back into bed, and Frank, to her surprise, had snuggled down into the blanket between her and Genie. He'd slept on the floor for the last couple of nights, and she found herself pleasantly surprised that he was already asking to get into bed. He loved his kennel, and he hated getting up early with Kate.

Her thoughts drifted back to Genie, and Kate decided she was pretty sure she already knew what Genie had been doing with Troy all night and was content to table that discussion until a more reasonable hour. As it stood, both CiCi and Genie were still sleeping, which meant that Kate could do her favorite thing ever—lie in bed and stare up at the ceiling. It was a luxury she rarely got anymore. It reminded her of mornings in bed at her father's house, the precious moments before her brothers were awake and stomping all over, leaving muddy work boots forgotten on the stairway and dirty towels in the bathroom.

Sometimes her friends would come over to spend the night, even though CiCi's house had a basement and a big television set and Laurie's foster parents kept the best snacks. At Kate's house, nobody ever bothered them, because nobody noticed them. Kate's father wasn't like CiCi's father—he didn't particularly care where Kate went or who she was with as long as she didn't get into trouble, and Kate always felt like her father had been pretty lucky to have a daughter who wasn't interested in trouble, anyway.

Beside her, Genie groaned and rolled over, nearly slapping Kate in the face with her hand. "Hey," Kate said. "Get off me."

"Why is it so cold in here?" Genie murmured. She snuggled in closer to Kate. "I'm freezing."

"Don't you put your cold toes on me," Kate warned her.

From the other bed, CiCi stirred. "Why is it so cold?" she echoed.

"Come get in bed with us," Genie replied. "It's warmer."

"No," Kate said, scooting as far as she could to the edge of the bed. "Don't come get in bed with us! Stay on your side of the room! In fact, both of you stay over there." She tried to push Genie away from her, but Genie held on like Velcro.

"Don't be so crabby," CiCi said. She pulled back the covers and got in. "Ahhh . . . it's so warm under here."

"I hate you both," Kate grumbled.

"Well, I love you both," Genie replied, snuggling in closer to Kate and allowing Frank to lick her face. "So much."

"Oh my God," CiCi said. "You had sex last night."

Genie covered her head with the blankets, and CiCi yanked them back, pulling them off Kate in the process.

"Hey!" Kate said, drawing the blankets back up.

"Tell us about it," CiCi said, ignoring Kate.

"No," Genie said. "That's private."

"It's only private when you aren't sneaking back into a hotel room in the middle of the night," CiCi replied.

"I didn't sneak in," Genie protested. "I was quiet, because you were both asleep."

Kate rolled over to face her friends. "Did you at least have a good time?" she asked. "Was he nice to you? Respectful?"

Genie grinned. "Yes," she said. "He was."

CiCi sat up. "Well, that's boring."

"Trust me," Genie replied. "It wasn't boring."

"I'm so jealous," CiCi said. "I'm going to go take a cold shower, but don't think I'm going to stop asking you about this."

"We need to get on the road, don't we?" Kate asked, glancing at the clock next to CiCi. "We've got to pick up the car before we can do anything else, and we want to check into the hotel and go to the casino before we head over to the concert."

"Sure," Genie replied. "Whatever you guys think."

Kate sat up and looked over at CiCi, who raised an eyebrow. "You don't have an opinion?" CiCi asked.

Genie shrugged from underneath the covers. "It's whatever you think. I'm too tired to make any decisions right now."

"Damn," Kate said. "We've got to get you laid more often."

Chapter 26

CiCi

By the time they'd all three showered and packed and were in the lobby waiting for an Uber to take them to the auto repair shop, it was nearly 10 A.M. CiCi figured Genie would have been upset about this, since they were supposed to be at the repair shop by then, but instead, Genie was staring off into space with a goofy grin on her face. CiCi wanted to be annoyed by this, especially since she hadn't quite forgiven her for the day before, but she couldn't help but be happy for Genie.

Just as the Uber pulled up to the front of the hotel, Troy sauntered out of the elevator and approached Genie. They spoke for a couple of minutes, and CiCi couldn't hear what they were saying, but just as she was about to tell Genie it was time to go, Troy leaned down and gave Genie a kiss so intimate that CiCi had to turn away and pretend to be looking at her phone until Genie came up to her and said she was ready.

Once Kate had convinced the skittish Uber driver that Frank was absolutely *not* vicious and was not going to bite him, and eventually provided his rabies vaccination, they made it to the repair shop. A man who looked like an older, more weather-worn version of Will and wearing a large turquoise belt buckle told Genie that if she ever wanted to sell the car to let him know. Then he pointed to a picture on the wall of him and Will and asked all three of them if they thought he could make it as a dancer if he were "just a little younger."

As they waited, CiCi resisted the urge to text Wade and ask how things were going back at the funeral home. It would be weird, she figured, to ask how business was, when business was dead people, and she really didn't have any other reason to text him. Lily, at least, *had* managed to answer a text earlier that morning. It was the first time she'd responded to a text from CiCi in days, and CiCi hoped that this meant there was some hope for repairing their relationship.

After they'd paid and were heading out to the car, Genie handed CiCi the keys and said, "I'm not going to tell you what happened with me and Troy. But I will let you drive to Vegas if you want to."

"After watching you to make out in the lobby," CiCi replied, "I don't think I need you to tell me anything. I think I've got a pretty good idea."

"Are we okay?" Genie asked.

"We're okay," CiCi replied after a pause. "It's not really you that I'm mad at. I'm mad at myself. I'm mad at Brent. I'm mad at the last twenty years, but I'm not mad at you."

"I wouldn't blame you if you were," Genie replied.

"I know," CiCi said. "That's why I'm not. I just want, more than anything, to enjoy the last part of our trip, so I can go home and face whatever it is that's waiting."

Genie reached out and gave CiCi's hand a squeeze. "We'll face it together, like always."

They loaded their luggage and Kate complained for only a minute about having to ride in the back seat again before they were finally, at long last, on their way.

"The show is completely sold-out," Kate said as they drove. "I'm glad we bought tickets in advance instead of expecting to get them when we got there."

"I've never understood why people do that," Genie replied. "Why take that chance? It's so much easier just to buy them beforehand."

"We used to buy Cardinals tickets from scalpers," CiCi said. "My parents never bought tickets until we got there."

"That's different," Kate replied. "I'm not sure why, but it is."

"Did you call the hotel and ask if they're dog friendly?" Genie asked Kate.

"I'm sure they will be," Kate replied. "Every other hotel has been."

"Yeah, but this is a casino and hotel in Vegas," Genie replied.

"Have you ever been to a casino and hotel in Vegas?" Kate asked.

"No, but . . ."

"It'll be fine," Kate said, waving her off. "Besides, who's gonna say no to Frank Sinatra?"

CiCi DIDN'T FIND driving the Lincoln as enjoyable as she thought she would. She felt a little bit like SpongeBob SquarePants in the episodes where he's driving a boat underwater. It was hard to accelerate and switch lanes. Honestly, she didn't know how Genie managed it this whole way.

Kate was snoring in the back seat, and CiCi knew her only choice for conversation was Genie, despite the fact that Genie had barely spoken four words since getting into the car. She kept getting text messages and giggling, and when she wasn't doing that, she was staring dreamily out the window. She wondered how Genie's life would have been if she'd met someone like Troy before now. CiCi knew all about Genie's college boyfriend, but she also knew how controlling and manipulative Genie's father had been. Still, even now, Genie worried about everything. Maybe this right here was the only way it could be for her. Maybe it was better, in the end, to meet someone now, when you're nearly forty and know who you are, and not when you're eighteen and still basically a pile of goo. CiCi didn't know. But she was happy for Genie. She wished

Laurie was here to see it, but she'd try to be happy enough for both of them.

"Are you excited about the concert tonight?" CiCi asked Genie after a few more minutes.

"Hmmm?" Genie glanced over at CiCi. "Oh, yeah. I can't wait."

"Do you think they'll still be any good?" CiCi continued. "I mean, they're all older than we are. Can you imagine any of the boys we went to high school with dancing and singing on a stage?"

Genie snorted. "Didn't Cory Shaw have a heart attack trying to sing karaoke at the last PTA fundraiser?"

CiCi thought for a second. "No, it wasn't a heart attack," she said. "It was really bad indigestion from the hot wings."

"God," Genie said. "When did we get so old?"

"To be fair, Cory has been balding since tenth grade and always carried Tums in his backpack," CiCi replied.

"Every year the parents of my kindergarteners just get younger and younger," Genie said. "I swear, most of them look like they could still be in high school."

"Some of them probably *are* in high school," CiCi quipped. "Did you know that there are at least three people in our graduating class who are *grandparents*?"

"Makayla Myers doesn't count," Genie replied. "She married a man who already had four."

"I know, but her oldest is in college," CiCi said.

"Your oldest will be in college next year," Genie reminded her.

"Ugh, don't remind me," CiCi said. "She wants to go to college all the way in Tennessee. She was accepted months ago, but I don't want her to go."

"Where?" Genie asked.

"Vanderbilt," CiCi replied. "She wants to get as far away from me as possible."

"As far away as possible would be Alaska. Anyway, she does not."

"Yes," CiCi said. "She does. She said, 'Mom, I want to get as far away from you as possible.'"

"Well, I'm sure she didn't mean it," Genie said.

"Trust me," CiCi said, her hands tightening around the steering wheel. "She meant it. I don't think there's any way I'll be able to convince her any different, especially now that Brent and I are headed for divorce."

"So, there's no chance you'll work it out?" Genie asked. "I'm not saying whether I think you should or you shouldn't. I'm just asking."

CiCi shook her head. "No," she said. "And even if we could, I don't think I want to."

"I always did think you were too good for him," Genie replied.

CiCi looked over at Genie. "Thanks," she said, wiping at an errant tear. "That means a lot."

Genie reached out and put her hand on CiCi's shoulder.

Before either one of them could say anything else, Genie's

phone rang. She looked down at it expectantly and then frowned. "It's the nursing home," she said. "I forgot to call this morning."

Genie pressed the green answer button and said, "Hello? Yes, this is Genie. I'm so sorry I forgot to call this morning, I had a . . . What? . . . When? . . . Why didn't anyone call me sooner? . . . No, I'm out of town. . . . No, there's no one else to call. . . ."

CiCi slowed the Lincoln and took an exit, parking on the side of a nearly deserted road. She waited while Genie finished the conversation with a knot in the pit of her stomach. What felt like hours later, Genie ended the call and put the phone in her lap.

"My dad died," was all she said.

CiCi brought her hands to her mouth. "Oh, Genie, I'm so sorry."

"They said he was fine last night," Genie continued. "Great, actually. Seemed better than he had in days. Then this morning when the shift changed and the nurses made their rounds . . . he was just gone. They think he died in his sleep during the early morning hours, but they're not sure. They said I can request an autopsy if I want one."

"We can catch the first flight home," CiCi suggested. She glanced to the back seat, wondering if she should wake Kate, who was still snoring.

"The car," Genie mumbled.

"Don't worry about the car," CiCi said. "We can get it back

safe and sound. One of us can fly home with you and the other can drive the car back."

"This fucking car." Genie pressed her shoulder hard into the passenger-side door and it flew open. She tumbled out and onto the ground, landing with a sickening thud.

CiCi pushed frantically at her own door until it opened, and she jumped out and hurried around to Genie's side. Genie was sitting back on the pavement, little bits of gravel mixed with blood stuck to her knees and the palms of her hands.

"Are you okay?" CiCi asked. "You're bleeding."

Genie ignored her. She grabbed onto the door handle and pulled herself up. She bent over the inside of the car and reached underneath the seat, straightening back up to reveal in her hands a large and rusted crowbar.

"My dad was always afraid someone would hurt his precious baby," Genie said, inclining her head toward the door. "He kept his guns locked up inside, but I guess he thought he could use this crowbar to intimidate people if he had to. He loved this car more than he loved me."

"He did not," CiCi said, banging on the back window to wake Kate. "You know that's not true."

Genie fixed CiCi with a stare that was so intense, CiCi had to look away. "*You* know he did," she said. "He could never let me have anything. Not even this trip. He resented me until the day he died, and now . . ." Genie paused to laugh. "Now everything he ever owned belongs to me, and there's nothing he can do about it. This car, *his favorite possession,* is mine now."

CiCi watched as Genie walked around to the front of the car. She stared at the car for a second, switching the crowbar from one hand to the other. Then, and to both CiCi's horror and amazement, Genie took the crowbar in both hands and plunged it into one of the car's headlights.

Genie stood back, gasping. "Wow. That felt good." She swung again, leveling the crowbar into the other headlight. "Really fucking good."

By now Kate was awake and had stumbled out of the car, bleary-eyed and confused. "What's going on?" she asked. "Did we have another blowout?"

"You could say that," muttered CiCi. She pointed to Genie, still standing in front of the car. "While you were asleep, she got a call that her dad died."

"Oh my God," Kate said.

"She's having a psychotic break, right?" CiCi asked. "We need to hold her down or something. She's going to destroy the car."

"I don't know," Kate said. She shielded her eyes from the sun and called to Genie, "Hey, Genie! Are you having a break-down?"

"No!" Genie screamed as she slammed the crowbar into the hood of the car. "I'm fucking pissed off!"

Kate shrugged. "Well, there you go."

"Kate!" CiCi exclaimed. "You can't just *ask* her that. She's clearly out of her mind."

Kate turned away from Genie to look at CiCi. "Were you

out of your mind when you burned all of Brent's clothes in your backyard and basically had a bonfire party?" she asked. "Or were you just angry that your husband, who was supposed to love you until death do you part, was cheating on you?"

"I was pissed," CiCi replied. "And maybe a little bit out of my mind."

"Did it feel good?"

"It felt amazing."

Kate walked toward Genie, who'd taken a break from smashing the hood and was doubled over gulping air.

"I'm sorry," Genie said.

Kate took the crowbar. "Don't be," she said. "It's okay."

Genie stood up. Tears were streaming down her face. "He never loved me," she said, falling into Kate. "He . . . he never . . ."

"It was his loss, you know," Kate said. "It was always his loss."

"I'm so angry," Genie said, hiccupping through her sobs. "I'm so angry with him."

CiCi reached out her hand and said to Kate, "Give me the crowbar."

"Why?" Kate asked, pulling back from Genie.

"I want to take a swing," CiCi said. "I mean, if it's okay with Genie."

Kate screwed up her face and said, "Of course it's not okay—"

"Go for it," Genie said, interrupting Kate. She took the crowbar from her and handed it to CiCi. "Beat the hell out of it."

CiCi curled her hands around the weapon. It was hot from the sun and from use. The weight of it made her feel powerful, and when she swung with all her strength into the passenger-side door of the car, she was nearly knocked off her feet. She righted herself and took another swing. And then another.

"I'm tired of being unhappy," she said, swinging. "I'm tired of pretending not to be unhappy. I'm tired of parent pickups and drop-offs. I'm tired of putting on makeup every morning for the stupid parent pickups and drop-offs, because if I don't, the bitches in the PTA will talk about it at the next meeting. I'M TIRED OF THE FUCKING PTA!"

With each grievance CiCi ticked off, the crowbar slammed harder and harder into the Lincoln, until she finally stepped back, exhausted. She handed it to Kate, who was watching beside Genie, wide-eyed. "Here," CiCi said, panting. "Try it."

Kate took the crowbar and handed Frank over to Genie. "Do I have to list off the things I hate?" she asked.

"I don't know," CiCi said, plopping down onto the grass just off the shoulder of the highway. "But it helps."

Kate tried it, landing the crowbar right in the middle of the back passenger window. When the glass began to pop and crack, CiCi and Genie cheered. "Okay," Kate said. "Here goes." She swung again. "I love my job." She swung again. "I love my kids." She swung again.

"I don't think she's doing this right," CiCi whispered to Genie.

"Shhh," Genie said. "She'll get there."

Kate held the crowbar high above her head with both hands. "I hate that spending time with my kids means I'm falling behind at work. I hate that falling behind at work means I'm failing my kids." She brought the crowbar down, hard, on the hood of the car. "There." *Thwack*. "Is." *Thwack*. "No." *Thwack*. "Such." *Thwack*. "Thing." *Thwack*. "As." *Thwack*. "Having." *Thwack*. "It." *Thwack*. "All." *Thwack*.

Kate threw the crowbar to the ground and collapsed next to CiCi. "I enjoyed that more than I thought I would," she said.

"Well, you are the woman who threw a frozen bag of peas at another person's head," CiCi replied.

"Wait, what?" Genie asked.

"She had it coming," was all Kate replied.

"Laurie would have appreciated this," CiCi said.

Kate grinned. "She would have, wouldn't she?"

"Do you think," Genie asked, "that wherever she is now, she can see us?"

CiCi took Genie's hand and then Kate's. They all three stared at the nearly demolished car as the rest of the world zipped along on the interstate just below them.

Chapter 27

Genie

"You know what nobody ever told me about getting older?" Kate asked, lying back in the grass, her arms behind her head.

"What?" CiCi and Genie asked in unison.

"That I'd have so much *chin hair.*"

"I swear I could grow a full beard," Genie replied, absently running the backs of her knuckles across her chin.

"And what is *with* the adult acne?" CiCi asked. "It's not fair to have wrinkles *and* acne."

"I have at least six different creams for my face," Kate replied. "Just for my face!"

"I have gray hair," Genie offered. "And not just a little bit. *A lot.*"

"I lose clumps of hair in the shower," Kate admitted. "I think I could probably make someone a wig out of all the hair I've lost."

"And I swear to God, I can't remember a damn thing," Genie

said. "Sometimes I'll be sitting in circle time with the kids and completely forget a song I've sung a thousand times before."

"Well, I've gained ten pounds this year, *and* I have to pee all the time," CiCi said.

Both Kate and Genie muttered, "Me too."

"But you know what?" Kate asked, sitting up. "I don't have a single problem telling those MLM 'boss babes' to stay away from me with their pyramid schemes. I used to feel so guilty about it, and now I don't care who unfriends me."

"They're not pyramid schemes," CiCi replied, and then, using air quotes, she continued, "They're 'working from home' so they can stay home with their kids instead of paying someone else to raise them in day care."

Kate rolled her eyes. "Yes, because all working moms are terrible, and clearly day care lowers IQ, and staying at home and hocking terrible-tasting vitamins is the only way your kid is going to get into Harvard."

"It's so ridiculous the way we judge each other," CiCi said. "I know I do it too, but I don't even understand *why* I do it."

"It's the vitamins," Kate replied. "They're tearing holes in our brains."

"Those vitamins were disgusting," CiCi agreed. "I'm glad I never sold those."

"Didn't you sell some of that weight loss stuff everyone was raving about a few years ago?" Genie asked CiCi. "I specifically remember getting a message from you on Facebook asking me to buy it."

"I bought five hundred dollars' worth of that crap," CiCi replied. "I never made a single sale."

"How long have we been sitting here?" Genie asked.

Kate pulled her phone out of her back pocket and said, "At least an hour."

"What are we going to do with the car?" CiCi asked. "It can't just stay here, can it?"

Genie shrugged. "I don't know. I wasn't really thinking clearly. I'm not sure what to do now."

"Well, we need to get a flight home," Kate said. "We should get you back to Orchard Grove as fast as possible."

"No," Genie replied.

"What do you mean, no?" Kate asked.

"No, I don't want to go back to Orchard Grove as fast as possible," Genie said. "I want to go to the concert."

"But your dad . . ."

Genie stood up. "I've spent my entire life doing everything my father has ever asked me to do. I never complained. I never argued. I've given him everything. I'm not giving him this trip too."

"Are you sure?" Kate asked.

"Yeah, you don't have to stay for us," CiCi agreed. "We'll do whatever you want us to do."

"I'm telling you what I want to do," Genie said. "I want to go to that concert. We can fly home tomorrow—I don't care—but we're sticking to the itinerary today."

"How far from Vegas are we?" CiCi asked. "We can't be that

far. I remember seeing several signs, and we've been on the road for a couple of hours."

"I'd say at least another hour or so," Genie replied. "Not that far, really."

"Do you think the car will still start?" Kate asked.

"I doubt it," CiCi said.

Genie stood up and walked back over to the car and got behind the wheel, and to everyone's surprise, it started right up.

"I guess it's just body damage," Genie said, trotting back over. "I mean, it's not great, but I think it'll get us there."

Kate stood up and took Frank from CiCi, who'd been holding him since the demolition. "Well, I guess if you drive slow and don't make eye contact with any other drivers on the road, we'll probably be able to get to the hotel. We can't drive it home, though. There's no way. There's a hole in at least three windows."

"Let's just get to Vegas," Genie said. "Then we can figure out what to do with the car."

As she drove, her head cocked to the side so she could see, praying that they weren't stopped by any police along the way, Genie knew she ought to feel guilty for destroying the car, but strangely, all she felt was relief. For her father, well, what she felt was complicated. On the one hand, she'd known his death was coming. Everything was in order. Her father had seen to that when he'd first been diagnosed with Alzheimer's three years ago. It surprised Genie when he gave her power of attorney and made her the executor of his estate, but really, who else did he have? He didn't have any friends or loved ones. It was just her. Still, it came as a surprise, and she'd done everything in her power to prove to him that she was worthy of such a task. During those first months, he'd finalized everything, down to the trim of his casket, even though the doctors told him he had years, maybe even a decade, to live.

Genie knew, despite the anger she currently felt, that she would grieve for him. She would do for him in death what she did for him in life—follow his orders, take care of him. Still, she couldn't believe he was gone. What would she do once she was free, once everything and everyone had been taken care of? The answer both thrilled and terrified her—whatever she wanted.

"Are you doing okay, Genie?" CiCi asked from the back seat. "My mom sent me a text a few minutes ago. She wanted me to tell you if there is anything she and Dad can do to help, they will."

"Tell them thank you for me," Genie replied.

"Are you sure you don't want to go back?"

Genie shook her head. "No. The nursing home knows the plan. He'll go to the funeral home. I know Wade will take care of him."

"I sent him a text," CiCi replied. "He sends you his love too."

Genie smiled. "Tell him I said thank you," she said.

"I will," CiCi said.

"So," Kate said, turning around in the front seat. "You're not cheating on Brent with Wade Collins?"

"No!" CiCi exclaimed. "God, I would never cheat on Brent. Not even now."

"But you're spending all that time at the funeral home," Genie said. "Why, if you're not going to see Wade?"

"I'm helping him," CiCi replied. "He sent out a request for a stylist to come to the funeral home and help with makeup and hair. Nobody would. They all acted like it was too creepy, so I offered. I've always been pretty good with that stuff. It's just volunteer right now, since I'm not a professional, but I want to make it full-time when I'm done learning."

"So you're not sleeping with Wade," Kate said, eyebrows furrowed. "You're just going there to make dead people look . . . less dead?"

CiCi nodded. "I guess you could put it like that. But nobody ever looks less dead once they *are* dead."

"I think I liked the idea of you cheating on Brent better," Kate replied.

"Don't be so judgmental," CiCi said. "It's a service, like anything else. It's a necessary service, by the way. And even if it wasn't necessary, don't you think it makes families feel better to be able to see their loved ones looking put together just one more time? It's psychological, sure, but death is psychological, isn't it?"

Kate stared at her. "Damn, CiCi. That was deep."

"Shut up," CiCi replied.

"No, I'm serious," Kate said. "No wonder Wade wants to jump you."

"He doesn't want to jump me," CiCi said, rolling her eyes.

"He does," Genie interjected. "You didn't see the way he was looking at you the other night."

"And he's so sexy," Kate replied, a grin spreading across her face. "A sexy undertaker!"

By the time they got to Las Vegas, Genie thought they all looked a little worse for the wear. Kate's red lipstick had settled into the creases of her mouth, and her linen pants were wrinkled. CiCi's hair was in various states of disarray, while Genie herself felt a little bit like she'd been run over by a truck. She was sure she looked it too. She wondered for a moment if maybe they should have just gone home.

The valet looked more than a little confused when Genie handed him the keys to the Lincoln, but didn't ask any questions after Kate pressed a twenty into his palm and said simply, "Crowbar."

"If we check in and get ready pretty quick, we can still have a nice dinner and do a little bit of gambling," Genie said, checking the time on her phone.

"I guess there's no time to work shopping into that schedule," Kate replied.

"Nope," Genie said. "But we could always just order room service and cut out the gambling."

"If we do that, then we won't get to gamble or eat at all before we leave tomorrow," CiCi said.

"No," Kate replied. She pursed her lips. "We're going to power through. If the members of Boyz United give a concert after knee-replacement surgery and rehab, then we can get through the rest of this day like the eighteen-year-olds we used to be."

"This is for Laurie," CiCi said. "She's the whole reason we're here."

Genie nodded. "Let's make her proud."

Chapter 28

CiCi

The young woman at the front desk in the hotel lobby took one look at them and said, "You're here for the Boyz United concert?"

"What gave it away?" CiCi asked.

"You all look like my mom," she said. "Every woman who's come in today reminds me of my mom. Boyz United was her favorite band in high school."

"How old are you?" Kate asked.

"Twenty-two," the woman, whose name tag read "Laiklynn," said. "My mom had me when she was sixteen."

"I guess technically we are old enough to be her mom," Genie whispered.

"Is your mom going to the concert?" CiCi asked.

Laiklynn nodded. "Yeah; she's super excited." She leaned over the desk and continued, "She thinks she's going to seduce one of them tonight. I can't remember which one . . . the only one who doesn't look totally old. Charlie, maybe?"

"Well, she's welcome to try," Kate replied. "But she'll have to go through me first."

"You ladies are so adorable," Laiklynn said with a giggle.

"You're dog friendly here, right?" Kate asked. Frank was tucked down into her purse, but his head popped up when Kate patted the bottom of her bag.

"Oh," Laiklynn said, furrowing her brow. "We're not really— only for the VIP guests who come to stay."

Genie shot daggers at Kate, but Kate ignored her and replied, "Is there any way we could be VIP just for the night? He's kind of a stowaway."

"He's so cute," Laiklynn said, leaning over the counter to rub Frank's head. "What's his name?"

"Frank Sinatra," Kate said without missing a beat.

"Well, Frank Sinatra would for sure be VIP, don't you think?" Laiklynn asked, deftly typing into her computer. "I think surely we can make an exception for Frank Sinatra."

"Oh, really?" Kate asked. "Thank you so much."

"I just need you to fill out some paperwork, and I need to make a copy of his rabies vaccination."

"Here," Kate said to CiCi, handing over her bag with Frank inside. "Hold on to this for a minute while I fill this stuff out. Oh, and hand me my wallet. All of the vaccination stuff is in there."

CiCi reached down into Kate's bag and was promptly licked

by Frank. "Here," she said, handing over the wallet. "I'm going to go look at the gift shop while you do that and see if I can find something for the girls."

Kate waved her off, and CiCi was getting ready to ask Genie to come when she saw that Genie was on her phone in the center of the lobby, sitting on one of the plush chairs and looking very serious. Figuring Genie was talking to someone about her father, CiCi wandered off alone, Frank in tow, to see what the gaudy hotel/casino gift shop had to offer. They hadn't really been anywhere for her to find a gift for the kids, with the exception of that shop in New Mexico where Genie bought the dress. She hadn't seen much in there for them, and to be honest, she hadn't really thought about it.

Even if they were angry with her right now, it had always been a tradition to bring home a little treasure when she was out of town without Lily and Sophie, and she hoped that bringing something home for them would restore a small portion of normalcy to their lives—and hers.

She set Kate's bag down to hold up a bright pink T-shirt with "Las Vegas" splattered across the chest in rhinestones. It looked like something Lily would love, but CiCi wondered if maybe the other parents in Orchard Grove would judge her for allowing her child to wear a bedazzled shirt basically glorifying gambling. She also wondered, looking at the sequined minidresses hanging beside the T-shirts, if anybody ever actually bought a wardrobe from a gift shop after losing everything while gambling like the movies always portrayed.

From the looks of the people shopping around her, the answer was yes.

It wasn't until she heard a startled squeal from the woman standing next to her that CiCi realized that Frank had jumped out of Kate's bag and was running through the store toward the exit.

"Frank!" CiCi yelled. "No! Frank!"

CiCi ran through the store and out into the lobby, chasing after Frank. For his part, Frank seemed to be enjoying the pursuit, and stopped only when a woman with a hot pretzel came into his view. For a dog with only three good legs, he sure was fast.

CiCi was nearly within reach when someone stepped in front of her and said, "Ma'am, I'm going to have to ask you to stop right there."

CiCi ignored the person and went to scoop up Frank, but she was intercepted and felt herself being jerked back by her arm to face whoever was speaking to her.

"I said STOP."

"Let go of me," CiCi demanded. "You're hurting me."

"Let go of the merchandise," the guard said. "Then we can talk."

CiCi realized to her horror that it was a casino security guard, and she was still holding, clutched in one of her hands, the pink bedazzled T-shirt from the gift shop.

"My friend's dog!" CiCi said, pointing furiously. "I was going to pay for this, I swear, but my friend's dog escaped, and I had to catch him!"

"You're going to have to come with me," the guard said, not at all moved by CiCi's excuse.

"Take it," CiCi said, shoving the shirt into the guard's chest. "I wasn't trying to steal it, I swear."

"Please don't make this any more difficult than it needs to be," the guard replied. "Come with me, and we'll get it sorted out."

"I'm not a thief!" CiCi nearly screamed. "It was an accident."

"Ma'am, I'm not going to ask you again."

Next to them, the woman with the pretzel had picked up Frank and was watching the scene unfold. She'd also given him half of her pretzel, and if CiCi hadn't been so incredibly upset about being busted for shoplifting, she might've laughed at the two of them, both eating the pretzel and watching her argue with the rent-a-cop.

"Fine," CiCi said with a sigh. She looked around for Kate and Genie, but they were all the way on the other side of the lobby, and neither one of them seemed to realize what was happening. "Excuse me," she said, as she was being led away, to the woman holding Frank. "That's my friend's dog." CiCi pointed across the lobby. "Please can you take him to her and tell her what happened? Her name is Kate!"

The woman nodded, but she didn't look as if she was in any kind of hurry to make it over to Kate, and CiCi hoped she wouldn't just walk off with Frank. Getting arrested was one thing, but Kate would never forgive her if CiCi lost the dog in the process.

The guard led CiCi through double doors that were nearly

hidden in the wall and then down three or four, CiCi couldn't keep count, flights of stairs. She was winded and even more irritated by the time the guard finally stopped at a thick door with a small window too high for anyone to actually see out of.

"You have to believe me," CiCi said as she entered a small room that smelled like disinfectant and mold. "I wasn't trying to steal that shirt. I just didn't want the dog to get lost."

"Do you know how many times I've heard that excuse?" the guard said, rolling his eyes. "At least four times this month."

"Really?" CiCi asked, genuinely impressed. "That's a line people have used before?"

"I'm going to need to see some ID," the guard said.

CiCi looked at him. "I don't have any ID," she said. "I put my wallet down in my friend's bag, and it's back up at the gift shop."

The guard made a noise in his throat that sounded a little bit like a sigh of exasperation and also like he was choking. He motioned for CiCi to follow him after she abjectly refused to let him grab her arm again, and he led her back to another, smaller room. The room was actually two holding cells, and on the other side, there was a man wrapped in a thin blanket with the casino moniker on it, and he appeared to be snoring.

"Stay here," the guard said. "I'll be back after I retrieve the bag."

"You can't leave me alone in here with . . . with that *guy*," CiCi said.

"He's asleep," the guard replied.

"What if he wakes up?"

"You're on the other side of the bars," the guard said and shrugged. "Maybe don't steal a shirt next time."

"You can't leave me in here!" CiCi called after him as the guard shut the door and locked it. "I have rights!"

"There are no rights in casino jail," came a voice from the other cell. "You might as well save your breath."

CiCi glared over at the man. "I *didn't* steal anything," she said, indignant.

The man stirred from his sleeping position and looked up at her. "Yeah, and I didn't get shitfaced and piss in the lobby ficus at four A.M. either."

"Gross," CiCi replied. "Why would you do that?"

The man shrugged and took off his baseball cap and rubbed his thinning hair. "You'd have to ask drunk me. Sober me is just as confused as you are."

CiCi couldn't help but laugh at that. She knew exactly what he meant, but she wasn't going to admit that to a stranger she met in a cell. She looked at the man. He'd walked a bit closer to the bars that separated them. He looked familiar to her in a way she couldn't describe. It was like she knew him from somewhere, but nowhere at the same time. She had the distinct feeling she'd known him, a younger version of him at least.

Her eyes widened when she finally realized who she was staring at. He didn't look the same way she remembered him. His hair was still bleached blond, but the graying five o'clock shadow on his face and the crow's-feet around his eyes gave away his age. "Oh my God," she said. "You're . . . you're Leo Lancer."

"In the flesh," he said, standing up and walking toward her. "Could you tell the guard that when he comes back, please? I've been arguing with him for hours about it, and he doesn't believe me."

"You didn't have your ID either?" CiCi asked. She could hardly believe she was standing just feet from the man behind the booming tenor of Boyz United.

"I had it," Leo replied. "But my legal name isn't Leo Lancer."

"Oh, that's right," CiCi said. "It's Leonardo Lanceramos."

"Nice," Leo replied. "I guess you're here for the concert."

"Sorry," CiCi said. "I guess knowing the full legal name of a stranger is creepy. I blame teen magazines of the late nineties."

Leo grinned. "It's okay. I'm used to it."

"I can't believe it's you," CiCi said. "My friends aren't going to believe this."

"I'd offer to give you an autograph, but I don't think that's allowed in jail," Leo replied.

"You've got to get out of here!" CiCi exclaimed. "You have a concert!"

"I tried telling that to RoboCop, but he doesn't believe me. Now I have to rely on my manager to figure it out, and I can tell you right now, the chances of him figuring *anything* out are slim."

"How come nobody has come looking for you yet?"

"I doubt they know I'm gone," Leo replied. "My wife and

kid are back home in Michigan. I don't have to be anywhere until sound check. The guys and I, well, we're not as close as we used to be."

CiCi nodded. "I understand. It's hard to maintain friendships. The women I'm here with have been my best friends since high school, but until recently, I wasn't sure how much we still had in common. I think it took losing our other best friend to figure it out."

"What did your other best friend do?" Leo asked. "Steal your husband or something? That's why Johnny and Joe don't talk anymore."

"No," CiCi said, stifling a laugh. "Laurie, our other best friend, died very suddenly a couple of weeks ago."

"Oh shit, I'm sorry," Leo said. "I didn't mean to sound insensitive."

"It's okay," CiCi replied. "I mean, it's not okay that she died, but I know what you mean. She's the whole reason we're even here." She glanced around the cell. "Well, she's the whole reason we're in Vegas to see you. We loved Boyz United in high school, and after she died, we just kind of thought . . . why not?"

"And now you're in casino jail with me," Leo replied. "Sorry about your luck."

"Aside from the fact that I *did not* steal that shirt, it's not too bad," CiCi replied. "You were Laurie's favorite, because, you know, every girl has to have her favorite boy band member."

"My daughter loves some ridiculous K-pop band," Leo said.

"She has a favorite guy. Has posters of him all over her room. I think she actually *kisses* a poster at night. I keep thinking, *Is this what girls do? Is this normal, or do I need to hire a shrink?*"

CiCi laughed. "Totally normal," she said. "In fact . . ."

She trailed off when she heard a jangling of the door and then a familiar voice waft through the cracks.

"If you don't let her out of here this absolute *instant*, you'll have a lawsuit so fast your head will spin!"

CiCi felt a wave of relief wash over her when Kate came barging through the door, nearly knocking the poor security guard down as he tried to open the door wide enough for her to enter. Genie followed behind her, looking confused and carrying Frank, who was still munching on the pretzel like it was a ham bone.

"Are you all right?" Kate asked CiCi. "I can't believe this. All for a T-shirt?" She turned to glare at the security guard.

"Ma'am, I was just doing my job," the security guard replied, chagrined. "I had to take her in."

"Didn't she explain to you that it was an accident?"

"She did, but . . ."

Kate looked like she was about to morph into full-blown lawyer mode, when she realized that CiCi wasn't alone in the holding cells. It took her less time than it had taken CiCi to recognize who it was, because, truth be told, Leo had been her favorite member of the band too, a fact that she and Laurie had argued over numerous times, *well* into their twenties, when they were supposed to be adults.

"Kate!" Genie whispered. "It's . . . it's . . ."

Kate cleared her throat. "And can you explain to me why you have Leo . . ."

CiCi waved her hands back and forth and mouthed the name "Leonardo" to her, and Kate nodded just slightly enough that only CiCi knew that she'd received the message.

"Can you tell me why you also have Leonardo Lanceramos behind bars?" Kate asked.

"You know him?" the guard asked. "I caught him pissing in the foliage this morning."

Genie let out a little giggle before receiving a stern look from Kate, which promptly shut her up. "Of course I know him," Kate said. "He's also my client."

The security guard looked confused and said, "Wow, heavy coincidence."

"Is there any way to get them both out of here?" Kate asked, switching tacks. "We just got here, and we've got plans to see that concert tonight. Please, we've driven halfway across the country."

"I'm supposed to wait until my supervisor gets here," the security guard said.

"Won't you be in trouble for keeping one of the casino's entertainers locked up down here?" Kate asked.

The guard rolled his eyes. "That guy is *not* an entertainer here," he said. "I know what those guys in that Boys America group look like. My daughter loved them when she was in high school."

"*Boyz United*," Leo corrected him.

"Whatever," the guard said. "I know what they look like, and you ain't one of 'em. You don't even have the right name."

"His legal name and his stage name are different," Kate said, her tone gentler. "Entertainers do that all the time. And you're probably thinking about the way they looked twenty years ago. Do *you* look the same as you did twenty years ago?"

"Not quite," the guard said, snorting.

Kate pulled out her phone and muttered something about the shitty service, and after what seemed like an eternity, she held the phone up for the guard to see. "Look," she said. "Isn't this the same man?"

The guard tilted his head like a dumbfounded dog and then squinted. "Well," he said. "I guess it could be."

"It *is*!" Leo exclaimed, exasperated. "That's *me*. I'm *him*."

The guard looked from the phone to Leo and back to the phone again. "Shit, man," the guard said. "You sure have aged."

"Thanks," Leo replied. "I appreciate you taking the time to notice that."

"You still pissed in the foliage," the guard said. His face was stern, but his resolve was crumbling, and CiCi knew that meant Kate was getting ready to move in for the kill.

"I'm sure you don't want to be responsible for holding up the biggest concert of the summer," Kate said. "I doubt your boss wants to be responsible for that either."

"I guess not."

"So," Kate said, putting her hand gently on the guard's arm.

"What if both my clients agree to pay for any damages they've caused, and then you let them both be on their way. You'd be doing the casino, and all of us, a great service if you could agree to that."

"I figure we could work something out," the guard replied. "If you think maybe this one over here"—he motioned to Leo—"could get me an autograph for my daughter. She lives in Ohio now, but I know she wanted to come tonight."

"Of course," Leo replied automatically. "I'd be happy to do that."

CiCi wanted to let out a whoop of joy, but she kept her excitement to herself. She didn't want the security guard to realize he'd just totally been had by Kate. He might change his mind and make them all wait for his supervisor.

"Wonderful," Kate said, clapping her hands together. "I knew you were a reasonable man."

The security guard blushed under Kate's approving gaze, and Kate, before anyone else could notice it at all, gave Genie a sly little wink.

Chapter 29

Kate

Kate was particularly proud of herself for having gotten CiCi and one of her lifelong crushes out of the hot water they'd managed to get themselves into, and it was hard for her not to brag on herself as they exited the security guard's quarters nearly an hour later.

As it turned out, Leo was equally impressed with her. "You're a rock star," he said to her. "I mean, I know rock stars. And you are totally a rock star."

"Thanks," Kate replied. "I'm not even licensed to practice in this state. Maybe I should be. I could make a killing."

Leo reached out and hugged each one of them, and Kate felt her eighteen-year-old self dying of happiness right there on the dirty casino carpet. "How can I repay you?" he asked. "You want front-row seats? Autographs? A shout-out on our podcast?"

"Please don't give me a shout-out if you're going to tell

anyone how we met," CiCi said. "I don't need my future ex-husband to know . . ."

"That you spent two hours in casino jail with a hungover member of a boy band?" Leo finished for her.

"Pretty much," CiCi replied. "No offense."

"None taken," Leo said. "Hey, give me your names, and I'll put you on my personal list. It might not actually be front row, but it'll be close."

"Thanks," Kate said. "I'm Kate."

"CiCi," CiCi replied.

Genie, who'd not uttered a word for quite some time, managed to squeak out, "I'm GenieandIthinkyou'reamazingandit's socooltomeetyou."

Kate wrote down their full names for him on the back of one of her business cards and handed it to him. She couldn't believe how lucky they were to have gotten put on two VIP lists in a matter of days. Of course, the circumstances leading up to those VIP lists had been pretty shitty, but maybe it was time to be more of a silver-linings kind of person.

"You three saved my life today," Leo replied, sliding the card into his back pocket. "I don't have my phone or my room key, and it would have been at least another hour before anyone realized where I was. Seriously, thanks again." He turned to leave, and then thought better of it and turned around and said to CiCi, "Hey, your friend—the one who . . . the one who died, what was her name again?"

"Laurie," CiCi replied. "Her name was Laurie."

THEY PICKED UP their new tickets at the will-call office, and Kate couldn't remember the last time she had actual, physical tickets to a show. Now, more often than not, she used her phone and a digital ticket that had to be scanned. It felt kind of nice to feel a real ticket in her hands. The new tickets weren't in the front row, but they were miles closer than the seats they already had. Not even Kate could keep her enthusiasm to herself.

"He was a lot nicer than I thought he'd be," Kate said. "I guess getting arrested while publicly urinating can be pretty humbling."

"Maybe he's just a nice guy," Genie said. "Maybe they all are."

"Seems too good to be true," Kate replied.

"Lots of things on this trip have been both too bad and too good to be true," CiCi said. "I'm not sure we haven't fallen through the looking glass or something."

"Or the pot we bought from that teenager in Oklahoma was laced with hallucinogenics," Genie said.

Kate laughed. Despite the anticipation building all around them for a show she was sure most of the people in the room had been waiting decades to see, she felt an overwhelming sense of peace to be where she was right at that moment. Sure, the day had started off worse than terrible with the news about Genie's father, and she knew that reality would be hard to come back to, especially for Genie and CiCi, when they returned to Orchard Grove. But none of that meant that they couldn't be together now, laughing and talking and simply enjoying whatever they had right now.

If Kate had learned anything at all during her divorce and, well, her nearly forty years on the planet, it was that everybody wanted their lives to be like an inspirational quote—everybody wanted to be gym selfies and humblebrags and coffee art, but real life was what happened in between the perfection. It was a bag of frozen peas, a bonfire in the backyard, and a crowbar against metal. It was divorce and loss and it was, at this very moment, friendship.

The lights went down and the entire auditorium started to scream. All six members of Boyz United took the stage, amid a spectacular light show that looked like something NASA could have created.

The first few songs were, of course, from their debut album, and everybody in the audience sang along. All around them, Kate realized, everyone was a teenager again. True, nobody moved quite as fast as they used to—boy band and audience alike—but everyone remembered the moves.

Toward the end of the concert, it was time for each of the men to sing their signature song—an experiment from their final album, when all of the members were attempting to flesh out solo careers in the early 2000s amid an industry that no longer favored choreographed moves and six-part harmonies.

Leo sauntered up to the front of the stage, his bad-boy persona on display for all to view. The rumor had always been that he was the ultimate reason for the breakup, and for a while, his life was tabloid fodder as his solo career and A-list celebrity status floundered and fizzled. He'd never addressed it publicly before.

"I know some of you blame me for the breakup of Boyz United," he said, sitting down in a chair provided for him by a roadie. "And maybe it was my fault." He paused and then laughed. "Yeah, it probably was."

There were a few muffled boos from the audience.

"Listen," he said, putting up his hands. "Listen, I know, I know. But if you're all true fans, and I think you are, then you also know that we were friends before the fame. We weren't like all the other boy bands out there—nobody manufactured us. Nobody answered an ad in the paper. We were all—the six of us—friends as kids."

The remaining members of the band appeared in a puff of smoke and sat next to him. The crowd roared.

"Fame was hard on us. Now, I'm not complaining. But this reunion has been five years in the making. We had to put all of our childish bullshit behind us, and trust me when I say there was a lot of bullshit. But we managed to work it out, and now we're here, together on a stage for the first time in nearly two decades."

More cheering.

"How many of you are here with your friends tonight?"

The house lights came on, and everyone cheered louder.

"That's what I thought," Leo said. "That's what I thought. Well, tonight, I met a woman . . . actually, I met three women . . ." He paused for dramatic effect while the crowd reacted, and then he laughed and continued. "Hold up, hold up,

I'm a married man! I met three women, and without revealing too much, let's just say they helped me out of a scrape I was in, and I'm grateful."

Kate, CiCi, and Genie all looked at each other.

"He's talking about us!" CiCi said. "He's talking about us!"

"So this song right here," Leo said as the music started to play, "this song right here is for Laurie and her friends."

Kate felt CiCi grab her hand. She looked over at CiCi, who was looking at Genie. Then they both looked over to Kate, and despite the tears in their eyes, all three burst out laughing.

"Laurie *hated* this song!" Genie yelled.

"Oh, you know she's so pissed," Kate yelled back.

"Of all the songs!" CiCi said. "It had to be this one!"

"It *had* to be this one," Kate agreed.

"I can't believe we're actually here," CiCi yelled as the song sped up and the crowd got louder. "It doesn't feel real."

"Me either," Genie replied. "I wasn't even sure if we'd make it."

"We were always going to make it," Kate said, grinning. She raised their intertwined hands in the air and cheered. "It just took us a little longer than everybody else."

Chapter 30

Genie

It was barely light outside when Genie, CiCi, and Kate arrived at the airport for their early morning flight. It was the only time they could find a flight together at such short notice. They'd considered flying in separately, but they were going to need to rent a car at the St. Louis airport to get home, and it didn't make any sense to waste an entire day waiting on each other or renting cars on their own. Besides, they wanted to be together. Even Frank couldn't decide which one of them he really belonged to, an issue that Kate was not exactly thrilled about.

Genie sat down in one of the gray plastic chairs next to the gate and tried to keep her eyelids from sticking every time she blinked. She'd forgotten to wash her mascara off the night before, and nothing she'd tried this morning seemed to do the trick. She was afraid if she kept her eyes closed for too long, she might just fall asleep where she was.

"I got you coffee," Kate said to her, handing her a cup. "It's black. I hope that's okay."

"It's perfect," Genie said, breathing in the steam. "Thanks. Where's CiCi?"

"She's getting a muffin," Kate replied.

"I hope she's getting us all muffins," Genie said.

"You better go and tell her," Kate said. "You know I don't really like breakfast. So I didn't want her to get me anything."

Sighing, Genie stood up and began to trudge toward the Starbucks kiosk. She was ready to be home, even if that meant planning a funeral. She knew the next few days were going to be rough once she was forced back into the reality of Orchard Grove, but CiCi had promised to help, and so had Kate, and she felt ready to face it. She wasn't going to be doing it alone. She'd already received phone calls and texts from well-wishers who'd heard the news. Leah at the nursing home had written a poem, and her daughter Simone had drawn a picture that Leah had posted on social media. There were similar tributes, similar messages of love that reminded Genie why a little town in the middle of nowhere wasn't necessarily the worst place she could think of to live. She was going to make it back in one piece— even if her father's beloved car was in more than a few pieces, living a new life in Flagstaff with the mechanic who'd replaced their blown-out tire. It needed a lot more than a new tire now. In more than one way, for more than one reason, Genie was glad to let the car go.

Deep in thought, Genie nearly missed the display sitting

front and center at the airport convenience store nestled beside the Starbucks. In fact, she had to stop and back up to see it—a shelf full of Laurie's newest book, along with a poster of praise for the book and for Laurie, and a note underneath it about her death. There were only a few copies left, and Genie picked one up and, setting down her coffee, looked the book over. She couldn't help it. She felt like the book, and Laurie, had been following her the whole trip, and touching it made her feel closer to Laurie somehow.

"It's a great read," said a voice from inside the store. "It's not my favorite of her books, but it's close."

Genie looked up to see the store attendant staring at her. She set the book down. "I've, uh, heard it's good," she said.

"Have you read any of her books?" the attendant asked, stepping around the register to approach Genie.

"Yes," Genie said. "She was very talented."

"I still can't believe she's dead," the attendant replied. "I met her once. Right here in this airport. She came to do a signing a couple of years ago."

"Oh really?"

The attendant nodded. "Yeah." She pulled her phone out of her pocket and said, "I've got the picture here somewhere. She was super nice."

"I've heard that," Genie said.

The attendant scrolled through her phone. "I know I've got it here somewhere. . . . Come on . . . where is it . . . oh, here it is."

Genie looked down at the picture the attendant had saved on her phone. In it, the attendant was bending down next to Laurie, who was seated at a table full of her books. They were both smiling.

"I'd never read any of her books before then," the attendant, whose name tag read "Nellie," said. "It was my first day on the job, and the manager quit that morning. I was really stressed-out, because I didn't know what to do, and only one other employee could come in to help me. I called a few of my friends to help. Laurie was so nice. She didn't let it bother her at all."

"I think I'll buy a copy," Genie said, picking up a book. She followed the attendant to the front of the store.

"She told me I was lucky to have such good friends who were willing to come in and help me on such short notice," Nellie continued. "Even though they complained about it the whole time." She laughed.

"You are lucky," Genie replied. "Friends are important."

"That's what Laurie said," Nellie said. She scanned the bar code on the book. "That'll be sixteen seventy-nine."

Genie handed her a twenty-dollar bill.

Nellie took the money and continued, "She said she had good friends like I did. She said they would have done just about anything for her, like hide a body." Nellie laughed. "I thought that was funny. My friends would probably call the cops."

"You'd be surprised," Genie replied, "what your friends will do for you if you need them."

"Would you hide a body?" Nellie asked. "Because I wouldn't."

Genie thought about it. "Well, I guess it depends on whose body."

"What about a body?" CiCi asked, handing over to Genie a lemon-poppy-seed muffin. "Here. This is all they had left."

"I was asking her," Nellie said, pointing to Genie, "if she'd help one of her friends hide a body."

"She wouldn't need any help," CiCi replied. "She's got a car with a really big trunk."

"There's a lot of junk in that trunk," Genie said.

While she and CiCi laughed, the cashier, who was at least a decade younger than they were, didn't seem to get the reference.

"What are you laughing about?" Kate asked. "Hey, where's my muffin?"

"You said you didn't want one," CiCi reminded her. "But you can have half of mine."

"Thanks," Kate replied. "So what were you two laughing about?"

"Hiding bodies in a trunk," Nellie the cashier said. "I'm not really sure why it's funny."

"I don't think I could help you hide a body," Kate replied, tearing off a piece of muffin and popping it into her mouth, chewing thoughtfully. "But I could represent you when the body is ultimately found and you go on trial for murder."

"Fine," CiCi said, slapping Kate's hands away from the

muffin. "But I'm not sharing my breakfast with you if you won't help me hide a body."

The cashier watched them go, wondering the whole time who those strange women were and how, maybe one day, she and her friends could be just like them.

Chapter 31

CiCi

Things were quieter when CiCi, Kate, and Genie returned to Orchard Grove. CiCi was relieved to find that most everyone in town had forgotten about, or at the very least gotten bored with, her marital crisis, and even Brent was more amiable than usual. She figured that was probably because she herself had become more amiable. After the trip, some things were just more important than others.

The first thing she did after unpacking was sit down with Lily and talk to her, really talk to her, for the first time in a long time. Then she called Genie, and they all three went out to lunch together. CiCi knew that she might never fully under-stand her daughter the way Genie did, but she also recognized the incredible gifts she'd been given in the two of them. Let-ting go, loosening her grip just a little, of the way CiCi thought things were supposed to be, allowed her to see new possibilities where she'd originally thought there were none.

Wade, of course, was a new possibility. He was calm and steady and patient and, when she was ready, hers.

She wasn't the only one with new possibilities on the horizon, and Genie made sure to remind both her and Kate at every turn that she and Troy had no plans to slow down. There was no calm and steady and patient with the two of them. Troy had already been to visit Genie twice in the months since their return, and boy howdy—did *that* create a stir. CiCi supposed it was easy for Orchard Grove to forget about her and Brent when there was the likes of a bronzed God like Troy hanging around Genie's house. Rumor had it that Genie's eighty-nine-year-old neighbor fell off the front porch and broke her hip trying to get a good look at Troy through a pair of her late husband's bird-watching binoculars.

Not even Kate, who'd been seeing an awful lot of that veterinarian from New Mexico, could help but swivel around to get a good look at Troy when the occasion called for it. She'd been coming down to Orchard Grove quite a lot lately, mostly to help her father renovate his house. Well, mostly to supervise the renovation. He'd flatly refused to move, but he hadn't disagreed when all three of them—Kate, CiCi, and Genie—appeared on his doorstep one morning with donuts and a plan to make his house a bit more inhabitable. Kate's boys, who'd been coming down a lot more to see their grandfather, had convinced him to come to St. Louis for a visit while the largest part of the renovation took place, and Kate reported that her father was having the time of his life in the city. He'd gone all the way up in the Gateway Arch on his first day and requested a full tour of the Budweiser brewery. Both of Kate's dogs—Frank Sinatra and Pat Sajak—were in every single picture, wearing tiny Budweiser shirts.

Perhaps the most surprising thing out of all the surprising things that had happened the week after their return to town was when Kitty showed up at CiCi's door clutching a copy of Laurie's will. As it turned out, Laurie left a large chunk of her estate to Kitty and Dan, which surprised absolutely nobody, but then there'd been a caveat that a portion of that large chunk be dedicated to a scholarship fund for graduating seniors at Orchard Grove High School. Laurie wanted her three best friends to make sure this final wish was carried out.

There were days when CiCi forgot that Laurie wasn't alive, and she'd reach for her phone to tell her something funny, or she'd be talking to someone and say, "My friend Laurie," and then she'd remember, and it was awful. There were days when she'd hear a song on the radio, and she'd be reduced to tears, because it was a song Laurie had loved. Sometimes Kitty would ask her out to lunch just to talk, because Kitty needed to be near someone who understood.

But there were other days, happy days, when CiCi and Kate and Genie would laugh at the memories, when they all felt a closeness to each other they hadn't felt since they were children—since that moment Laurie appeared in Orchard Grove, and the days and months and years that would come after that were so much more than most people got in an entire lifetime.

CiCi didn't regret a single second.

Epilogue

Genie

One year later

The Orchard Grove High School gymnasium didn't look much different than it had more than two decades ago. There were still folding chairs on the gym floor for the graduates to perch on while wearing their blue-and-white graduation gowns. The bleachers were full of parents and family members and friends all on the verge of tears over their "babies" graduating from high school.

Genie went to graduation every year, but this year was different. This year, instead of sitting with the rest of the staff members, she was up onstage sandwiched in between the principal and the superintendent. She couldn't help but nervously bounce her legs up and down as she waited to be introduced by the school board president, even though she knew that Kate was shooting daggers at her from across the gym in a vain attempt to get her to sit still.

She couldn't, wouldn't, didn't *want* to sit still. She felt like she'd spent half her life sitting still, and now that she'd figured out that sitting still had never actually been a requirement, Genie hadn't quit moving.

Beside her, the high school principal gave her a little nudge. "I think you're on," he whispered.

Genie stood and walked to the podium that had been placed in the center of the stage. She was very nearly too short for it, and she took a second to adjust the microphone before she began to speak.

"Good evening, graduates," she said, smiling at the fresh young faces staring up at her. "And welcome, family and friends. Most of you already know me—I'm a lifelong resident of Orchard Grove and one of the kindergarten teachers at the elementary school. In fact, I had nearly half of the graduates in my classroom thirteen years ago. I'm so proud of every single one of you." Genie paused and adjusted the papers she'd brought with her, just in case she forgot any of her lines. "But tonight, I'm not here as a kindergarten teacher. Tonight, I'm here on behalf of the Laurie Lawson Memorial Foundation for the Arts, a nonprofit organization based in St. Louis. The goal of the foundation is to foster and encourage young people to take an interest in creative professions such as writing, music, and drama. This year, the foundation is awarding more than a hundred thousand dollars in scholarships across the state of Missouri."

There was a round of impressed cheering throughout the gymnasium, and Genie cleared her throat.

"Laurie Lawson was a graduate of Orchard Grove High School, and she was one of my three best friends. She was a prolific author. She came to our little town as a foster child to Kitty and Dan Scott, and she walked across this stage to receive her diploma just like you are all doing tonight. She always said that Orchard Grove was her home, and the people in this town were her family. Tonight, two Orchard Grove seniors will be the first ever to receive the scholarship, and I know if Laurie were here, she couldn't have picked two more deserving candidates."

AFTER THE CEREMONY, Genie and Kate walked around the gym in an attempt to find CiCi.

"I don't know where she is," Kate said. "I said I had to go to the bathroom, and she said she'd wait for me, but when I came out, she was gone."

"I bet I know where she is," Genie said. She pointed toward the playground. "Let's go check."

Sure enough, CiCi was sitting on the swings, swaying back and forth, dragging a patent-leather toe in the gravel.

"What are you doing back here?" Genie asked. "We've been looking for you."

"I thought I'd give Brent some space to get pictures with his family," CiCi said. "We got ours first."

"Are you okay?" Kate asked, sitting down on a swing beside her.

CiCi looked up at her friends. "I'm okay," she said. "I'm so proud of Sophie. Salutatorian. Can you believe it?"

"Yes," Genie replied automatically. "I had her in kindergarten, remember?"

"And you knew then that she was going to graduate at the top of her class?" CiCi asked.

"Well, I knew she was the only kid who didn't try to shove crayons up her nose during naptime," Genie replied.

"Close enough," Kate said.

"I can't believe you're not going to be teaching kindergarten next year," CiCi said. "You're so good at it."

"I'll miss it," Genie replied. It was the truth. In fact, she'd cried when, a month earlier, she'd handed in her resignation and then promptly gone to the only real estate office in town and put her father's house on the market.

But it was the right thing to do and the right time to do it. She was ready.

"Well, I can't believe you're moving *away from us* to live with a *boy*," Kate said, pretending to cry.

"Yeah," CiCi agreed. "Just when the two of us are single and ready to mingle."

"First of all, nobody says that anymore," Kate said.

"And second of all?"

"And second of all," Genie replied, "neither one of you is really single, are you? CiCi, you're practically living with Wade."

"*He's* practically living with *me*," CiCi corrected her. "It's my house."

The fact that CiCi had gotten nearly everything in the divorce was a particular source of pride for her, especially since Brent had practically begged to come home to avoid financial ruin. Despite CiCi's win, she played nice with Brent for the kids, and everyone was surprised about how cordial they'd managed to be over the last few months.

"Do you remember the last time we were here?" Genie asked. "Sitting on these swings?"

"I do," Kate said with a grin. She reached into her purse and pulled out a flask. "I remember well."

"No way," Genie said.

"You have to," Kate replied. "For nostalgia."

Genie held out her hand. "Give it."

Kate unscrewed the top, took a swig, and handed it to Genie. "That's so disgusting," she said. "I can't believe I ever thought it was good."

"You didn't think it was good," Genie replied. "You thought it was cool."

"God, we were so young," Kate said. "Did you see how young all of those kids looked tonight? They're all babies, really."

"They'll be all right," Genie said. "We're all right, aren't we?"

"If you'd told me at our high school graduation that this is where we'd be right now, I would have laughed," CiCi said. "But I don't hate it."

"I don't hate it either," Kate replied. "I do miss Laurie, though."

"What do you think she'd say if she were here right now?" CiCi asked.

"That you still can't hold your liquor," Kate replied with a smirk.

"I'm serious! What do you think she'd say, Genie?" CiCi asked. "If she were here right now?"

"I don't know," Genie said. She dug her feet into the gravel. "But I think she'd say she was glad that we're together." She pushed herself backward, and then propelled forward into the air, pumping her legs back and forth. "And she'd also say CiCi can't hold her liquor."

"Well, I'm a better swinger than you are," CiCi replied, swinging herself backward and forward. She threw her head back into the air and laughed as Genie worked to keep up.

"Well, you did learn from the best," Kate replied. "How are your parents, anyway?" The three dissolved into giggles, soaring into the air. Eventually their rhythm synched, and Genie held out her hand, a lifeline thrown out into the darkness, and all any one of them had to do was be ready to catch it.

Acknowledgments

It is with sincere affection and admiration that I'd like to thank the following:

Priya Doraswamy—For loving me even when I have six stories in my head and only one outlet (her).

Lucia Macro—For being the editing genius that she is. You somehow always know what I mean to say, even when I don't know how to say it.

Asanté Simons—For being kind and gentle with the reminders. I'm sorry I'm annoying. It's genetic.

My husband—For being the muscle behind my big, fat mouth.

Jude—For telling me on a regular basis that I am not nearly as cool as I think I am.

My mom and dad—For telling me the story of my conception while we were sitting in a Taco Bell drive-thru at 10 P.M.

when I could not escape, thus solidifying my need for many sessions of therapy.

Robert and Matt—For never letting me forget that I've yet to make them central characters in a novel, which means I have lots more work to do.

About the author

About the book

Insights,
Interviews
& More . . .

Meet
Annie England Noblin

ANNIE ENGLAND NOBLIN lives with her son, husband, and four rescued bulldogs in the Missouri Ozarks. She graduated with an MA in creative writing from Missouri State University and currently teaches English at Arkansas State University. Her poetry has been featured in such publications as the *Red Booth Review* and the *Moon City Review,* and she coedited and coauthored the coffee-table book *The Gillioz: "Theatre Beautiful."* ⌒

A Very Nineties Road Trip Playlist

Genie

1. "Loser" by Beck

2. "Breakfast at Tiffany's" by Deep Blue Something

3. "Show Me the Meaning of Being Lonely" by the Backstreet Boys

4. "Everybody Hurts" by R.E.M.

5. "No Rain" by Blind Melon

6. "Fantasy" by Mariah Carey

7. "My Own Worst Enemy" by Lit

8. "The Freshmen" by The Verve Pipe

9. "Everything You Want" by Vertical Horizon

10. "Foolish Games" by Jewel

CiCi

1. "Barbie Girl" by Aqua

2. "Wannabe" by the Spice Girls

3. "C'est la Vie" by B*Witched

4. "Show Me Love" by Robyn

5. "Truly, Madly, Deeply" by Savage Garden ▶

A Very Nineties Road Trip Playlist
(continued)

6. "Livin' la Vida Loca" by
   Ricky Martin

7. "Tearin' Up My Heart" by
   *NSYNC

8. "Genie in a Bottle" by
   Christina Aguilera

9. "Summer Girls" by LFO

10. "MMMBop" by Hanson

Kate

1. "Torn" by Natalie Imbruglia

2. "Wonderwall" by Oasis

3. "Bitch" by Meredith Brooks

4. "Stay (I Missed You)" by Lisa Loeb

5. "Strong Enough" by Sheryl Crow

6. "Short Skirt/Long Jacket" by Cake

7. "Crash Into Me" by
   Dave Matthews Band

8. "Steal My Sunshine" by Len

9. "Linger" by the Cranberries

10. "Building a Mystery" by
    Sarah McLachlan

Laurie

1. "No Scrubs" by TLC
2. "Virtual Insanity" by Jamiroquai
3. "Butterfly" by Crazy Town
4. "My Name Is" [Explicit] by Eminem
5. "Pump Up the Jam" by Technotronic
6. "This Is How We Do It" by Montell Jordan
7. "Fly" by Sugar Ray
8. "Sex and Candy" by Marcy Playground
9. "I'll Be Missing You" by Puff Daddy (feat. Faith Evans and 112)
10. "Tonight, Tonight" by the Smashing Pumpkins

BONUS TRACK: "Independent Women, Pt. 1" by Destiny's Child ✌

Boyz United Reunion Tour Set List

1. "I Want to Be Inside (Your Heart)"

2. "Y2K Kind of Lonely"

3. "Give Me a Taste"

4. "Wide Open Love"

5. "Lick It (Ice Cream Remix)" ∿

Reading Group Guide

1. Laurie, Genie, CiCi, and Kate were best friends in high school. Who were your best friends in high school and are you still in touch with them today?

2. So much of the novel deals with impossible appearances—Kate and CiCi with perfect marriages, Laurie and her never talking about her past, Genie with her feelings of inadequacy about her weight. How much effort do you feel women, in general, put into creating the appearance of perfection and why?

3. Kate often thinks of herself as a bad mother. Is she too hard on herself? If she were a man, would she be judged as a bad parent?

4. Cici's work at the funeral home seems unexpected, given her personality. What unexpected traits did you discover in each of the main characters as you read the novel?

5. The Wigwam Motel is real. What is the craziest/worst/most interesting place you have ever stayed? Haunted hotels count! ▶

Reading Group Guide *(continued)*

6. The friends all loved a band called Boyz United as teenagers. Discuss your most embarrassing band loves of your teenage years.

7. The "road trip" is popular trope in American fiction. Why do you think this is the case? Care to share any of your own road trip experiences?

8. Laurie means different things to different people. How do you feel different friends bring different types of emotional nourishment to your life?

9. Pets, especially dogs, always take center stage in Annie England Noblin's books. Here she explains how dogs often name themselves. Is this true? Have any of your pets "named" themselves?

10. What are some of your favorite driving songs and why?

11. Do you think each of the main characters ended up where she needed to be by the book's end? ❧

Discover great authors, exclusive offers, and more at hc.com.